I0846776

International Incident

A Crown & Heart Novel

Book 1

By

Nikki Davenport

Content Notes:

References to cancer and childhood trauma

Profanity

Explicit sexual content

Kidnapping and non-gory physical danger

Copyright © 2023 by Nikki Davenport

All rights reserved.

No part of this publication may be reproduced, distributed, or transmitted in any form or by any means, including photocopying, recording, or other electronic or mechanical methods, without the prior written permission of the publisher, except as permitted by U.S. copyright law.

The story, all names, characters, and incidents portrayed in this work are fictitious. No identification with actual persons (living or deceased), places, buildings, and products is intended or should be inferred.

Library of Congress Control Number: 2023916702.

ISBNs

Ebook: 979-8-9890545-4-1

Print: 979-8-9890545-0-3

Cover design by GetCovers.

Published by Granite Clover Publishing, LLC

www.nikkidavenport.com

First Edition: November 2023

Chapter One

Washington, DC

Khara Therin, the reigning Queen of the island kingdom of Lytua, was once again facing off against her formidable assistant Joanne.

And losing. Again.

"The Speaker of the House has been holding for a full five minutes." The arch in Joanne Mosley's eyebrow dared Khara to refuse her.

Khara looked down at her lap and cleared her throat. She plucked a piece of lint from the hem of her knee-length skirt, pausing to admire the deep wine color in the plaid. "I'm not feeling very well." Keeping her words light didn't keep her hands from shaking as she fought the urge to pull at where the collar of her blouse felt tight.

"I'm sorry to hear that."

Whew. "Perhaps I should just—"

"You're still attending the Speaker's party."

"Well, then I don't really need to speak to her, do I?" The words tumbled out more harshly than Khara intended.

Joanne folded her arms, tapping her foot impatiently. Her petite frame was silhouetted against the conference room floor-to-ceiling window, the afternoon sunlight glinting off her jewelry. Ever the professor scolding her recalcitrant student, Joanne pointed at the telephone sitting innocently on the side table. "She's on line two." With that, she swept out of the room without a backward glance. Onto the next task, knowing full well she'd already won the argument, and leaving Khara alone to her disappointment.

How did she always do that?

Khara heaved an exasperated sigh and leaned back in her chair at the head of the massive table. Joanne wasn't buying any of her stalling today. They were still a bit testy with each other after Khara's perceived snubbing of a suitor at the previous day's luncheon.

She could refuse to talk to the Speaker. She spent a few moments contemplating if this was a battle worth fighting... it wasn't.

Best to get this over with, Khara thought. After stealing a few moments for some deep breaths, she picked up the line gingerly. She injected enthusiasm into her voice, even as she rubbed at the throbbing spot between her eyebrows. "Good afternoon, Speaker Crosby. My apologies for keeping you waiting. How may I help you?"

Speaker Lana Crosby was close to gushing with excitement as she greeted the Queen. "I just wanted to let you know how honored I am that you'll be attending my little soirée tonight. My son will be there, and I'm positive the two of you will hit it right off. He's an investment banker, you know. Single, too, if you can believe it. Did I mention that?"

Only three or four times since we met yesterday. Khara made a face at the receiver, then stole a glance around the room to make sure Joanne wasn't there to see it. As if Khara would ever get involved with an American politician's family member. That could spark an international incident if things didn't work out. Had the woman even heard a word she'd said, or had she been too busy plotting? Even though the meeting had been to discuss an important multinational ecological initiative, all the Speaker could focus on was trying to set Khara up with her son. Khara's patience had already been stretched to the limit from the luncheon that had preceded the meeting.

"Queen Lillianna?"

The use of her regnal name brought Khara's attention back from where it had wandered. "Yes, Speaker Crosby, thank you for the kind invitation. Your son sounds delightful. I am looking forward to attending." *There*. That was just ambiguous enough—an acknowledgment without a commitment.

Khara wrinkled her nose when they rang off soon after. It was a sure bet that the Speaker's son would be seated next to her tonight. Pretending not to understand English well had previously helped in sticky suitor situations, but it wasn't an option here. The Speaker knew she was fluent. Ah, well, she'd figure something out. She always did.

Massaging her fingertips into where the muscles in the back of her neck were tightening up, Khara considered her predicament. She had long since learned how to say no to pushy matchmakers with grace. This situation with the Speaker was no different. It was a bit of an ongoing nuisance to correct the misconception about how Lytuan royalty worked. People's eyes tended to glaze over when Khara explained that if she married while in office, her husband would be Consort, not king by default as many assumed. The same way her predecessor's wife had never held the title of Queen. This concept just never seemed to resonate. Such odd ideas about royalty. And it wasn't just in the States, it was nearly everywhere they went.

People were quick to assume that Khara must be in the market for a husband. The joke was on them though, for she had no intention of *ever* getting married.

Not that she opposed marriage. Quite the contrary. Khara believed in love deeply and saw evidence of its existence and effects every day with her team. After she'd sworn her oath and ascended the throne, she'd become a prize. No longer a woman with normal needs and wants. It didn't take long for Khara to recognize that her crown, and its influence, were what men desired now, not her. It was all about how she could improve someone else's standing. That trade-off was one she hadn't expected.

Humbling didn't even begin to describe it.

What she wanted was a cup of tea and a book. Instead, she would be getting dressed up and put on parade, regardless of her personal feelings on the matter. Again.

Annoyance at the Speaker's presumptuousness stuck with Khara as she worked her way through a handful of administrative tasks—initialing edits to an op-ed she was writing, signing off on a few letters. Her heart lurched when she came upon the baby item catalog, where Joanne had marked a few tasteful gift suggestions for her best friend, who was getting close to her due date. Khara was thrilled about becoming an honorary auntie, and her fingertips lingered over a state-of-the-art pram pictured on one of the pages. It was perfect. It even came with teal accents, Yvanda's favorite color. A quick pen stroke approved the purchases. Joanne would see to the rest.

Khara was in DC to strengthen diplomatic ties, and the trip was a success so far. She rotated visits to each of the cities where Lytua maintained embassies. Last year, it was Sydney, and next year, would be Nairobi. Beyond the ecological initiative, the other main priority for this trip was solidifying a medical research collaboration. Most of the work had been done in setting things up, but there were city and national leaders to call on. Meeting with the Speaker of the House had been a courtesy, one Khara very much now regretted extending.

The throbbing in her head intensified. Khara massaged small circles on her temples.

The political theater and posturing Khara could have done without, but she bit back her indignation. This was about what was best for the citizens of Lytua, not her.

Suck it up, Buttercup.

A groan slipped out when Khara saw that the blue *Embassy* folder had made its way into the stack of action items again. What should have been a simple decision had stretched on for days because of her lack of concentration. Why was this vexing her so?

The front of the folder blurred a little before her eyes. Hearing Joanne bustle in, Khara blinked and schooled her face. Joanne set a small tea service tray next to her and poured out. "Hibiscus, your favorite."

A distracted smile of thanks was all Khara could manage.

A frown pinched Joanne's brow when she saw the grilled chicken salad languishing untouched on the sideboard. "You've not eaten."

Khara picked at the edge of the offending folder. She'd forgotten all about lunch. "I'm not hungry." Her stomach chose that moment to make its emptiness known with a pronounced growl.

Joanne cocked her head, her sleek gray bob dancing with the movement. "You're not still sulking over yesterday, are you?"

With the rebuke still smarting, Khara was feeling rebellious. "You accused me of being rude to that gentleman sitting next to me at the luncheon."

"Bah, 'accused' is going a bit far, don't you think?" With quick, efficient motions, Joanne replaced the silver dome cover over the wilted salad and collected Khara's place setting.

"Those were your exact words. And it was an unfair accusation." Khara swiped at an errant coil of hair that was tickling her cheek.

"Come now, you're being dramatic. Would it have been so difficult to feign interest for a few minutes?" Joanne turned to face her, the room service tray held aloft in her sturdy hands.

Khara narrowed her eyes. "That stodgy bureaucrat was interrupting. He is not entitled to my time by virtue of having a penis. I actually *was* interested in what Dr. Huffman was sharing about her research project."

Joanne was pinning her with that signature no-nonsense look, quiet disapproval in the firm set of her mouth. "Queen Lillianna, you know very well that the social obligations—"

"*Of overseas travel supersede my personal feelings about them.*" Khara threw her hands up. "I know. You've drilled it into me."

The dishes gave an ominous rattle as Joanne thunked the tray down on the conference room table. "That sounds as though you're mocking me, young lady."

"I'm not mocking you, I just—" Khara broke off to swallow hard around the lump in her throat, her face burning. Ashamed of her impertinence, she tried to rein in her temper.

She shoved back from the table and got to her feet, taking her tea over to the small side table by the window. Everything about this trendy hotel conference room felt wrong. The furniture was too dark, too heavy. And the black marble table for twenty at the center—far too large. It overwhelmed the long room, made it feel crowded and authoritarian, which wasn't the Lytuan way. A square or round table would have been a better choice for discussion and cooperation. Right now, the whole setup irritated her. Everything about it was rubbing her the wrong way.

"You're a brick wall of etiquette." Khara faced her assistant. "It never does me any good to argue with you about these things."

"Have you learned nothing in our six years together, my Queen? Perhaps you should stop trying." The sympathy in Joanne's expression softened her curt tone. "I know this is your least favorite part. Just a few weeks more, then we'll be back home where you won't have to worry about such things."

"Until the next trip." Khara unclenched the forceful grip she had around the delicate teacup handle. "I bet an unmarried king wouldn't attract this level of scrutiny."

"I assure you, he would."

At Khara's scoff, Joanne straightened to her full five-foot height, her lips pressed together in a grim line. "What's gotten into you? Your behavior this trip has bordered on erratic."

Khara squeezed the bridge of her nose with her thumb and forefinger. "I'm weary of people foisting their single family members upon me, as though I would accept just anyone, with no regard for compatibility. Honestly, being an unmarried monarch is akin to waving a red flag in front of a bull. Some kind of tragic situation in need of fixing. I hate being cornered by men I don't want to talk to. And why does no one use any color in this forsaken place?"

Joanne's brow furrowed. "What are you on about?"

If she'd decorated this room, Khara would have capitalized on that sunshine spilling in and used bright, bold color everywhere. Such a waste. She missed the light, airy feel of her island. Khara gave an expansive gesture to indicate their surroundings. "This place has no character at all. It's austere. Boring, uninspiring, and stifling. Even the curtains are stuffy." Khara pinched the stiff, beige brocade, gave it a shake. "These hideous things belong in a funeral parlor."

"I agree." Folding her hands before her, Joanne was the picture of calm. "They are quite somber. But we both know you're talking about more than drapery."

Khara plucked the weighty material away from her. It barely moved. "Why should I have to pretend to be interested in anyone placed before me?"

"It's polite."

"It's demeaning. No one is interested in Khara—just what Queen Lillianna can do for their image. That's why I gave up on dating in the first place. I derive greater satisfaction from my work." Khara tilted her chin up and put her shoulders back.

"You might be surprised if you get out there again. Why not let the suitors court you and enjoy yourself? Use it to your advantage?"

With a forlorn shake of her head, Khara said, "It's not enjoyable to know I'm just a commodity. I will not put myself in that situation ever again."

"Queen Lillianna, don't say that." Joanne rushed to her side, alarm in each of her quick steps. "You have no idea what the future will hold."

Khara gave a derisive snort. "I can tell you what it *doesn't* hold. A man who sees me as more than merely a means to an end. The best I can hope for is a fulfilling distraction." She sat the saucer down on the side table so hard it shattered and sent the pretty teacup teetering.

Both women scrambled to right it. They worked together without speaking to clean up and dispose of the shards. As quickly as it came on, Khara's anger receded. She had to look away from the concern in Joanne's eyes, mortified to feel her throat burning. "I'm going out on the terrace."

"Good idea." Joanne scooped up the *Embassy* file and offered it to her. "Take these with you and make a decision already. You've put it off for days." She held on when Khara tried to take it.

For someone so small, Joanne had a will of iron and no compunction in using it. But the unexpected softness in her assistant's eyes surprised Khara. "Joanne?"

The older woman released her hold. "I know you believe I'm being too hard on you. Please know that my only wish is for your continued success." She held up a hand for silence when Khara opened her mouth to speak. "I confess, I had my doubts about a twenty-six-year-old taking the crown. But for being the youngest Queen ever elected, you've shown wisdom beyond your years. You should be proud, Khara. I certainly am. You are so much more than your title. More than any one man could ever deserve."

Now tears were truly threatening. Khara bit her lip and gave a shaky laugh. "That may be the most you've ever said to me at one time."

A ghost of a smile played across Joanne's features as she waved at the file Khara now held clutched to her chest. "Choose an architect. Please. Then we can carry on with the next thing. I will check on you later."

Khara watched her assistant take the tray and leave, then headed for the sanctuary of the sparsely furnished stone terrace. Some of the tension drained away with her first step outside. Closing her eyes briefly, Khara breathed in a deep lungful of the crisp, refreshing air before tossing the folder onto the tiny patio table. The hoteliers had done a better job infusing the narrow outdoor space with character—cheerful potted plants and flowers in colorful pots were in abundance. Nothing would ever replace the sun and balmy breezes of her island home, but the colorful fall leaves in Washington, DC, did enchant Khara. Considering Joanne's words, she absently rubbed the scar on her chest as she leaned on the wide-columned balustrade. She let the hustle and bustle of M Street, twenty stories below, soothe her.

When her head was clearer, Khara went back to the little table and sat. She readjusted the neckline of her blouse to cover the marred skin near her collarbone.

Joanne was right. Khara was feeling restless on this trip. She scowled at the folder with the architectural samples but didn't feel moved to open it. Cursing softly, she slid down in the chair, so her head rested against the back and interlaced her fingers over her belly. The underside of the balcony above offered no insight.

Now her stomach was actually upset. Lytuans revered their elders. She'd been disrespectful to Joanne and would need to apologize for it. Her assistant had children older than her, and Khara wondered if Joanne thought of her as a child. It didn't help that she did childish things, like throw tantrums about being scolded or bemoaning her duty. Joanne had never addressed her by her given name before today. It had taken her aback almost as much as the encouraging words.

Joanne was so integral to her success. She could barely remember how contentiously their relationship started out. Joanne had served her predecessor and been reluctant to join Khara's staff. Every day, Khara was thankful for her.

Joanne's confidence in her reminded her of her mother, who'd believed in Khara when she didn't even believe in herself. Faye Therin was taken too soon by heart disease while Khara was in her second year at university. That dull, familiar ache pulsed within at the memory of her warm smile. Not a day went by that Khara wasn't acutely aware of the Faye-shaped hole in her heart. Khara didn't want to let either woman down. She couldn't.

But sometimes she felt like a fly caught in a spider's web.

There were random times when Khara longed for someone to share her day with—perhaps over a glass of wine after a challenging week—as well as her dreams, her fears, her bed. A partnership. It was foolish to yearn for what she'd never have, yet the hope sparkled like a mirage.

She felt grateful for what she had and knew very well she had no right to complain. And still... wouldn't it be lovely to have someone hold her close while they looked up at the night sky together?

Disgusted with her unproductive musings, Khara snatched the folder up and all but stomped back inside to the conference room. Joanne glanced up at her from where she was working at her laptop on the other side of the oversized table. *Enough dragging your feet.* Khara sat and decided she wasn't doing anything else until she made a choice. *No more excuses.* This was one thing within her sphere of control today and, dammit, it was getting done.

Perhaps thinking music would help, as it often did. Khara scrolled through the varied curated playlists she kept stored on her phone to find a match for her mood. Connecting the device to the wireless speakers around the room was one of the first things Khara had done when they arrived.

An aria from a nineteenth-century opera swelled in the background as she opened the folder and slid out a small stack of photographs. When a rogue thought about the coming evening cropped up, Khara shook it off and refocused her attention. She spread the black and white photos out on the table before her. Four beautiful buildings by four talented architects, one of whom would receive an offer to design the new Lytuan embassy building. Joanne had chosen a representative sample from their respective online portfolios.

One photo commanded her attention right away, but Khara wasn't one for impulsive decisions. After studying each of the four buildings, she rearranged them for a different perspective. That same picture of an inviting four-story mixed-use building with a courtyard full of lush gardens kept drawing her eye, no matter where she situated it. This was a place Khara could easily imagine music and laughter in the air as families, friends, and colleagues gathered to celebrate milestones or holidays. It had the look and feel of a home.

The other pictures were of three different multi-family homes. One so modern it could have been part of the hotel they were in now. Another was a beautiful design but with no compelling features, it was almost soulless. The last one was interesting, with quaint landscaping around the perimeter. Doors to units were spaced far apart and adjacent to the parking area, though. Residents would hardly ever see one another.

Family was important to Lytuans, as was the sense of connection to one's community. Khara returned to the first photograph. Whoever designed this must have thought the same thing. The doors all faced the courtyard. Benches and pretty pathways abounded. Neighbors could greet one another, keep an eye on children playing, help one another garden, get together to celebrate. Why fight her gut instinct?

"This one," Khara decided, tapping a manicured fingernail against the photo. "This has passion." The label on the back was an unrecognizable jumble. "I can't read your handwriting here. What does this say?"

Joanne came to stand beside her and flipped it over with quick fingers, setting her sparkly bracelets clinking. When she squinted, Khara reminded her, "In your pocket."

"Ah, thank you, dear." Joanne extracted the reading glasses from the pocket of her peacock blue cardigan and slipped them on. "Joshua Riddick of Riddick & Sloane Architecture. I'm assuming you'd like a briefing file on him before you call, as always?"

"Yes, please." Khara took note when Joanne sat her glasses down near one of the lamps. She added Mr. Riddick's name to the afternoon's growing to-call list. "Thank you."

Joanne walked over to the far side of the conference room, where she'd set up a makeshift desk of sorts. Khara was pouring herself a new cup of tea, pondering notes she wanted to make on an upcoming university convocation speech, when Joanne returned with a folder and gave it to her. The label read *Joshua Riddick*. Khara accepted it with a chuckle. "You prepared a briefing on all four of them?"

Nodding, Joanne winked at her. "I knew you wouldn't have time to read it, so there's a summary right on top."

The neat, bulleted list of highlights and notable accomplishments clipped to the inside cover made Khara smile. "Joanne, have I mentioned how wonderful you are?"

The assistant smirked. "Not today."

Khara's full laugh rang out. "You're wonderful, and I appreciate you. I could not have gotten through these six years without you."

"I know," Joanne called over her shoulder as she left the room.

Watching her go, Khara thought of the advice the outgoing Queen imparted to her on her first day. *Keep people around you whom you can depend upon to tell you the truth, no matter how difficult it may be to hear.* Khara and Joanne didn't always agree, but nobody could ask for a better assistant.

Khara finished the email she'd been working on earlier and captured a few thoughts for the speech before turning her attention to the information Joanne brought. Preparation was the key to successful relationships and negotiations, Khara believed. Knowing what motivated someone, what kept them up at night. What put that gray in their hair. These were things Khara tried to puzzle out before meeting someone.

When the ethereal strains of the "Flower Duet" from *Lakmé* began, Khara closed her eyes to let them wash over her. Her heart lifted. It was one of her very favorites, one she always stopped to appreciate because of how light and buoyed it made her feel. This exquisite rendition by native French speakers had an incomparable lilt to it and made her think of angels singing. It was only once the piece finished that she continued her perusal.

Khara sipped while she skimmed the briefing info on Joshua Riddick. *Owner and managing partner of Riddick & Sloane Architecture. Nine years in the U.S. Army. Graduate degree from Howard University. Ran a foundation that mentored underserved students with special emphasis on youth in foster care.* She saw that Mr. Riddick's birthday was January first. New Year's babies were wonderful luck in Lytua. It was their most celebrated holiday, signifying rebirth, renewal, and liberation from past difficulties.

A quote from a recent profile article read, "I'm lucky enough to do what I love. Every Black and brown child needs to get that opportunity."

The file continued with the mission, vision, and values from the company website and an extensive list of references.

An unexpected frisson of excitement sizzled through Khara, and she froze with the teacup halfway to her mouth. She was suddenly reminded of that life-changing dream of her mother she'd had years ago. Left with a curious feeling she couldn't quite identify, she gulped and knocked the rest of her lukewarm tea back. Her hand was shaking.

Chastising herself for being silly, Khara slammed the file shut. Joshua Riddick was simply an architect she wanted to hire, no more. She hoped he lived up to the information in his file.

Chapter Two

EVEN THOUGH HE RARELY enjoyed surprises, Joshua Riddick appreciated a good prank as much as the next person. This, however, went so far beyond a prank he thought he could hear his blood pressure rising.

"Lena," he called out to his assistant. She wasn't at her desk outside his office, though, and her phone continued to jangle. Was that ringer always so annoying?

Knowing it was probably another dupe, calling in response to the prank classifieds post, seeking "another royal soul at heart," Riddick let it ring and tried to get back to the newsletter he was drafting. Crackpots of every stripe were calling to make offers to help the Nigerian prince slumming it in DC because his government mistakenly exiled him. If it wasn't such a pain in the ass, Riddick would have found it funny. As it was, he wondered how people were still falling for this outlandish scam.

The bothersome calls had started three days ago. Lena had thought it was a harmless misprint in the newspaper.

"I'm not answering anymore." His fireball of an assistant was adamant, glaring at him from the doorway to his office with her arms crossed. She'd had enough three days ago. "These people are obnoxious."

Yes, they were, and he knew he'd better get this under control, or she'd leave him. Lena's very low tolerance for bullshit was a trait they shared and the main reason they gelled so well. Riddick wasn't about to let anyone drive off the best assistant he'd ever had. "I don't blame you. Just roll all the lines over to my cell and I'll deal with it. Sorry you had to put up with this."

It would be a hassle, but he wouldn't lose her over it. It'd die down at some point if he just rode it out. He was able to get the online ad taken down with a few veiled threats and a sizable donation to the editor's favorite charity. Unethical, but he was desperate. The wording in the actual ad didn't give any clues as to who was pranking him this way.

The jig was up, though, when the young man he mentored couldn't contain himself when they met up for lunch the next day. They'd done their usual catch-up conversation over pancakes until Dion burst out with, "So, have you gotten any *royal* calls lately?"

"Royal?" Riddick sipped his coffee, calm as could be. He'd pegged his frat brothers for the culprits and was already planning to give them hell at their next function. Now the pieces were falling into place. He should have suspected the kid's mischievous streak from the beginning. "What do you mean, royal?"

Dion Wilcox sat there with his mouth hanging open until Riddick took pity on him.

"Several hundred at last count. They better not cost me my assistant, or you'll be answering my telephone after school every day until you graduate."

Dion's eyes grew wide as saucers. "Hundreds?"

"Yeah. And still coming. Lena is through."

Panic flared in Dion's eyes, distress clouding his features. For a second, it looked like he might cry. "I'm sorry. I... I just thought you'd get a few calls, and we'd laugh about it. Please don't stop mentoring me."

Riddick's irritation faded some. Dion was still so sensitive to criticism, and Riddick hated seeing the teenager shut down. He patted him on the shoulder. "Pick your head up, Dee. You hang your head for no one." Once he was looking at him again, Riddick continued. "I'm not going to stop mentoring you. Everyone, including me, has fluffed it at least a few times. No big."

"Is Lena really mad at me?"

"She's okay. More annoyed than mad. I know you didn't mean for it to get out of hand. But it did, and it's jammed our phone lines to where legit folks are having a hard time getting through. That's been rough." He decided not to add that the prank could have cost him business. The correction was only supposed to sting, not demoralize the kid.

Dion grimaced, pulled his navy jacket tighter around his thin shoulders, and mumbled something to the ground.

"One more time?" Riddick prompted.

Dion looked him in the eye and said he was sorry.

Riddick felt a sliver of pride thinking about the young man's progress. He'd been a skittish, distrustful child who wouldn't even look at him during their first few visits. He was as tall as a grown man now at fourteen. In no time, he'd probably surpass Riddick's considerable height. It was easy to forget that he was still just a kid, doing what teens do: dumb shit. "Good. The next question should be...?"

Dion pursed his lips as he thought about it. "What can I do to fix it?"

"Exactly."

Once he helped Dion draft an email to Lena, apologizing for the inconvenience he caused, their day was back on track.

Riddick declined a coffee refill with dessert but returned the flirtatious smile their favorite server aimed at him and let his gaze follow when she sashayed away.

"You should ask her out." Dion looked up from his phone long enough to observe. He was pushing an ice cube from his lemonade around his mouth. "She's cute. Been all about you for a while."

It was true, the young woman had made it clear with her body language that she was interested, and Riddick did like curvaceous women with something to hold onto. If they'd met under different circumstances, perhaps. "Maybe so. Just because a woman's interested doesn't obligate you to make a move." He had a firm no-macking rule when he and Dion were together, but he didn't tell him that part.

"The ad was funny," Riddick admitted as they left the diner and walked back to where his car was parked on the street. "People are offering some wacky stuff to get that exiled prince back on his throne."

Dion offered him a crooked smile. "Can you believe people are still falling for that sh—that stuff?"

It was such a fine line to walk—Dion needed his confidence encouraged but also needed firm guidance and boundaries. How did parents navigate this minefield every day without losing their damn minds?

On their way to the Frederick Douglass National Historic Site, Dion leafed through a well-worn copy of the statesman's first autobiography. They'd read it together in the weeks leading up to the outing. It surprised Riddick how much excitement this trip had generated. Dion held up the list of questions he planned to ask the park rangers. Such a far cry from his bitter complaints about being dragged to "crusty, dusty" museums at the start of their relationship. The two of them had struck a bargain: if Dion took part, he could have an input in deciding where they'd go. Riddick was adamant that each field trip have an educational component. Then they could do fun stuff, like the mini golf they had planned for later. Most of the fun stuff had educational elements mixed in, but Dion hadn't cottoned on to it.

The rich history was one of the things Riddick liked best about living in the DC area. There were endless excursion options of all kinds. Mini golf was Dion's chosen activity this time.

Riddick's heart swelled as he watched Dion hesitate for only a moment before approaching the docent at the end of the tour. The kid was getting much more comfortable speaking up and advocating for himself. Good for him.

By the time he dropped Dion off, Riddick was ready for a drink. Maybe two.

"How was mini golf?" The teen's foster dad was waiting for them at the front door.

Dion jerked a thumb at Riddick and snorted. "He has weird ideas about pool."

The older man turned questioning eyes to Riddick after Dion called out goodbye and jogged up the stairs into the rowhouse.

Riddick shook his head and grinned. "We argued about plane geometry and physics while we played. Pool came up."

As he always did after dropping Dion off, Riddick reviewed their day together on the way home. He tried to see things through the lens of his younger self. What would Riddick have needed or wanted when he was in similar situations? That kept the impulse to buy everything for Dion at bay. It was tempting to throw money at the problem, but Dion didn't need stuff. He needed positive male role models who would stick around. Riddick questioned himself after every meeting, even after two years paired together. Did he use the kindest words, smile enough, ask the right questions? Maintain boundaries?

Riddick stifled a groan when he turned his cell phone back on. Twenty-eight missed calls and another full voice-mail box. Even though he'd changed his outgoing greeting to say that there was no prince at this number, folks ignored it and still left messages imploring His Highness to return their calls. Ridiculous. His mailbox reached capacity several times a day, prompting him to grit his teeth and answer the phone. Offers of seed money, a place to lie low, and the "best blow job he'd ever have" came pouring in until Riddick lost his patience. Explaining the situation to the hapless callers only convinced them he *was* the prince, testing their loyalty. Hopeful candidates were calling at all hours from around the world.

He'd given up on the explaining and started hustling people off the phone. Inconvenient, sure, but in the end, not a gigantic deal. No longer upset about the prank, Riddick chuckled as he merged onto the interstate. That ad was hilarious. Dion was a clever kid.

The calls tapered off significantly by the following morning, but other disasters piled up, wreaking havoc with his schedule. Disorganization and last-minute changes annoyed Riddick, for he had a deep-seated need for order to be able to function at his best. He didn't require perfection, but he did like things neat. It didn't take a rocket scientist to figure out his crappy childhood was responsible for the desire to feel in control most of the time. Some people got stuck in their past. Riddick used his past to fuel his work.

It was well into the afternoon before Riddick found some peace to work on his latest project, the renovation of a warehouse downtown. It was being transformed into a co-located human services building, next door to a new elementary school. Part of a city initiative to increase access to supportive services for their most vulnerable residents. Riddick was all for removing barriers and doing what he could from an architectural perspective to make things easier for those who needed it. His design was full of thoughtful features like plentiful integrated seating and counter space. He'd worked closely with his favorite interior designer. The delivery date was approaching fast. He preferred to leave enough space in the timeline for the finished product to rest before the final review. He was absorbed in the task quickly.

By the time he reached a good stopping point, hours had passed, and everyone had gone home. By then, he needed to stand and stretch to loosen his back muscles. He was clearing his drafting table off, debating between making dinner or having it delivered, when his cell phone rang again. Damn, he forgot to turn it off after the last spate of calls an hour ago. Riddick rolled his shoulders and used the remote to lower the volume on the Mozart station he'd been streaming. The caller ID read the Ritz-Carlton Hotel.

Yeah, right.

He'd had enough of this shit for tonight. Riddick jabbed the button to accept the call. "Yes?"

"Oh. Good evening," a female voice responded. "I'm looking for Mr. Joshua Riddick."

Here we go again. "Who is this?"

"A potential client. I represent the government of a small island nation in—"

Riddick let out a derisive snort at the phony accent. "Not interested." Then he clicked off.

Chapter Three

K HARA INSISTED ON MAKING her own telephone calls, figuring that leaving a message when necessary was better and much more personal than having her assistant do it. Joanne would screen the return calls, certainly, but there was just something satisfying about doing the dialing herself. Plus, it tended to throw people off balance. Disrupting a rehearsed spiel gave her glimpses of how a person handled surprise, how they regrouped.

This call, she'd saved for last, even though it dominated her thoughts all afternoon. Why she was nervous about it was no mystery. She vacillated between being eager to talk to Joshua Riddick and feeling uncomfortable with that eagerness. The anticipation was disconcerting.

Khara hadn't thought of the dream in years. When she caught herself pacing, fidgeting, and tapping her pencil on the table, she reached for calm detachment to master her nerves.

The dream occurred the night Khara had decided to withdraw from the election when her confidence had been at an all-time low. Her opponent, a senator with some antiquated views, was much older than she. He was the only other candidate running after the previous Queen had stepped down to care for her ailing spouse. Khara couldn't tolerate him winning the throne by default. Fresh out of law school and a senator herself at the time, she entered the race hoping to force Senator Richardson to broaden his thinking. It hadn't been her intention to make a serious bid for the monarchy until he started being condescending to her. He'd taken her candidacy as a personal insult and ran a horrible smear campaign against her.

Home again after a debate where he'd been particularly brutal, Khara reminded herself she didn't have to do this. Perhaps she'd been hasty in believing she could make a difference. Dejected, she decided not to do anything drastic while her emotions were running so high. Everything would look more reasonable after sleeping on it.

Khara lay tossing and turning for hours with her thoughts racing. When at last she dropped off, her mother's spirit visited her. She collapsed in tears in her mother's arms, the familiar scent of her perfume bringing memories rushing back.

Rise, my dear daughter. Rise and see what is in the balance.

Khara stood astounded while Faye showed her the improvements she would make as Queen, the pathways and opportunities she would create. Beautiful new buildings would spring up around the capital city of Augustus—more schools and libraries, health care, and recreation facilities. Khara saw herself welcoming collaboration with community members, signing documents before the High Court, speaking on the floor in Parliament. Images swirled around them with dizzying speed and filled Khara with wonder. *She* would bring about all this? The sheer potential made her laugh with pure joy and fascination.

A tall figure off to the side caught Khara's attention. Something stirred deep inside, not unpleasant, but a peculiar, all-consuming pull. *Who is that?*

Her mother's hand squeezed hers, and Faye gave her a smile so radiant it made Khara's heart hurt. *Your paths are destined to cross if you have the strength to do what Lytua needs. If you are strong enough to keep fear and anger from getting the best of you now.*

The feminist in Khara balked. *I should fight because I need to find true love and live happily ever after?*

Faye Therin's smile grew. *Goodness, no. You will fight because you are the Queen Lytua must have. You need no man. Although you will love each other more than either of you thought possible. The love you share will change you both.*

Khara woke up with renewed determination. Heedless of the early hour, she called her best friend, who was acting as her campaign manager and told her she was ready to fight for her throne.

She didn't believe in superstitious twaddle, but Khara could recall with absolute clarity the pounding of her heart, the sense of rightness and belonging she experienced when she looked upon that faceless figure.

It was a dream from long ago, with no bearing on her life now. *Hokum*, she rationalized to herself. She wasn't religious, but she couldn't deny that the dream affected her deeply. Surely, she didn't really believe she'd meet this shadowy man one day. All this time she thought of the dream as a metaphor, her subconscious giving her extra motivation to get through a difficult time. Not an actual man.

Then why was she so unsettled about making this call?

A glance at the suite's ornate wall clock urged her to stop procrastinating. Joanne would cluck at her like a mother hen in forty-five minutes to tell her it was time to get ready for the ball. *Just like Cinderella*, Khara thought as she stabbed at the phone's buttons. Enough stalling. She was thirty-two years old and would fear no man, whether or not he might have been part of a dream that changed her entire professional trajectory. What did a man in a dream mean, anyway? Nothing.

"Yes?" A deep voice snapped into the phone on the fourth ring, surprising her.

"Oh. Good evening. I'm looking for Mr. Joshua Riddick."

"Who is this?"

"A potential client. I represent the government of a small island nation in—"

"Not interested." *Click.*

Khara looked at the phone receiver in confusion, then re-dialed. The same voice answered, this time right away.

"Look, lady, I told you—"

"*Excuse* me, sir," she cut in. "I will ask you to do me the courtesy of actually hearing my proposal before hanging up on me. That was unforgivably rude."

Silence, followed by a heavy sigh. "Go ahead, then."

"Am I speaking to one Mr. Joshua Riddick?" What was that metallic-sounding clinking in the background?

"It's just Riddick, but yes, you are."

"As I tried to say a moment ago, I represent the government of a small island nation in the Caribbean. We wish to engage your services for an upcoming project."

"Which services are those? You'll have to be more specific."

Now Khara sighed and muttered something uncharitable in Lytuan. "This was obviously a mistake—"

"Wait," Mr. Riddick said, his tone losing some of its abrasive edge. "You've got me. I apologize, it's been a long day in a week of long days. How can I help you, Ms.—?"

"Therin," she supplied.

"Ms. Therin. How can I help you, Ms. Therin?"

"If you're going to continue to be insufferable, we should end this call here."

"Hmm. No, we're good." The sound of his low harrumph zinged right up her spine. "So, what've you got?"

Khara made the mistake of wondering what Mr. Riddick looked like, and her face heated. She gritted her teeth, smoothed a palm down over her thigh. It was a dream. Nothing more. "The lease will be expiring on the building where our embassy is currently housed. We believe it makes more sense to build a new modern one rather than to renew. One that the government will own. We've already purchased a plot of land."

"Smart. Where?"

"In Georgetown."

"You found land to buy in Georgetown?"

A light laugh escaped Khara at his awestruck tone. "Oh, no, that's in Arlington. The current embassy is located in Georgetown. It's quite beautiful, but it does get crowded, and the parking is—"

"Atrocious?"

"Ah, so you've been there."

"A time or two. You should see it in the summer."

"Let me guess. Overrun with tourists?" A smile was tugging at her lips.

"Packed in like sardines." His deep laugh was infectious. "Even Sequoia isn't worth wading through that, and I love Sequoia."

It was on the tip of Khara's tongue to let him know she, too, loved the waterside eatery. She just barely stopped herself. How on earth were they talking about a restaurant?

"Alright, so besides the crowds and the parking, what else isn't working with your current setup?"

Puzzled, Khara paused in sliding her pearl pendant back and forth along its silver chain. "You wish to know what we dislike? Not what we envision for the new building?"

"Eventually. Your current concerns tell me what issues I'd want to address in a new design. Like if you said you'd always hated how dark the lobby is, I'd be sure to incorporate lots of natural light."

"Ah, that's quite brilliant. And I don't believe one can ever have too much natural light."

"You see? We're on the same page already. Now tell me what gets on your nerves."

Khara didn't spend a great deal of time at the Lytuan embassy, but she shared what she remembered from conversations with the Ambassador and her staff. Before she knew it, twenty minutes passed. "Are you available to come by tomorrow morning at nine to discuss the project in-depth?"

"I am."

"Marvelous. Let me get the address for you."

"The Ritz-Carlton? No worries, I know it."

How? Khara almost blurted the question. Unwelcome visuals of a handsome, dark-skinned man lying naked in bed at the Ritz-Carlton flooded her imagination, alarming Khara with the heat that spread through her. What was going on with her? She had to get off this phone. "Wonderful. Well, we'll see you tomorrow morning, then. Thank—"

"Wait. Who should I ask for?"

His voice made her think of a rich, full-bodied merlot and the most decadent chocolate. Her mouth was dry. "You'll be met in the lobby and receive further details there, Mr. Riddick. Goodbye."

Khara clicked off and found herself flustered and frowning. She couldn't even remember the last time someone hung up on her. For someone with a reputation for generosity, Joshua Riddick sounded downright curmudgeonly at first. Or did it just seem that way because *she* was unnerved? Heavens, was she blushing?

To be fair, he said it had been a long day. Goodness knows, she'd had more than her share of long days and must sound out of sorts on occasion herself. The rest of their unusual conversation was... surprisingly pleasant. And she'd be seeing him tomorrow, though she wasn't entirely sure how she felt about that. Even after that powerful reaction to reading his file, she hadn't expected to enjoy herself.

Khara blew out a breath and broke into a smile when she glanced at her watch. She'd have just enough time for a cup of tea and a chapter of the thriller she was reading. Things might be looking up.

If luck was with her tonight, she'd be able to avoid the Speaker's son altogether. Then an answer came to her. She could mention feeling a headache coming on when she arrived, then it wouldn't be a surprise when she needed to leave early. Perfect. She could live with that. Even Joanne wouldn't fault her for that one.

Riddick had more questions, but the prickly Ms. Therin was gone, having rushed him off the phone. What just happened? A vague feeling of guilt seeped into him. He was used to hush-hush requests with short turnaround times from people who preferred to stay low-key. It was the DC area, after all. Politicians, lobbyists, diplomats, and wealthy people with more money than taste—or common sense—made all sorts of bizarre requests.

The cultured, softly accented female voice he'd just spoken to threw Riddick for a loop. There was an imperiousness in the lilting accent that caused Riddick to pause in cleaning up his drafting tools. She was ever so slightly bossy, as though she were used to being in charge. Like she had every expectation of her wishes being carried out or her orders obeyed. That came from wielding true authority. Well, she did say foreign government.

Riddick liked that she called him out on being a dick. It took balls to call him back to do so. He deserved that. There was some fearlessness there. Some steel in that spine. The woman still sounded put out, even after he apologized, but her accent sure was sexy as hell.

He imagined her saying his name under different circumstances. Was she bossy in bed? That could be fun. Jeez, Riddick thought, interrupting that train of thought before it got him in trouble.

The call stayed on his mind as he locked up the office, grabbed his jacket from the mahogany coat rack and headed down to his car.

She wasn't a native English speaker—the careful way she'd placed her words was a dead giveaway. Then she'd muttered under her breath in a language he didn't recognize. And what did he do? Acted like a smartass, Riddick thought with some remorse. Not cool. Getting off on the wrong foot with a potential client could damage the reputation he'd worked so hard to cultivate. He'd smooth things over tomorrow.

Riddick couldn't stop thinking about that voice, even much later listening to the distinctive twang of John Lee Hooker's guitar as he whipped up a quick dinner of pasta and vegetables. If this was some kind of setup, he was going to be pissed.

Chapter Four

R IDDICK COULD STILL SPOT a cop. Everything about the tall, stern-looking woman who approached him in the hotel lobby the next morning screamed law enforcement. Wearing glasses and a tailored pantsuit, she tagged him right away, even though he was almost an hour early. He was unsure what the traffic or Metro would be like on the overcast September morning. Anytime weather was a factor, he built in plenty of travel time. He ended up arriving far sooner than he'd expected. After he'd parked in the hotel garage, he faced two choices—he could either stall or just go in early. It made little sense to wait in the car, looking suspicious, like he might be "casing the joint". Riddick grabbed his work bag and went inside.

"Mr. Riddick. This way, please," she spoke with the same accent as Ms. Therin.

The woman led Riddick to a small conference room and invited him to sit. "Your appointment is with the head of the Lytuan government, Queen Lillianna. Before we can bring you to meet with her, we need to explain a few protocols."

Riddick listened to the long list of protocols.

"Do you have any questions before we continue?"

The woman folded her hands on the table in front of her and looked at him expectantly. Her hair was very short, with light brown highlights. With her bone structure and confidence, the look didn't seem as severe. She was working it.

"Just one." Riddick rested his ankle on his other knee. "Am I being punked?"

She frowned. "No, Mr. Riddick. Certainly not."

"This is disturbingly mysterious," he mused.

"We take our Queen's safety seriously."

"Of course. And you would be...?"

"Cenn."

"Just one name, like Prince or Madonna?"

She didn't crack a smile. Or give a surname. Riddick cleared his throat. "Right. Sorry, go on." He'd worked with royals before, and they were some of his least favorite client interactions. Most were pretentious and typically fell into one of two categories: the "more is more" crowd and the "even *more* is more" crowd. Honestly, they were more trouble than they were worth. Many wanted over-the-top monstrosities to showcase their wealth and status. Riddick wanted no part of that. He didn't do gaudy, no matter how much the job paid. His firm was in a position where they could turn down requests, and he didn't take that for granted.

"I've never heard of Lytua."

"Most people haven't. We're quite insular. Lytua is a long, narrow island situated in the Atlantic, but considered part of the Caribbean."

"Ah, like Bermuda."

"Yes, similar to Bermuda."

Once he'd agreed to follow the protocols, including signing a standard non-disclosure agreement, Cenn escorted Riddick up to a lavish conference room and instructed him to wait. Queen Lillianna would be with him shortly.

How long had single-name Cenn been waiting for him, and how did she recognize him?

As far as he could tell, there were at least two ways this could play out. This "meeting" could be an elaborate part of the prank. But the woman on the phone used his full name, whereas the ad didn't list a point of contact. It could be completely legit. Or he could wake up in a tub of ice, with a missing kidney. Riddick was pretty sure that was an urban legend, but he didn't want to risk his organs to find out. Then again, who would run a body parts black market scheme from the Ritz-Carlton?

Choosing to sit by the window instead of the table, Riddick set his messenger bag down and fished out his laptop, thinking he'd immerse himself in responding to emails to kill time. They were on the twentieth floor, and the view was spectacular. Fog still partially obscured the city streets, but downtown was bustling.

He looked up when a woman backed into the room from the far side. She was humming a cheerful tune, a coffee mug in one hand and a stack of files in the other. A half-eaten bagel perched on top. She was oblivious to his presence, absorbed in the task of sorting through the files. Still humming, she leaned over the table and took a sip from her mug. Ah, this must be the Queen's assistant. Assistants were the best—influential and often more knowledgeable than the identified client. They set the tone, even as they toiled away in under-appreciated roles.

Riddick studied the woman—pretty in a ruby-colored blouse and gray skirt. Her skin was a lovely shade of brown, somewhere between desert sand and bronze. Understated jewelry, what looked to be curly hair pinned back into a no-nonsense chignon. He watched her take a dainty bite of the bagel, then balance the uneaten part back on top of the mug. Shapely calves, he noted. Nice curvy hips and ass, too. Meat on her bones, just the way he liked. Curiously, the woman wasn't wearing any shoes. She startled badly when Riddick said hello and sloshed hot coffee over her hand. He hurried over when she gave a cry of pain.

"Here," he said, taking the mug from her and sitting it on the table. "I'm sorry. I didn't mean to startle you. Are you alright?"

He took her hand in both of his to examine her thumb and wrist. Before she could say anything, he'd grabbed a napkin from the sideboard and was drying her hand with gentle dabs.

The woman looked up at him with wide eyes. "Oh, Mr. Riddick. You're quite early."

Her eyes were arresting—a soft hazel, framed with long lashes.

"Guilty. I'm guessing I caught you setting up. Ms. Therin, right?" He'd recognize that sexy voice anywhere. The woman matched the voice. *Shit*. What was with him today?

She nodded and pulled her hand free. "I'm fine, thank you."

He retrieved the bagel from where it had fallen on the floor in the hubbub.

"And I ruined your breakfast, too. Sorry about that." He chucked it into the nearby wastebasket.

She was staring at him, unmoving. Then she seemed to shake herself.

"Don't give it another thought. Please have a seat. May I offer you some coffee?"

"After I made you scald yourself? Hardly. You sure you're alright?"

"I am, yes, thank you."

He took another look at her hand. Her skin was already turning red. "This may need burn cream if you have any."

Her hand was small in his. Standing next to her this way, he couldn't help but notice how he was damn near towering over her. This woman didn't seem intimidated, though. Or if she was, she didn't show it. As the Queen's gatekeeper, she must be used to staring all kinds of people down, from the merely curious to the overzealous. She was giving off the vibe of someone who could hold her own in any battle of wits.

When she tugged her hand out of his for the second time, he almost held on.

Chapter Five

Mr. Riddick's unexpected touch sent a thrill skittering up Khara's spine, but it was quickly overshadowed by a sense of befuddlement. No one just *touched* her—it was an enormous breach of decorum. It just wasn't done. It would scandalize Joanne. She wasn't even fully dressed. Jaden, the head of her six-person personal security detail—the Elite Guard—would have been furious and would likely have tackled him.

Did he not know? Had he not been briefed? Khara dismissed those thoughts immediately, knowing Cenn was a stickler for observing the formalities. Not even on her worst day would she forget to communicate the protocols to a visitor. What was going on? She could only conclude that it was an oversight. No harm done, though. She'd blundered her way through many a faux pas of her own and would never purposely embarrass someone for a mistake. Khara let it go and offered a magnanimous smile.

He was almost a foot taller than her in her stocking-clad feet, had to be at least six-two or three. She'd planned to sit down with the files for a few minutes to organize them, then go put on her blazer and pumps right after. Well, she couldn't very well leave to get them now. "As we weren't expecting you so soon, Mr. Riddick, I must ask you to kindly excuse my disarrayed state." She'd just carry on as though this were nothing out of the ordinary.

"No problem. You do have me at a bit of a disadvantage, though."

"How so?" His well-defined lips demanded her attention.

"You know my full name, but I don't know yours."

Was he...*flirting* with her? Gracious. She offered her hand. "I'm Khara, Mr. Riddick."

A zing of awareness fired through her when their hands touched. *Finally*, some part of her breathed. An otherworldly sense of déjà vu struck Khara, as though her soul recognized him, which was preposterous. She was positive she'd never met the man. Last night's dream making her feel off-kilter was surely to blame.

"It's a pleasure to meet you, Khara Therin. I'm sorry about the misunderstanding on the phone."

At this, Khara raised an eyebrow. "'Misunderstanding?'"

"I was an ass," he conceded. "There you were just trying to do your job and set up an appointment for the Queen."

"For the Queen," she echoed, thrown. *What on Earth?*

She watched as he collected his belongings from the chair by the window. Joshua Riddick had the most beautiful dark skin, rich brown like the Bermuda cedars she'd fallen in love with on a trip there. Her imagination hadn't done him any justice, Khara thought, as they sat across from one another at the expansive marble table.

"A good assistant is worth their weight in gold. Truly invaluable. I didn't mean to make things difficult for you."

Khara shook her head. "I'm sorry, Mr. Riddick, I believe you have me confused with my assistant, Joanne." Come to think of it, where was Joanne? She always received the visitors.

"Ah, I see. You have your own assistant. I bet between the two of you, the Queen's operations run as smooth as glass."

She was poised to correct him when the gravity of the situation sunk in. He had no idea *she* was the Queen. It was the only plausible explanation.

Khara cleared her throat and decided to test the theory. "As I said, the Queen wasn't expecting you so soon. And as she's currently engaged, how about I...." Her heart thudded when he smiled at her. Goodness, but he had a pleasant smile. "Ah... get you situated until she's ready? I can try to answer some of your questions in the meantime." Reflexively, Khara checked that her scar was covered. She was noticing everything, like the faint laugh lines around his mouth and eyes. And didn't he just have the nerve to smell good too? His woodsy fragrance was spicy, crisp, and understated. No wedding ring, either. *Get it together, girl,* she admonished herself.

"I'd like that," Mr. Riddick said. "Gives me a chance to redeem myself."

Mr. Riddick's face was striking—a high, noble forehead and broad cheekbones. Framed by thin locs that brushed his collar. He gave the distinct impression of a man who worked hard and was not to be trifled with. It was accompanied by an unexpected hint of vulnerability in those dark eyes.

Khara scrambled to marshal her thoughts. She was supposed to be hiring an architect for the new embassy building, not drooling over the architect. Oh, there were more handsome men somewhere, she supposed, but something about *this* man's undeniable masculinity made all of her sit up and take notice. Blood started rushing to places it hadn't rushed to in a while.

The broad shoulders and muscular frame were evident in the well-cut three-piece suit of slate gray. She knew enough about fashion to know the suit had not come off any rack. He seemed at ease in it, whereas she'd seen plenty of men who looked like the suit was wearing *them.* This was a man who dressed well on a regular basis, a characteristic Khara appreciated. The measured confidence he carried himself with was right there—unmistakable and unapologetic. He was what he was, and that was *fine.* All full, sculpted lips and glorious chestnut complexion. Why did she have the sudden urge to crawl into this man's lap and get her... *well.*

His velvety voice interrupted her libidinous thoughts. Khara suppressed a shiver. "Have you been cooped up in here with meeting after meeting?"

Yes, small talk. That she could do. "Endless meetings."

"Have you gotten to see any of the city?"

"Not yet. There hasn't been time."

"She doesn't give you any time off?"

"Who?"

"The Queen."

"Oh, yes, of course, she does. I just worry about keeping everything in order. Let me just, ah—" *Stay in character*, she reminded herself as she pulled out her phone to turn it off. There was Cenn's text advising her and Joanne that Mr. Riddick had arrived early and was waiting for her in the conference room. As was her new habit once she had her schedule set for the morning, she'd turned off the notifications since she didn't want them to interrupt her thoughts. She was trying to curb her addiction to her smartphone.

When she'd gone into the conference room, Khara's mind had been on the email she was drafting to the Speaker's son, who'd sent an apology for missing his mother's dinner last night. What a surprise Mr. Riddick's sonorous voice had been, setting her heart pounding hard.

"How did you hear about us?" the beautiful man asked. "Riddick and Sloane don't advertise, and I'd like to know whom to thank." Those locs were sexy on him, too. Soft-looking. They beckoned her fingers.

It took her brain a second to catch up. Her heart was hammering. "We reached out to a local contact at Howard University. A Dr. Jackson recommended you." When her attention wandered again, this time to admire those long, thick fingers, Khara all but leaped to her feet and took her time at the sideboard. She must need more coffee, obviously. Yes, that must be it. Lord, her face felt hot. "We support Black-owned businesses as often as we can. Veteran-owned, as well."

"Thank you for that."

It was rude to give him her back, she knew, but Khara needed a second to get herself under control. What was going on with her? Why was she reacting this way? Because the man was *gorgeous*, that's why, she answered herself. She could feel a trickle of sweat along her hairline. A quick steadying breath and a reminder that she'd dealt with many good-looking men without losing it bolstered her.

She turned to face her visitor, smiled, and sat her ass down with a fresh cup of coffee.

A minute later, the door to the conference room burst open and Joanne spilled in, out of breath as though she'd run there as fast as her kitten heels would carry her. "*I'm so sorry!*" She stopped short, seeing the two of them already in discussion. "*So sorry. I didn't see Cenn's text. I didn't know he was here until just now.*"

"*Everything is under control here, Joanne,*" Khara answered the older woman in Lytuan. "*We're fine.*"

Joanne's bright eyes swung between the two of them as she switched to English. "Ah, then I'll just see myself out. Excuse me for interrupting." She beat a hasty retreat and closed the door behind her.

Riddick must have understood the distressed tone. "Is she okay?"

"Yes. Just flustered." *Like me.*

"What language was that?"

"It was Lytuan, the language of our island."

"It was beautiful. Melodic almost. So, back to business. Tell me more about this project. Now let's hear what the Queen is looking for."

Time evaporated as they spoke about the new embassy building the Kingdom of Lytua was commissioning. The small community of Lytuan ex-pats in the DC area would be growing soon, as several multinational collaborations in medical research were in the pipeline. "In short, we are in need of a better base of operations."

Riddick listened attentively, jotting in a spiral-bound notebook. He summarized as they talked, clarifying a few points along the way. Khara was fascinated by his tidy notetaking. "Forgive my intrusiveness, but I can't help but notice you don't use your laptop to take notes." It mystified Khara.

"I used to." Riddick sat his pen down and stretched his fingers out before him. "I used to be obsessed with typing every single word, until I forgot the thing one morning before a big meeting. It ended up being one of the best meetings I ever had."

Khara cocked her head and wrapped both hands around her coffee cup. "How so?"

"Surprisingly, it was much more productive with a conversational style. I stayed tuned in to the moment instead of being focused on my furious typing. Game-changer. Haven't used my laptop in a meeting since. I just type my notes up at the end of each meeting, while everything is still fresh."

"You may be onto something there." Khara nodded in agreement. "Not competing with the clacking of a keyboard has been refreshing, I must say."

Khara pretended to check her phone. "My apologies, Mr. Riddick. It looks as though the Queen hasn't been able to shake loose. I don't want to take up any more of your valuable time. I'll review our discussion with her later and follow up if there are questions."

"Great, thank you. I'm available any time." Riddick closed his notebook and packed it away, along with the unopened laptop. "I enjoyed talking to you, Ms. Therin."

"Khara, please, and likewise."

"If I call you Khara, then you'll just call me Riddick? None of that Mister stuff."

"As you wish... *Riddick.*"

"Again, I'm sorry about the phone call. Let me change gears now that we've gotten the business out of the way. Are you free for dinner tonight?"

Khara paused in gathering her materials together. "You'd like to talk more about the project?"

"No, not at all."

Her brow furrowed. "I don't understand."

"I'd like to take you to dinner."

Khara's mouth popped open. She couldn't speak right away. Those dark eyes of his were so intense. "You're... asking me out?"

"Yes, I am."

He was all business during their meeting while she was busy trying to keep inopportune daydreams at bay. Now he was turning on the charm, and honestly, she was here for it. It had been a long time since an attractive man showed genuine interest in her. She wasn't about to just fall into his arms, though. "Is this because you were an ass last night?"

"No. Well, maybe a little. But mostly because you're the most interesting woman I've met in a long time."

Khara could only stare, wide-eyed. She felt something happening to her ovaries.

When she hesitated, Riddick blew out a breath. "Damn. Are you married? In a relationship? I should've asked first."

"I'm single." She twisted her fingers together to stop them from trembling.

"Not sure how that's even possible. You have a lovely smile. I'd like to see more of it."

He was definitely flirting with her! *Oh, my.* Her heart rate kicked up to a gallop. "Thank you."

"Interested?"

"Maybe."

"What will it take to get you to a 'yes'?"

"What's the first thing you did this morning?"

"*That* will get you to go to dinner with me?"

That smile again. Lethal. Mercy, he could have been in a toothpaste commercial. She'd buy two of whatever he was selling. "Maybe."

"Tough crowd. Okay, I'll play. The first thing I did this morning was go to the gym, like most mornings."

"Oh, God, are you a morning person?" The horrified question popped out before she could stop it. *Drat.* Her brain could not seem to function well around this man.

Riddick laughed, and the chocolaty sound tingled right through her. "Not at all. But too much can happen during the day to throw off my gym time if I try to do it later. Best to do it first. What about you?"

"I have an intense dislike for mornings."

"A-ha, a card-carrying morning hater. So, the first thing you did was hit the snooze button, then?"

"Something like that."

He laughed again. "Duly noted. And after that?"

"Coffee. A very large cup of strong coffee in silence."

"Why silence?"

"It's very rare to get quiet time to myself during the day."

"Ah, so you fill up on it first thing."

"Yes, that's it."

"So, dinner? Did I pass?"

"I'd love to have dinner with you."

The grin he gave her made her stomach feel jittery. Had she just gotten out of her own way to flirt successfully? She barely suppressed a fist pump.

They exchanged telephone numbers and agreed on a meeting time. He'd text her about the location later, after he made reservations. Khara only remembered she still had no shoes on when she rose to walk him out. Too late now. She was laughing as she opened the door. Cenn was there, ready to escort him back to the lobby. It was a good thing Cenn was experienced enough to keep any surprise off her face, for Khara knew the sight of her smiling, laughing, and telling a man that she'd see him at seven was unusual. She was probably wondering where her shoes were, too.

Khara closed the door behind them and did a happy little victory dance. She had a date. Now, to just get through the rest of this day....

Maybe, just maybe, she could pull this off.

Khara was busy signing paperwork for Joanne when the head of her six-person personal security detail—the Elite Guard—came in a few minutes later to ask how the meeting went.

"Very well," Khara said. "He asked excellent questions. We'll hire him for the project once we see to the details."

"That's great news."

"And we're going out to dinner tonight."

Both Jaden and Joanne froze at this casual announcement. Joanne was the first to recover. "A date?"

Khara smiled and nodded. "A date," she confirmed.

Joanne beamed at her. "Good on you!"

Khara continued signing documents but felt Jaden's gaze on her. Besides acting as the Captain of her Elites, Jaden Everly was a friend since childhood. It was his job to be suspicious. He was protective and perceptive and was probably already looking at all the angles. "He mistook me for Joanne, thinks I'm the Queen's assistant. I didn't correct him. I know what you're thinking. But this is just a date. Harmless fun."

Jaden crossed his arms over his broad chest, biceps bulging against the fabric of his dark suit jacket. He was around the same height as Riddick and heart-breakingly handsome, too, with his neatly trimmed beard and mustache. Once upon a time, Khara had a difficult time functioning around him. Then again, he'd been her first crush, even though he'd only ever thought of her as the pesky little sister he never had. She'd take that bit of knowledge to the grave.

"So, you didn't notice Mr. Riddick was muscular and good-looking? Because that's not harmless." Jaden arched a questioning eyebrow at her.

"He *is* good-looking, isn't he?"

"Yes, he is," Joanne chimed in under her breath, earning a conspiratorial smile from Khara and a scowl from Jaden.

"I'm serious, *Avlah*."

Even after all this time, the affectionate honorific of *Avlah*—exalted Queen—still humbled her. "I know. Let me have this, Jaden. It's not like I'm going to fall in love with him."

"Famous last words. I seem to remember saying something similar about Aimee."

"That's true, you did. The next thing any of us knew, you were skipping to the altar. How is she feeling, by the way? Still having morning sickness?"

His features softened a fraction. "Yes. Not as bad as with Dorian, but don't change the subject. I don't like this."

"Understood."

Jaden left her to the paperwork.

Khara glanced out the window to see the sun hadn't burned the morning fog off. It made her long for the perfect beach weather of home.

The overwhelming urge to do another little victory dance hit her. Where would they go? What on earth was she going to wear?

Chapter Six

THEY WERE A FEW minutes into their conversation when Riddick decided he was going to ask Khara out. It pleased him that the Queen wasn't able to meet. It gave him more time with Khara and more time to figure out how he could ask her out without sounding like a creep. She probably got hit on all the time, but she'd seemed pleased—surprised, even—when he'd made his move. Had he seen a moment of uncertainty flash in her eyes?

Riddick left the fancy hotel in good spirits. A successful meeting and a date with an alluring island girl? Score and score. As soon as Khara spoke, he wished he hadn't stuck his foot in his mouth the night before. That imperious tone of voice was there again. Steel drums and turquoise waves sounded in her accent. Hot sand, sun-soaked days. He liked her sass, that she didn't let him off the hook right away for his poor behavior. He would have been less gracious if the roles were reversed. Riddick made a mental note to explain the prank.

He was so deep in thought he got to his office garage on autopilot. "Still think the Nats are going all the way this year?" Riddick asked the baseball-loving parking attendant when he stepped out of his car. They spent a few moments shooting the shit about the hometown team's chances of getting into the playoffs, both optimistic.

A stop at the desk of the building information clerk got him the latest on how the planning for her son's wedding was going. Her station was in the very center of the building's airy atrium, where she could monitor lobby traffic. Unable to resist the divine smells coming from the cafe, Riddick scooped up a couple of orange cranberry muffins and left a generous tip, as he always did, for the college student barista. He remembered what it was like to be a starving college student.

The view from the elevator never failed to lift his spirits. Trailing plants lined the low balcony-style walls around each level, creating a curtain-like effect of greenery. It was one thing that attracted him when they were scouting for a bigger office. Up on the sixteenth floor, where Riddick & Sloane occupied the entire space, the young fill-in receptionist stammered a hello in response to his cheery greeting. He pretended not to notice when she knocked over her pencil cup. Their regular receptionist went on maternity leave two weeks early, and they hadn't found her long-term fill-in yet.

Relief filled him when he saw Lena back on duty at her desk outside his office. He was cautious when he greeted her. Braced himself. She must have read the prank call question on his face, for she shook her head and told him, "Just a few more this morning. I told Dion I accept his apology."

The smidgen of tension in Riddick's shoulders eased. "How's Nick doing at rehearsals?" He asked as he sorted through the stack of mail waiting for him. "Is he loving his first big role? I still can't believe he's in tenth grade already."

His no-nonsense assistant shot him a megawatt smile at the mention of her son. "He's rehearsing all the time. Going method on us. I certainly wouldn't be mad if I never hear that 'Emerald City Sequence' again."

"He's a good egg. It'll be great seeing him shine again, and I love seeing you and Sophie in full stage-mom mode. Brought you a muffin." Riddick sat the white bakery bag on the corner of her desk.

Lena peered at him over the tops of her cat-eye glasses. "You're buttering me up."

"Shamelessly. Would you kindly make a dinner reservation for me? It's short notice, but I know you can work magic."

"Ha, make threats is more like it." Lena picked up a lime green sticky note and pencil. "And what miracle will you be needing today?"

"Tonight, at seven, for two. Someplace on the upscale side, but not like I'm trying too hard. Romantic, but not in-your-face about it."

Her eyebrows shot up.

"She's from out of town, and I don't have a clue what she likes to eat. Someplace fun."

Lena's gaze went to the ceiling as she pondered. "Sounds like a job for Georgia Brown's. I'll see to it."

"Perfect. Thanks, Lena. You really are the best. Will you also get me an appointment with the staffing agency? We need a more permanent receptionist solution."

The corner of Lena's mouth twitched as she tried not to laugh. "Good gravy, is that poor girl still dropping stuff every time she sees you? I swear, you make her so nervous she can hardly get your name out when she answers the phone. I'll set something up."

"Hey, don't blame it on me. I'm not doing anything special." Despite his best efforts to put her at ease, the temp couldn't even look him in the eye. "Got a question for you. Am I misremembering, or was it really tedious dealing with those royals for that project?"

Lena made a face and gave an exaggerated shudder. "The one where the snooty Prince snapped his fingers and tried to order me around like a servant? He totally deserved the earful you gave him."

Riddick had forgotten about that dude. Sheesh.

"The assistant smoothed things over when Prince High-and-Mighty threatened to press charges. Killed me with that long-suffering, 'It won't look good for the Queen if you try to have an American arrested for objecting to how you spoke to his secretary. First Amendment and all that.' He even winked at me when he said it."

Now Riddick remembered. "That was a whole scene. But I was actually thinking of that King who kept insisting on all those weird, over-the-top features. Like his face sculpted into the bathroom walls."

"Yes, the vacation home reno for the precious son's wedding gift. I doubt anyone ever told him no before. I'll never forget when that King called you a short-sighted peasant for not bowing down to his hideous design, you just looked him dead in the eye and said—" In a perfect imitation of his voice, Lena intoned, "'*I might be a short-sighted peasant, sir, but I don't need tacky monuments to convince everyone my dick is bigger than it is.*' I still can't believe you said that. It was epic. The King looked like he was going to have a stroke."

"The Queen thought it was funny, though. She seemed like the only halfway decent one among them. The rest were condescending as hell to their staff. Or am I remembering it wrong?"

"Oh, no, they were completely obnoxious. The poor put-upon assistants were the only ones who had a clue about anything. Just trying to keep the peace, smooth the ruffled feathers. I wanted to stage a revolution. The royals just wanted everyone to make a fuss and roll over for whatever they wanted. So full of hot air. I doubt they're paid nearly enough to put up with all the bullshit shenanigans. What makes you ask?"

Riddick was quiet as he considered how much to disclose about the morning's appointment. The build Lytua was requesting was pretty modest—no ridiculous flourishes. The staff he'd met hadn't seemed downtrodden or unappreciated. Khara had been positively... luminous. No affectation or inordinate swagger that came with knowing their employer had clout. "We might have another one, but they seem a lot more reasonable and down to earth in what they're asking for. Once again, it's the assistant who's on top of things. We'll see how it goes."

Lena cocked her head. Maybe picking up on something in his voice he hadn't intended to reveal. At times, she was far too perceptive with her employer. He felt exposed.

"Anyway, let me dive in." Riddick started toward his office, then turned and walked backward so he could call out, "Don't let me forget graduation and wedding presents for Norma and Jesse."

Eyes full of good humor, Lena wagged a finger in his direction. "Don't let it go to your head, mister, but I love having a boss who celebrates things like the building supervisor's daughter finishing dental school."

"You taught me well."

"Nice try, but that's all you."

After spending years parked at desks in dreary, unimaginative surroundings, Riddick had taken pains to make his workspace match his flow. He needed options for whatever the task at hand required. If he needed to read, he tended to use the sitting area with its cushy sofa and chairs. Informal meetings he took at a small round conference table. With his drafting table and desk parallel to the two walls of windows, he made the most of the view without having his back to the room. Years ago, he'd made the mistake of saying something to Lena about the possibility of adding some greenery. A mind-boggling number of potted plants and ornamental trees appeared soon thereafter. The effect was oasis-like and exactly what he didn't know he needed.

Riddick got settled and tried to get on with the morning's work, but all he could think about was one Khara Therin. From the moment he'd heard her voice, it intrigued him. Seeing how poised and beautiful she was just added to the unexpected attraction.

Could she have been any more charming with asking about what he did first thing in the morning? She'd sounded appalled at the thought of him being a morning person.

Riddick chuckled to himself. After sending Khara a text with the name and address of Georgia Brown's, he set a reminder on his calendar to leave on time. It was something he hadn't paid attention to in years. Maybe he'd slip out early to get an edge up and shave before heading home.

He called his favorite barber and made an appointment.

Chapter Seven

WELL, THAT MAN WAS anything but harmless, Jaden thought, remembering Khara's words. He called a team meeting once Khara told him where they'd be going to dinner. He was the first one to the conference room.

The rest of the Queen's Elite Guard trickled in, taking their seats around the big table in their temporary command center. Jaden watched the three women and two men and reflected on how, for better and sometimes for worse, they were a family. There were quirks, pet peeves, and bickering, but their unit was tight, as a good team should be. They'd worked together in some combination for almost ten years. There was no one he'd rather have at his back or safeguarding their leader.

Their own families were part of a larger tapestry now. The entire team had fallen in love and gotten married within the last few years, himself included. The circle grew with spouses and children. Partying had easily given way to playdates and barbecues. They were interwoven into each other's lives, and he wouldn't have it any other way.

But their *Avlah* was alone. She didn't complain about being lonely. In fact, she loved the Elites' families like they were her own. But was it enough? *Was* she lonely? Jaden considered his home life. That sweetness he felt when his young son threw his arms around him in greeting when he came in the door. The way his wife searched his entire face for clues to where his head was. He wished the same for everyone. Connection, devotion. Was this Khara's time, her chance? Maybe instead of officiating over a wedding, she'd have one herself?

He and Khara had known each other most of their lives, as their mothers had been good friends. Just three years apart, they'd always been close—squabbling like siblings as they'd grown up and gone to school together. They'd taken turns comforting each other in their grief over the deaths of loved ones. Jaden had been the first person Khara confided in when she thought of running for election.

Jaden sighed, weighing duty against friendship. Didn't Khara deserve a chance at having some "normal" time? Companionship? It was easy to forget that she was a single woman when she worked so tirelessly in her duties as Queen. The press enthusiastically deemed her as being married to her work. Jaden had doubts about it being a good thing. She needed restorative downtime just like everybody else, though it was rare she took it.

It's just a date. When was the last time she'd even *been* on a date? Maybe she'd be daring and sow her wild oats. But the deception....

He had a strict moral code, and that black and white thinking had almost alienated the love of his life.

One thing was for certain: if this Mr. Riddick was a wolf in disguise, there was going to be trouble. He'd better be nothing but the real deal. Jaden never wanted to see such complete devastation in Khara's eyes again, as he had when that dumbass fiancé broke things off. He still couldn't think of that fool without wanting to flatten him. How Khara managed to be civil when he was in her presence was beyond him.

It took Jaden a moment to realize that everyone was waiting for him. Notebooks open at the ready, coffee and teacups nudged aside. He'd gotten lost in his thoughts—all broody, as his wife would say. Might as well cut right to the chase, no matter his misgivings.

"Heads up, folks, we have a unique situation here. Our *Avlah* is going on a date this evening with Mr. Riddick."

The table was full of smiles, murmurs, nods, and general surprise.

"Mr. Riddick doesn't know *Avlah* is the Queen, and she has requested it stay that way. Apparently, he thinks *Avlah* is the Queen's assistant. It will make things a little more challenging for us, but nothing we can't handle. Let's set her up for success."

More murmurs.

"Cenn, you met him. Impressions?"

Cenn considered this before answering. It was a trait of hers he admired. She'd been judicious with her words the entire time they'd worked together. As usual, she was flipping one of her ever-present throwing knives through her nimble fingers. "Prepared, respectful, good manners."

Jaden smiled, a bit of his concern subsiding. "That's a good start. Let's talk logistics."

Jaden was leaving when he heard his name behind him. He slowed, turning to find a tech rushing down the hall to meet him, her long braids swinging.

"Do you have a moment?"

"Of course, Melanie. What's up?"

Surprise lit in her youthful face, perhaps at him remembering her name. She was new and eager, an ace who'd come with the personal recommendation of the Guard trainer and former Elite, Darius Marchand, for her excellent tech skills. This was her first assignment, and she was living up to the hype.

Jaden took her to the conference room his team had just vacated.

"I have the report you asked for on the compromised laptop."

The IT team did regular inspections of all their tech to make sure they were secure. Over the years, they'd prevented ransomware attacks, hacking, and a number of other things. A routine sweep uncovered a listening device program embedded in a virus on a laptop. The Guard it belonged to didn't have access to any particularly sensitive info and hadn't known it was even there.

"Still appears it was an isolated incident. I wasn't able to pinpoint exactly how long it had been there, but it wasn't there at the last check-up. Nobody's device has anything like that on it. I scrubbed the machine and re-imaged it."

Jaden debated whether or not to tell Khara. In the end, he decided against it. There was no need to cause her undue stress. It wasn't the first time something like this had happened and surely wouldn't be the last. They'd done everything they could to protect themselves. He signed off on Melanie's report and thanked her.

"Keep me posted."

Chapter Eight

THIS WAS AN OCCASION for the Get Pumped playlist, so Khara cranked it up until the music filled the suite and surrounded her. The upbeat mix was a holdover from cancer treatment, for whenever she'd needed extra motivation—to get to chemo or through a radiation session, to get out there and combat fatigue with a walk. Now she used it whenever she needed to get up her gumption.

What if she threw caution to the wind just once? Heck, she was halfway there with Riddick not knowing who she was. The very thought of anonymity made her think reckless thoughts, like running away with him to a beach retreat somewhere. Or spending a weekend tucked inside a cozy mountain cabin together. He thought she was interesting, not her influence. The Queen's assistant couldn't do anything for his position or profile.

She'd taken a chance dating a few fellas earlier in her tenure but was dismayed to find that they weren't truly interested in her, just excellent actors. It wasn't worth the effort to extend herself, only to feel insulted and used in the end. So, she'd withdrawn and focused on work. The discreet occasional lover and quality adult toys kept her satiated. Mostly, anyway.

Casting her mind back to her last lover, Khara gave a dreamy sigh. It had been a very short-term arrangement during a climate change conference in Bruges. She'd made the dashing military officer's acquaintance several years ago, but there was no way it would go farther than a few satisfying days in bed together. No emotional risk, no surprises. He had a similar issue—public figure problems, they'd joked before he returned to Zambia. It had pleased her to learn of his recent marriage. She wished him well.

Joanne had gotten too close for comfort with her observation earlier about her being restless. How could Khara tell her assistant that, yes, she felt different since Link, the last singleton of her Elite Guards, found the love of his life? How sadness tinged the joy she felt when congratulating Wyn—another Guard—upon the recent announcement of his wife's pregnancy? She could never tell Joanne how dread settled in the pit of her stomach with the devastating realization that love wasn't meant for her. How sometimes the ache for it—when she let herself feel it—was so sharp, so deep, it stole her breath.

Happy couples surrounded Khara, from her older sister, Shanna, and her wife to every one of her Elite Guards. She was feeling like the old saying—always the bridesmaid, never a bride. At the ripe old age of thirty-two, she was in a dating desert.

Or had been until this morning.

She couldn't keep the excited smile away. Whitney's energetic vocals on "I'm Your Baby Tonight" got Khara shaking her hips and moving her body with conviction.

Khara fretted over what to wear. Not since before she'd ascended the throne had she been on a simple date. She lamented not having anything *fun*. Her stylist, Maxine, designed most of her clothing choices for magisterial business. She didn't have any reason to include something suitable for a carefree date. Now, wasn't that a sad state of affairs? Khara hated shopping and wasn't naïve enough to think she could go find something on her own. It was why Khara placed her sartorial decisions in Maxine's capable hands—she didn't miss.

Joanne had the foresight to get Khara connected with the stylist during her very first days on the throne. The brilliant Maxine breezed into Khara's life with a sketchbook and a vision. Khara was resistant at first, arguing that it seemed wholly unnecessary to have someone dress her, but Maxine broke down how it was so much more than that. It was building her brand, her image, as well as saving her time and energy. Although she was skeptical, Khara spent an endless afternoon doing initial fittings for Maxine's team to judge styles, colors, and fabrics. It had been excruciating, yet worth every single minute of discomfort. Maxine kept her looking marvelous with minimal effort on her part.

Once again, Joanne came to the rescue. She plucked an elegant black cocktail dress from the back of the closet. Khara recognized it right away as the dress she'd worn to a friend's gallery opening last year. "I've packed this every trip since Cape Town, hoping you might find a reason to wear it." Joanne held the hanger aloft. "You're going on a proper date with a handsome man. A little drama is in order."

Khara felt a rush of affection for her assistant as she fingered the soft fabric of the dress' flared skirt.

Out of habit, she spent a few moments fussing to make sure the top part lay just right, but she needn't have worried. Maxine was careful to keep her port scar concealed as requested, although she suggested more than once that Khara show off where they'd delivered the chemo drugs as a badge of honor. Khara slid the sweetheart neckline aside a little to see the puckered flesh in the full-length mirror. Not quite an inch long, the horizontal incision mark could have come from anywhere or anything and had faded noticeably after four years. It didn't scream "cancer patient" the way she once thought it did. At the start of her breast cancer treatment, she was so self-conscious she swore everyone was staring at her port.

No one stared at her port any more than they'd stared at her bald head. Lots of women went bald in Lytua, and she'd blended right in. When her beloved kinky coils started falling out from chemo, Khara channeled her heartbreak into defiance and shaved the rest of her hair off. That minor act of rebellion, even with tears streaming down her face, had made her feel powerful. Like she was snatching some measure of control back. The coils hadn't come back quite the same, but she'd adapted and had been supplementing with wigs and hairpieces and an array of fashionable turbans and headwraps since then. It was fun to change up her look often.

Khara was feeling pretty damn good about how she looked by the time she stepped into her silver pumps and was ready to go. She'd forgotten just how much she loved this dress. But then doubts crept in, making her stomach feel a little fluttery, almost queasy. What if Riddick was running a scam, trying to get her to lower her defenses? It wouldn't be the first time someone resorted to trickery. Khara couldn't bear the thought of dealing with yet another opportunist. It dimmed her enthusiasm a little. It would crush her if he were just another greedy charlatan. How would she be able to tell?

She wasn't going to be fooled and disappointed again, as she had been with her fiancée. Thinking of the circumstances of her broken engagement didn't sting as much as it used to. Time had given her perspective.

If she kept going like this, she would end up bitter and suspicious of everyone. It couldn't be healthy.

Maybe she should cancel and avoid the possibility of looking like a fool altogether.

Khara took a deep breath, determined to manage her expectations. It was only dinner, that was all. Dinner. Not an elopement. Nothing for him to take advantage of. It was fine to be attracted to Riddick. The man was sexy as hell, and she was a hot-blooded woman. He was interested in her, wasn't he? She didn't imagine how he'd looked at her. There was nothing to gain by pursuing her when he thought she was a member of the Queen's support staff.

If she had any nerve at all, Khara thought, she'd seize the opportunity and act on that delicious pull she felt towards Riddick and have a fling. The wild, unrestrained thought sent a little sizzling zip of excitement through her. Previous lovers had all been men she'd known for years, even though they didn't go on regular dates.

Perhaps this was the time to do something outrageous, like turn off her brain and just take him to bed. Khara couldn't believe she was having thoughts like this about someone she'd just met a few hours ago.

Just then, the introductory organ solo of "Let's Go Crazy" started. Deciding to take it as a sign, she sang right along with Prince.

If she could stay in the moment, she could enjoy some harmless fun. She wanted to believe she could pull this off. How hard could it be to pretend to be someone else for a night?

Yes, a fling could be perfect. Khara didn't have time for anything else, certainly not falling in love.

Chapter Nine

ENTERING THE RESTAURANT LOBBY without being announced or exclaimed over was like a dream come true for Khara. It was a guilty pleasure to arrive unnoticed, with no flashbulbs going off in her face or a long receiving line of dignitaries to greet. All while her stomach was growling, and her feet were killing her. She sighed in pure pleasure as people drifted right by her. Here at Georgia Brown's, she was just another woman on a first date. The muscles between her shoulder blades were in a tense knot. With effort, she forced them to relax. She hadn't been this nervous in years.

"Wow, you look beautiful."

She turned to see Riddick coming towards her, wearing that devastating smile again. The term "weak in the knees" never applied to her until then. He looked good enough to eat in a black jacket and crisp white shirt. His tie was unexpected—lavender paisley that hinted at a playful side. He looked so appealing that Khara knew he was in danger of shorting her circuits. "Thank you. I don't get out on my own a lot, so it's nice to have a reason to do it up. I like your tie." She hoped she sounded more casual than she felt.

The restaurant was lively, teeming with activity and the excited buzz of conversation. It smelled like heaven in here—there was a tempting mixture of yeasty, deep-fried goodness floating in the air. Khara sucked in a breath when Riddick put his hand at the base of her spine to guide her to the table after the maître d'. A small cutout there in the dress design allowed her to feel his fingers on her bare skin. That did something to her pulse. She hoped she didn't trip over her own feet as she walked before him.

Once seated, with drinks and an appetizer ordered, Riddick turned his full attention to her, and she felt almost naked under his gaze. When he asked after her hand, she blanked.

"From this morning? The coffee?"

"Oh, right. It's fine." That penetrating gaze was making it difficult to string two sentences together. Not her finest moment.

"Why don't you get out on your own?"

His voice was just as deep and chocolaty as she remembered. "There are many work obligations. Not much time left for Khara."

"She keeps you busy, huh?"

"Who does?"

"The Queen."

Khara cleared her throat. "Ah, yes. Yes, she does." Oh, mercy, she was going to blow it in the first five minutes if she didn't pay better attention. Subterfuge didn't come naturally to her.

"Typical."

Khara stiffened with her hand reaching for the breadbasket. "I beg your pardon?"

"How long have you been in town?"

"Nearly three weeks."

"See? And you haven't even gotten to see the city. Typical royal be-havior—expecting the world to cater to their whims. Like their assistants should automatically have no life of their own while toiling away to make *them* look good."

Her smile faltered, the wine souring in her stomach. "Have you known many monarchs?"

"I've worked with royals before and, sorry to say, but they were pretty much useless. Completely out of touch and lost without the assistants they worked half to death. They took the credit for their hard work."

"And is that the reason you dislike them? You see them as useless?"

"I don't like the thought of a hereditary monarch having a cushy lifestyle of ease from exploiting ordinary people. They deserve no special treatment because of the circumstances of their birth. They take it for granted. It's outdated and unnecessary."

Khara was appalled. She'd never taken Joanne for granted. Had she? She wasn't the Queen tonight, she reminded herself. Why was she feeling defensive? "The Queen is one of the hardest working people I know. She's not exploiting anyone."

"That you know of." He snorted. "You might be a little biased."

Indignation flared within Khara, leaving her cheeks feeling hot. "I'd appreciate it if you'd refrain from disparaging someone I happen to care about a great deal. You're insulting my employer and, by extension, my judgment." Her accent was more pronounced when her emotion was high. It was thick now.

He looked at her across the table, his expression inscrutable. A muscle ticked in his jaw. Khara met his gaze with a level one of her own.

Their server came by but sensed the discord and hurried off without a word.

After a tense moment that felt endless, Riddick bit out, "I don't believe in blind loyalty."

"On that, we can agree. If not the rest."

Riddick huffed out a breath and straightened his tie. His expression softened. "I apologize. I've only had limited and unpleasant interactions with royals, but here I am spouting off like I know more about your livelihood than you do. You strike me as a woman with integrity. I doubt you would follow the orders of someone you didn't respect."

Khara fought the urge to defend herself further from his unfair assumptions. She wasn't the Queen tonight, so what did it matter if he had an unfavorable opinion of her? Only then did she realize how hard her heart was pounding. "I also apologize. I'm protective of her."

"Truce?" Riddick lifted his cocktail, and she touched her glass to his with a quiet clink.

Khara took a deep breath to let her annoyance fade. "Truce." She could count on one hand the number of times she'd faced negative initial impressions about her position. Most people peppered her with questions. She'd never experienced outright derision, and she didn't care for it.

"I should start by clearing the air about last night," Riddick said, then explained about the classifieds prank that kept his phone ringing off the hook the last few days.

That put his surly mood in context. "Even in Lytua, we've heard about the Nigerian prince scam. It's hard to believe people are still falling for that. You are forgiven. Dion sounds like quite a character."

"He is. He's also a fantastic artist. Have a look."

"Oh, wow." The artwork pictured on his phone was so vibrant it seemed to jump out at her. Khara studied the abstract art for a few moments, drawn in by its creative color and composition. "That is impressive. What medium is this?"

"Oil on canvas. Not his favorite, though. Takes so long to dry."

The server presented their first course with a flourish. "We're world famous for our fried green tomatoes. A Low Country specialty."

"Where is the Low Country?" Khara asked him.

"The coastal region of South Carolina, ma'am. Enjoy."

The delicacy deserved its reputation. They were divine. Khara knew right away she'd be trying to replicate this dish at home.

Chapter Ten

D ESPITE THE TRUCE ON the subject, Khara couldn't help but try to repair Lillianna's image. "The Queen is... she has many redeeming qualities. She's also an educator and philanthropist. The citizens call her the People's Queen."

Khara thought she was doing well with obscuring her identity in her answer to Riddick's question about liking her work until he frowned at her.

"Khara," he interrupted. "I came to learn more about *you*, not hear about your boss. You don't have to convince me the Queen is good people. In any case, my feelings about royals have nothing to do with you. She's not here."

But she *was* here. For a moment Khara was perplexed, then realized her mistake: she'd been couching almost everything she said in terms of what the Queen thought and did, in an attempt to separate herself. She'd have to get better at this if she wanted to pull off this ruse. She managed to keep the tremor out of her hand as she lifted her wineglass and took a sip. Forced herself to relax a little and tried again. It sounded more natural this time. She was still trying to change his mind about the Queen. Her. Whomever.

"I love it. It's hard work, but important. Very rewarding. Even as a child, I wanted to go into the government. What about you?"

"It's not what I pictured myself doing, but after trying on a couple different careers to see what fit, I knew it was the right place to be from the first. Haven't looked back since."

"What other careers did you try?"

"I was good at drawing and visual arts from a young age, but never considered it a career, though. Had a good head for numbers. Did a couple of hitches in the army right out of high school, trying to figure out what I wanted to do with my life."

"A Ranger, right?"

Riddick's brows knitted together. "How did you—"

Khara's face heated with embarrassment. She was *dreadful* at this. "I apologize, that was rude. It was in the security briefing on you." Maybe she should have another glass of wine? Would it make things better or worse?

"Yeah?" His eyes sparkled with amusement. "What else was in there?"

"Details I wouldn't already know on a first date. Please, go on."

"What would be in a security briefing on you?"

She gave an uneasy laugh. "Not much of interest, I'm afraid."

"I doubt that. Seems only fair I should know something about you that would be in a dossier."

Wracking her brain for a nugget of information about herself that didn't tie to her position was impossible. Finally, she hit on something. "Young people complete two sets of compulsory service before being considered adults and full citizens: civics and military. As I said, I was always interested in government. My civic service was in government and my military service was in law and government. My mother said it was inevitable, I would watch hearings and other legal proceedings like other children watched cartoons. She said I was bossy and opinionated from a young age."

"Does she still say that?"

That pinch of permanent grief flared inside her. Would it ever go away completely? "I'm afraid she passed away when I was at university and my father not long after."

"Damn, I'm sorry. That must have been brutal."

"It was. It was quite messy there for some time. But my sister and I had each other, lots of friends and support."

"I'm glad to hear that. Are you and your sister close?"

"In some ways. She's much older than I am and travels extensively for her work. How about you? Your parents? Family?"

"My mother lives here. She's retired."

Once her initial anxiousness burned off, Khara felt more at ease, even after deciding against that second glass of wine.

Riddick confessed, "I'd wanted to do some research before tonight, but I ran out of time. Being honest here, I'd never heard of Lytua before this morning."

"Most people haven't. We maintain a low profile and keep to ourselves. We don't allow large numbers of tourists all at once. It was settled by freedmen, freed and escaped enslaved people. According to legend, they concealed the island through magic."

To her horror, Riddick got out his phone and entered Lytua into the online search engine. The roaring in her ears and sudden thundering of her heart made it hard for Khara to concoct a quick response. She'd insisted years ago on a strategic website design that didn't put information about her on Lytua's landing page. The focus should remain squarely on the people she served. A general web inquiry, though—that was another matter.

A frown wrinkled Riddick's high forehead, and Khara's heart plummeted, for she knew right away what was confounding him. Riddick held up his phone, showing her official state portrait. *Queen Lillianna of Lytua* read the caption. "This looks a lot like you."

It was pretty damning evidence, Khara had to admit. "Oh, that. You won't believe it." She paused to take a healthy swig of her wine, her mind racing. "That's from a costume party years ago that somehow got circulated as being Queen Lillianna. I *am* wearing her vestments and crown, but that was for a gag. The foreign press got hold of it and it made the rounds. We've since given up trying to correct the mistake. You can't imagine the headache it's caused being misidentified so often."

Khara held her breath and willed the jitters in her stomach away. The story was fairly flimsy and wouldn't hold up to serious scrutiny, but she wouldn't need to worry about that.

Riddick's frown gave way to a wry smile. "Having just been on the receiving end of erroneous press, I absolutely *can* imagine. You and the Queen must favor each other."

"Actually, we do. We've had a bit of fun with it, though. The press mixes us up constantly and has even thought I must be her daughter." This last point was the truth. Many people did just assume a ruler couldn't be young.

If she'd believed in hell, Khara was sure she was well on her way there. The elegance of Riddick's long, tapered fingers momentarily distracted her as he gave his Old Fashioned a gentle swirl, rolling the amber liquid across the single oversized cube of ice. His nails were clean and neat, well cared for. She approved. "Let me give you some highlights."

He leaned forward, those soulful eyes alight with curiosity. "On Lytua? Please do."

"We've a Matrilineal society. We elect our leader, most recently, a Queen. The last several have been Queens."

Now Riddick paused. "You *elect* your Queen? Why didn't you say so earlier?"

She lifted an eyebrow at him. "You weren't in a place to hear it then."

"Ouch." He acknowledged the zinger with a small tilt of his head. "That's fair, though. How does that work?"

"It's not a hereditary monarchy. Our monarchs have always been elected democratically. Any citizen can run for the election. Similar to your president, they act as the executive branch. We have a bicameral parliament and High Court."

"Interesting. Tell me more."

Khara chewed and considered what she could say without giving too much away. "Only full citizens are eligible to vote or own property. Every adult is a reservist and qualifies every year with weapons, even the Queen."

Between bites of a pillowy-soft dinner roll, she shared with him about island life—some history, some of the things she liked best. He was quite a thoughtful listener, giving her his undivided attention, asking for further detail and drawing connections. His phone was nowhere in sight, which she found refreshing.

"How long will you be in town for?"

"Close to three weeks. We were supposed to have returned to Lytua nearly a week ago but had unexpected business in New York. There was no need to fly back and forth when we can do plenty remotely. After a few days in New York, it'll be back home to Lytua."

"When will you be stateside again?"

"I'm not certain. Depends on the Queen's schedule. She'll be quite busy once the Parliament session starts."

Their entrées' arrival commanded their attention and Khara decided, after tucking into her Creole-blackened salmon, that she needed to get to the Low Country.

When she raved over the delicate pineapple butter sauce and sautéed spinach, Riddick laughed and offered her some of his grilled red snapper. He seemed amused by her robust enjoyment of the cuisine.

Riddick told her about starting up his firm with his good friend Eric as his partner. It was important to both of them to connect to the local community and do philanthropic work from the very beginning. They provided internships, scholarships, and mentoring to youth in foster care. Listening to the many ways Riddick & Sloane were involved prompted Khara to ask, "You seem to have an affinity for this group. What drew you to working with them?"

He was silent for an endless moment. So long Khara worried she'd somehow offended him with the question. Something in his eyes put her on the defensive and made her want to backpedal and apologize for prying. She was always so interested in the "whys" of people's actions, it was easy to forget that not everyone cared to delve deep into their motivations. At length, he said, "I've seen a lot."

Chapter Eleven

T HEY STAYED AT THE restaurant for three hours. With talk of the Queen firmly behind them, they laughed as they talked about their time at university, discussing books, movies, music, travel, hobbies, politics, and friends. He taught graduate-level classes at two nearby schools. She also taught but didn't say so. What personal assistant taught courses at law school? They were in such deep conversation that they didn't even notice the restaurant emptying around them.

Riddick asked over dessert, "There's a great jazz club not too far away if you're up for some live music."

Khara nearly leaped out of her seat, for she didn't want the night to end yet, nor did she want to come across as needy or desperate. It wouldn't have surprised her if she caused a great deal of scrambling and swearing when she texted that they were going to take the Metro to Blues Alley. She tried to stall a bit to give the team time to reorganize and get moving. Oh, she'd hear about it tomorrow, for sure.

When the bill came, he waved Khara off when she reached for her beaded handbag. "Absolutely not. I did the asking. I pay."

"Fine, I'll ask you next time, then I'll pay."

Riddick sat back in the booth and regarded her for a moment, tapping his index finger on the table. "You wouldn't want my mother to think she'd raised a heathen son, would you?"

"Oh, no, certainly not. You've been nothing but a gentleman."

"Then let the gentleman pay." He must have read the exasperation in her expression. "Is this going to be a problem? Is it done differently in Lytua?"

"No, it's not that. The assumption is that I would pay for things."

"Because of who you work for?"

She nodded, causing her curls to sway.

"When we're together, I pay. Doesn't matter if you were the Queen herself. It's how my mother raised me—to make a date feel like she's taken care of when we go out, that she doesn't have to worry about anything. I don't want someone worried about who will pay the bill. Are you okay with that?"

"I am. But you should know two things about me."

Riddick sat back and put his arm across the top of the booth. "Let's hear 'em."

"First, I'm not any sort of gold-digging damsel in distress. For the past fifteen years, I've had the means to buy whatever I wish. I've known—and I'm certain you have, as well—people out to get whatever they can from someone else, even when it would be more appropriate for them to buy it themselves."

"I've offended you. My apologies."

"You haven't. Let me finish, please. Second, I've also known—and, again, I'm certain you have, as well—people who use money to control others' behaviors in dating situations. I'll never be at someone's financial mercy. You can pay, but I won't accept anything I can't obtain on my own. That's how my mother raised me."

"Understood."

"Are you okay with that?" she asked.

"I am. Our two philosophies are not mutually exclusive. I suspect we've both put off some dates with them, though."

"Yes, and good riddance. Never compromise your beliefs."

It was a piano jazz night, and Khara felt pretty and feminine as her dress swirled and swished around her knees when they danced. Khara made a mental note to let Joanne know that the dress was perfect. More than once, she caught Riddick's eyes on her generous curves, and it excited her. Riddick smelled so good it was distracting.

Khara's smartwatch vibrated with two quick bursts followed by a longer one, signaling an overdue check-in. That never happened. She excused herself and found Alene Devereaux, another one of her Elites, was already in the line for the ladies' room. She was dressed in date night attire to blend in, her micro braids piled up on her head. Khara hurried up behind her. *"I lost track of time. I apologize."*

"Just checking that all is well, Avlah?"

"Yes, it is. You look fantastic, by the way."

Alene lit up and thanked her. Like Khara, Alene was curvy, bordering on voluptuous. One would never have guessed she'd given birth to her first baby just a year ago. Washington was such a cosmopolitan city—no one gave the unfamiliar language any notice.

Check-in completed, Khara took the time to refresh. She smiled at her reflection in the mirror over the sink and hummed as she washed her hands and straightened her hair. Riddick was funny and interesting and a fun dance partner. His hand felt hot on her bare lower back. Capable. There was strength and power in his firm touch. Khara imagined those sizeable hands on more than her lower back. He'd leave her breathless, she was sure of it.

She was used to studying people, sizing them up quickly. As long as it didn't involve her own dismal romantic life, she was pretty good at it. Riddick moved with effortless confidence, only a hint of swagger. He had no trouble laughing at himself and was a good listener.

She liked him. Liked him a lot. Khara was excited, but nowhere near as nervous as she was at the evening's start. She was having the time of her life.

The man was splendid. Her heart rate picked up again when he saw her coming back to the table; she aimed a smile at him. The rational part of her piped up and warned against getting too comfortable.

Somehow, it felt like they were alone in the hotel lobby as they said goodnight. Riddick had fallen into step beside her as they walked from the Metro. It was one thing that outed him as former military, right along with that proud bearing. He carried a quiet, unmistakable authority, like he'd be the person everyone looked to for leadership in a crisis.

"Can I see you again? Tomorrow?"

Khara's stomach flipped. She'd already been feeling pure exhilaration at the end of the best date she'd ever had. He sounded almost shy. "I'd like that." Should she have said no? Would it have been better if she'd played hard to get? She stunk at playing dating games.

"Maybe a little sightseeing this time?"

"Sure. I'm attending a function in the evening, but I could do early after-noon." She couldn't remember what function it was at the moment.

"That'll work."

There was enough heat and interest in Riddick's gaze to make her cheeks feel a little warm.

Another flash of imagination had those piercing eyes locked on hers as she lay beneath him, taking him deep, her limbs wrapped around him tight. Khara fiddled with the chain strap of her purse. Her heart skipped when his gaze fell to her mouth. Oh, if he kissed her now, she might embarrass herself. She wanted that mouth of his all over her body.

"I've never kissed on the first date, Khara," he said at last, his voice low and enticing. "But I am tempted tonight." He pressed a soft, lingering kiss to her knuckles, his eyes never leaving hers. "Goodnight."

"Goodnight, Riddick."

Khara was grinning as she made her way to the elevator where another Elite, this time Link Trymble, awaited her with a huge grin plastered on his lean face. She'd never kissed on the first date either, but oh, Riddick's succulent lips were so very kissable. And what a lovely surprise that he'd bent over to her hand instead of bringing it up to him. That proper etiquette had seemingly been lost over the years, but not with Riddick.

She'd had so much fun tonight. Not only did she pull it off, but she'd felt funny, engaging, and beautiful while doing so. Riddick liked *her*, Khara. And wasn't that just grand?

This time, when the doubts tried to assert themselves, Khara shoved them aside, riding high on the evening's success.

Chapter Twelve

S**O WHAT IF HE'D** had to return to the restaurant to collect his forgotten car from the valet? Riddick didn't mind.

Too wired to get to sleep, he grabbed the notepad he kept on his nightstand. He'd intended to jot a few notes for the next day, but his mind kept returning to how the evening had gone.

They almost didn't make it past the first course, and the blame for that lay squarely with him. He'd nearly blown it big time with his preconceived notions.

The fire that sprang into her eyes when he'd cast aspersions at Lytua's Queen had given him pause. She'd clapped back so eloquently that it was clear she wouldn't be having any of that nonsense whatsoever. He couldn't blame her. How kindly would *he* take it if someone questioned his profession, his entire way of life?

There was no predicting what Khara would say. She had no problem standing up for herself and making sure he knew the score from the outset. Just as she'd done on the telephone last night. That was something he respected. This was a woman who was passionate about what she believed in.

He didn't mention going to the jazz club earlier in the evening on purpose. As someone who liked having options, he always planned something for later, but kept the knowledge to himself. That way, there wouldn't be another event to suffer through if a date tanked over dinner. The woman never knew about it. Riddick was having such a good time with Khara, he congratulated himself on having something ready to extend their time together. No floundering.

Spending time with the Queen's assistant was the most fun he'd had in a long time. Khara was easy to talk to and listened like she was paying attention with all of her senses. She asked insightful questions and was interested in both the restaurant's and jazz club's rich histories. They spent so much of the evening laughing and talking that he didn't even realize how long they stayed in the restaurant.

She'd had a little trouble separating herself from her work at first, which Riddick suspected happened a lot. He wondered if she had many conversations that didn't revolve around her employer. Was that why she'd been surprised when he asked her out?

Khara's tawny skin shone like velvet in the evening's light. He couldn't stop watching her trace her fingertip through the condensation on her water glass. She'd painted her nails a deep purple, and it mesmerized him.

He liked her quick, clever mind. When she asked why he went by just Riddick, she probed beyond his standard answer of, "Nobody calls me by my first name except for my mother." The speculative look she'd given him told him she'd never be one for pat answers. She was definitely a thread-puller. He could see her following a line of questioning until she got the whole truth.

"That didn't answer the question, though."

Few people dug into the origin of his name. He could now include her in that group. "She's special. That's just for her."

Somehow, she'd caught him off guard when she asked what drew him to his work with youth in foster care, even though it was a question he was used to getting frequently.

Riddick evaluated how much to tell her. The fact that he'd experienced foster care and adoption firsthand was information he guarded jealously. He never just up and disclosed his hardscrabble childhood. Yet here he was, giving it real consideration. Something about Khara made him want to open up. In the end, he'd given his standard answer and could tell right away she wasn't buying it.

She gave him another speculative look with her head cocked a little, sensing more. He was relieved that she didn't press with any follow-up questions.

What he didn't say about his time in the Army was that there'd been a lot to figure out for a kid who'd been through so much. One who'd only barely graduated from high school. The Army discipline and clarity of purpose had been life-changing for him. He'd needed order in his life while he figured out what he wanted to do. Riddick liked order, needed it to function at his best. He'd felt a little bereft losing that when he came home to care for his mother when she'd been ill.

While he appreciated her intellect and sense of humor, he'd be lying through his teeth if he said he wasn't aware of Khara's va-va-voom curves all night. When he arrived at the restaurant and saw her standing there waiting for him, he thought, *whoa*. Her dress was sexy as all get out. Fitted without being too tight and showing just hints of smooth golden-brown skin. Her body was lush with mouthwatering curves that felt like heaven against him. The cutout that bared her lower back to both his gaze and touch fascinated him. When he'd put a hand on the naked base of her spine to guide her through the crowds at the restaurant and club, he could have sworn he felt her shiver.

In heels, she'd still been about six inches shorter than him. He wouldn't get a crick in his neck whenever he kissed her. And, oh, he would kiss her at some point. She smelled delicious—something subtle, not too sweet, but seductive just the same. Dancing to the mellow piano music, they could talk without shouting. They'd laughed about how her mother insisted she learn social dance as a teenager. Despite being a graceful dancer now, she'd been tall and uncoordinated—no one wanted to partner with her. "You wouldn't know it now," he'd told her.

Riddick appreciated all shades of brown, had dated beautiful Black women in a wide variety of hues, heights, sizes, and shapes. At thirty-four years old, he was pretty open-minded. His only real type was intelligent and funny. Khara was both and a great deal more.

The cute spray of golden freckles across the bridge of her nose seemed to brighten when she blushed. He'd thought it might have been an illusion when he saw it during their morning meeting. It wasn't a trick of the light. The rosy pink darkened her cheeks prettily several times tonight. It was adorable.

He liked her freckles and told her so. "Born and raised on a Caribbean island," she'd said, lifting her shoulders in a shrug. "Yet sensitive to the sun. They resist all my attempts to disguise them." Both blush and freckles disappeared into the neckline of her dress. He wanted to trace them down, however far they went. With a single fingertip. With his tongue.

Her hair was free of its earlier updo, and he'd been right. It was curly. Her natural, chin-length curls were delightfully unruly. A sumptuous shade of sable, pinned back from her face with a jeweled headband. Just long enough to get his hands in. With her round, expressive face, large hazel eyes, and wide smile, it wasn't a hardship looking at her all night.

Everything about her screamed class and refinement. It was oozing out of her pores.

Riddick tossed the pad back on the nightstand and was reaching to turn out the lamp when he saw he'd doodled next to his notes without even realizing it. He froze, the smile slipping from his face. Huh. That was unexpected.

Chapter Thirteen

J ADEN NEEDED A DRINK by the time his charge was safely in her rooms for the night, and he was back in his. He couldn't deny seeing her relaxed and so lighthearted was well worth the logistical headaches. His Queen—on the subway. The *subway*. They'd need to talk about that spur-of-the-moment change in the morning.

For someone who lamented they didn't flirt very well, Khara did a bang-up job as far as he could tell. She'd danced, and she *never* danced if she could avoid it. The tinkle of her unselfconscious laughter was like music to Jaden's ears.

She needs more of this in her life, Jaden mused. She tried not to show it, but he knew trying to separate genuine interest from fake had taken a toll on her. He wasn't even upset when she missed a check-in later in the evening. One drink didn't worry him. Jaden wasn't concerned about that. What made him uneasy was... well, he wasn't exactly sure.

The evening kicked off well. When she'd emerged from her bedroom ready to head out, Jaden raised his eyebrows at the dramatic transformation. "Well, you look fantastic, kid."

Khara brightened, gave him a brilliant smile, and thanked him.

Jaden had to give it to her. Even as she was all but bouncing with excitement, she gave his security spiel her full attention. They always reviewed panic buttons and protocol for breaches prior to testing the signals on her communications devices.

He even made her repeat it back to him. "If security is compromised in any way, I will be alerted, and I am to shelter in place until one of the Guards retrieves me. We will evacuate to the rendezvous point."

Nodding, Jaden returned her jewelry and watched as she fastened it on with trembling fingers and smoothed her dress down. If he didn't know her so well, he would have missed the little signs of her nervousness. She was gesturing with her hands, something she was usually quite disciplined about. It brought a smile to his lips as he remembered how antsy he'd been on his first date with his wife.

It was so unusual to see her this excited about an outing, even his customary scowl wouldn't stay in place.

"I wish you'd let us clear the restaurant, or at least secure it."

"You know how I feel about this. People shouldn't be inconvenienced because of me. They could be in the middle of an anniversary dinner or about to propose for all I know. Who am I to spoil that?"

She was unfailingly considerate, especially compared to her predecessor, who would have thought nothing of mucking up someone else's plans. Jaden disliked the inherent risk of unknown variables, though. Khara was every bit as headstrong as she'd always been, and they'd bumped heads continuously at the beginning of her reign. She'd been so hard to guard at first, made his job nearly impossible. She preferred unseen security to discourage people from thinking she was unapproachable. He could laugh about it now, but at the time, he hadn't been sure their friendship would survive.

Ensuring the Queen's safety was an enormous undertaking, with a multitude of moving parts. Like any world leader, there were disgruntled malcontents who sought to hurt her personally and professionally. They'd dealt with threats big and small, intruders, sabotage, arson, and a suspicious fall into a busy Hong Kong street Jaden still wasn't entirely convinced was an accident. Then there was the bombing at Parliament that still made his blood run cold whenever he thought about it. No matter the evidence suggesting the contrary, Jaden's gut told him Khara had actually been the target. And it was scenarios like that that kept him up at night.

Threats to her life didn't seem to faze Khara, and the team worked diligently to keep her out of harm's way. She trusted them, despite some early missteps, and although she conscientiously attended to her part, she refused to wall herself off. She was a public servant, and she was determined to serve *in* public, not locked away in safety somewhere. It may have made for exasperation and creative problem-solving on occasion, but Jaden respected it. So did the people of Lytua.

"Sometimes I think you're too much the people's Queen."

The look she flashed him was full of mischief, reminiscent of their days as children when she was trying to talk him into some ridiculous scheme that was sure to get them both in trouble. She'd excelled at that. God help the man who was actually her equal. "Relax," she told him. "It's just a date."

She might believe that, but Jaden had his doubts about the "just" part. He kept his own counsel about it for now, though. This whole thing was unusual enough without making wild predictions.

He saw her into the car, where Cenn was waiting, then hopped into the front seat of the chase car. The remaining team members had taken their positions. Two were already in place at the restaurant, posing as a couple. Jaden held his breath when the restaurant valet opened Khara's door and extended a hand to help her out. She was only out in the open for a few seconds, but it still carried a risk. He didn't take a full breath until the team inside reported through their earpieces that they had her covered.

The team's voices were a jumble throughout the date.

"I can't even remember the last time I saw *Avlah* actually eat in public or laugh so much."

"She seems to be having a great time."

"She's flirting effectively, that's for sure."

"Good for her."

"She looks quite happy."

"Comms, people!" Jaden had chastised half-heartedly, but it was impossible to rein in the excited chatter about all the novelty unfolding before them.

"They've ordered dessert." Link sounded incredulous.

Dessert? Jaden frowned. She never ordered dessert, so this was a major indulgence for her. This Mr. Riddick was getting less harmless by the minute. He sure hoped Khara knew what she was doing.

Once he'd made arrangements for which Guard members would be posted outside Khara's bedroom in the suite, Jaden ran through his nightly security routine.

It was too late to call home, but he wanted to hear his wife's voice. Jaden started to dial, then changed his mind, remembering that she had an early morning meeting with her staff. He was tempted to send a text instead, knowing it wouldn't wake her if she was already asleep. No, he wouldn't disturb her much-needed rest. Jaden imagined her in bed with their son knocked out next to her, probably sprawled out like a starfish. The image brought a smile to his face. Dorian liked to keep Aimee company when Jaden was on travel and had become extra protective now that he was going to be a big brother. He hoped the kids would be close, like he and his younger brother were.

Jaden found he couldn't sleep and wandered down to the hotel's gym to blow off some steam. He'd been working at the heavy bag for twenty minutes or so when he heard someone come in.

"Ah, so it's not just me that's unable to sleep," Wyn Gregoire called out.

Concern swept through Jaden, for his team's well-being was one of his top priorities. He wiped sweat from his brow and noted Wyn was dressed in workout clothes too, a frown marring the younger man's features. "What's on your mind? Is it about Sam?" Jaden asked.

Jaden felt the tension in Wyn's sigh. Of course, it was Sam. How could it not be? He gulped down some water while waiting for Wyn to gather his thoughts.

Wyn scrubbed a hand over the back of his neck and made a face. "I wouldn't admit it to anyone else, but I'm scared to death. I'm so worried about her all the time I can't get any rest. How did you do this the first time?"

"Handle my wife being pregnant? Shit, I was scared to death too."

Wyn's eyebrows shot up. "You were?"

"Hell, yes. It's a big deal. And the fear doesn't magically go away, not even when it's the second time around. I worry every day."

The two men spent a few minutes in deep discussion about first-time pregnancy and impending fatherhood until Wyn was visibly more at ease.

Jaden rolled his shoulders, trying to loosen some of the tension lodged there. "Let me ask you this. What are your thoughts on *Avlah* dating this Mr. Riddick?"

Wyn's eyebrows rose. "Officially or unofficially?"

"No punches pulled."

"I think it's great."

Interesting. Wyn hadn't been with the Elites yet when Khara's engagement imploded. He'd only ever known her as determinedly single. "What makes you say that?"

Tilting his face up to the ceiling, Wyn closed his eyes for a moment before putting his hands on his hips. "It has to suck that she can't trust anyone to be sincere when they know who she is. She's been different lately, not quite the same. Since around Link's wedding, I think. Lonely, maybe."

"That's exactly what I thought." As much as she shrugged off matchmaking and suitors, Jaden had seen how wistful she'd been during the festivities. Jaden did not add his suspicions that the spate of recent babies and pregnancies were magnifying things for Khara. Wyn had his hands full with his own worry about that.

"Anyway, I've never seen her smile like she did tonight. She seemed... lighter. More like herself when she's not 'on', you know?"

Jaden knew, and he agreed. He clapped Wyn on the shoulder. "Tell Sam how you're feeling. She's probably scared, too, and you'll rest better."

Once Wyn left, Jaden chuckled. Wyn and Sam had come a long way from the constant sniping and snarling at one another that marked their early interactions. Sparks had flown when Wyn—a baby Elite at the time—confronted Sam publicly about a newspaper article she'd written. The journalist and the Guard had gone from adversaries to love birds to newlyweds in no time flat. And now soon-to-be parents. He'd wait until closer to Sam's due date to advise Wyn not to puke in the delivery room like he did.

He was puttering around in the command center when the new tech came rushing in.

"There you are, sir. I was looking for you."

Jaden frowned and checked the wall clock. It was well past one in the morning. "What's up?"

She didn't sit when he invited her to, instead continued to stand, tapping a pencil against the folder in her hands and looking decidedly uncomfortable. An unpleasant feeling settled in Jaden's gut. Whatever was coming, it wasn't good.

"You told me to let you know if anything was unusual and I may have found something. It could be nothing. It probably *is* nothing, but it just feels weird. And I wanted to run it by you."

"Always trust your gut, Melanie. What've you got?"

"Feels like someone is always testing our security and they never get anywhere, but there was a bizarre... not even an attack, more like a probe. Like poking around for weaknesses."

Melanie walked him through the small breach their advanced protective software had discovered. She'd shut it down right away and tried to trace it, but the perpetrator was just a hair faster and disconnected everything. It tracked back to a large telemarketing business overseas. A front, certainly. On the surface, it presented like any other run-of-the-mill cyberattack. They were often targeted just as so many other businesses were.

Whoever was behind this, they'd tried to access flight information from the island, which left Jaden feeling uneasy. Why would someone be rummaging through official government flight records? If a hacker was really after causing trouble, they would have gone for something juicier, like the financials. What were they looking for? And to what end?

"Could be random," Melanie mused as she took off her glasses and cleaned them with the hem of her shirt. "A bored kid, maybe."

That was certainly a possibility, but Jaden had seen too much in his career to believe in random anything. *Was this a one-off, or was someone scouting for weaknesses in their electronic defenses in preparation for something bigger?* "You sent this to the Municipal Police, too?"

"Yes sir, as per procedure." Anything related to national security went to him, as well as Lytua's main law enforcement office.

"Good. I'll follow up with the chief tomorrow. I'd like to know her thoughts. Good work, Melanie."

The young tech beamed up at him.

By the time Jaden was finally drifting off to sleep, he'd worked through a handful of possible outcomes, each more alarming than the last. He admonished himself to stop blowing things out of proportion. The breach wasn't anything unusual, and he had no reason to be overly suspicious. But why flights? What were they looking for?

He was going to drive himself around the bend. It must be this whole un-dercover Queen business adding an extra layer of worry. Khara was bound to be recognized at some point. What would happen when she was inevitably caught out? How would she keep this charade up?

Chapter Fourteen

A T LAST. THE OPPORTUNITY Trina Krove had been waiting for had finally arrived.

Trina had to do some sleuthing to uncover where in the world the bitch Queen was staying this time. She was a top-notch hacker, even though her position already allowed her the highest level of access. This task required disappointingly little use of her true talents. Her last real challenge was hacking into the FBI and MI6 databases just to see if she could do it. It was all about that thrill, that rush she got knowing she faced jail time and steep fines for accessing prohibited information.

She usually kept tabs on when Lillianna was off the island, but she'd been quite busy at work, and both her husband and son had been brought low with a wicked case of food poisoning. Now that she was getting caught up, serendipity seemed to be smiling upon her.

The Guard always filed three flight plans when the Queen traveled, ostensibly to avoid tracking her location like Trina was doing now. Try as she might, Trina couldn't break through the traps and triggers embedded in the Elite Guard's closed-loop communications. It was a waste of several days' effort to get into the Guard secretary's email, only to discover he didn't have access to anything juicy.

But Joanne Mosley did.

She probably knew more about the Queen than the Queen did. Joanne was diligent about keeping a historical diary that detailed the Queen's activities.

The diary was public record, but in the wake of the Parliament bombing, it was published on a delay system to prevent compromises in security. She used a cloud-based platform, and Trina had hacked into Joanne's working draft of current details quite a few times. With some research and cobbling together of specifics, Trina could usually figure out where the Queen was or was going to be. Sabotaging the schedule was a temptation she avoided, for the Guard would certainly close a breach if they suspected one. That would leave Trina without this virtual back door that gained her insider knowledge.

It would break Joanne's heart to know Trina used her to gain access to her beloved boss. *How unfortunate.* Trina liked Joanne. They'd worked together on a number of committee and community projects throughout the years, long before Lillianna arrived. She'd always respected Joanne's work ethic and devotion.

Trina scrolled through mundane details like which special dish the Queen preferred at a local restaurant—bougie bitch that she was. Which gown she wore to whatever event. Which raincoat she preferred. There was a small snafu with the hotel catering staff, but the head chef took care of it right away and sent the Queen her favorite treat as an apology: cheesecake. *Suck up.* As the entry listed the head chef by name, Trina cross-referenced it with the cities in the registered flight plans. *Bingo.* Within minutes, she learned the hotel name and location.

A smile spread across her face. This was it.

She'd been laying the groundwork for nearly a year, gathering intel and fine-tuning her plan. It was time to finally put it into action, and Trina was almost lightheaded with giddiness.

Lillianna was going down this time. No more near misses.

Trina maintained contacts around the world who performed all manner of skullduggery for her. She paid substantial sums of money for their discretion and gave wide latitude. Having decided this well in advance, she used one of her many burner phones to connect with one of her outlier contacts. They'd known each other for years, but she had never fully utilized all of her unique skill sets. The Intermediary excelled at recon and undercover work. She was the best operative Trina had, which was why she used her as infrequently as possible. Now was the time. She could be counted upon to follow her instructions to the letter.

The message she typed out was short:

DC. Await further instructions.

The Intermediary was usually fairly swift in her responses. It would largely depend on her location, though, and who knew what time zone she was in. Trina settled in to wait.

If she hadn't ruined her family's life, Trina probably would have liked Lillianna. She'd proved to be a decent leader, but it would never be enough to make up for the damage she'd done. Trina was going to enjoy every single moment of what she had planned for her.

Lillianna was finally going to pay for her repeated insults. She was going to hurt. To *bleed*. The thought filled Trina with dark, effervescent glee.

An alarm popped up in the middle of her screen. Trina muttered a curse and moved quickly to close out and cover her tracks. The Guard's sharp new tech had reversed things and was trying to track her. That little bitch had gotten pretty close, but Trina was smart enough to route her hacking through multiple fronts. She was confident she hadn't snooped enough to raise significant suspicion, but she knew she'd have to be even more careful from now on. Maybe she should recruit the new tech.

Her husband's voice called down the stairs, "Honey, it's late. Close that thing and come on to bed."

Trina smiled at the cranky edge in his voice. If only he knew what she was up to. He'd never know the lengths to which she'd gone to ensure his success. "I'll be up in a minute."

"That's what you said two hours ago!"

A laugh bubbled out of her. "Okay, okay. I'm coming now."

The burner phone buzzed from where she'd sat it on the corner of her desk, and Trina snatched it up so fast she nearly dropped it. The Intermediary's answering text was even briefer:

Acknowledged.

Yes.

Grinning, Trina powered down her untraceable laptop, returning it and the phone to the concealed compartment in her office wall. Heavens no, she'd never use her work or personal laptop for such things; that was a rookie mistake. She chuckled to herself, her mood lifting even more.

Corey was waiting for her in bed with the covers thrown back for her, as usual. As soon as she appeared in the doorway, he marked the page in the paperback he was reading and set it aside on the nightstand. A smile curved his lips as he patted the spot next to him.

He was just as handsome as the day she'd met him more than thirty years ago at a social club dance. His face was leaner, his body tougher. A touch more salt than pepper in the hair now, but it suited him and lent an air of distinction. Trina slid into bed for their nightly ritual of debriefing about the day.

"Cyrus has been writing the Queen poetry again. Can you imagine how much sweeter on her he'd be if they'd been in the same class in school instead of a year apart?"

Their gentle-souled son was many things, but a poet was not one of them.

Trina sighed. She wasn't sure what her sweet boy saw in the haughty bitch, but it didn't matter. She'd do anything for her only child to have what he wanted. For whatever reason, he wanted Lillianna, and Trina would make sure he got her. For a while, at least.

Once again, she considered if it was worth the trouble to just go ahead and dispose of the Queen and deal with any fallout from her son later. It was a favorite fantasy. Watching that self-righteous light in her eyes die as she choked the life out of her. These violent thoughts had concerned her at first, for Trina had never been particularly bloodthirsty up until that point.

Eliminating Lillianna would force another election, one that would turn out more favorably for her family than the last.

Patience, Trina. Patience. She was almost there.

Corey touched the frown line between her eyebrows, startling her. "Let it go, Trina. I don't like what it's doing to you. I know you blame her...."

Hot fury flashed through Trina. "If she hadn't humiliated you—"

His voice was soft, like a remorseful caress. "I got behind the wheel of that car, Trina. No one made me."

Trina bit back her resentment. Corey had been sober for over two years now and with it had come a startling clarity and self-awareness. The four years before that had been hell as he looked for validation at the bottom of a bottle. Violent, unpredictable mood swings had everyone walking on eggshells, but he refused all treatment. She'd held the family together and done everything she could to help, but in the end, it wasn't her love that turned things around for him, it had been a near-fatal car wreck.

It had been Trina who'd kept her cool, swung into action, and used her influence to keep the accident out of the press. It would have ruined his career. She'd paid off the victims and ensured their silence, then arranged to have them taken out overseas when their greed got the better of them and they demanded money. She could vividly remember the scene of twisted wreckage, the crumpled car chassis still smoldering.

Corey gave her knee a pat, and Trina focused on his confident smile. She cupped his face and gave him a peck on the lips. "I love you," she blurted. "I'm so proud of you."

She might never forgive Lillianna for being the reason he fell apart in the first place, but her husband had done all the work to put himself back together.

Chapter Fifteen

"T HERE'S A LADY HERE to see you."

Riddick looked up from his computer monitor at his friend and business partner, Eric Sloane. He wasn't expecting anyone, and he was busy, dammit. Work needed to get done before he met up with Khara. "Who is it?"

"Dunno, man." Eric leaned against the door frame and slipped a hand into his pocket. "She's proper—feels like I ought to offer her tea or curtsy or something. Elegant-like. Real pretty. Got an accent."

Riddick's eyes widened, his annoyance at the interruption vanishing. Was Khara here? No one else fit Eric's description. He got to his feet with a flicker of apprehension settling in his stomach. His glance in the mirror was a reflexive one. Good, no crumbs or stray pencil shavings on his cashmere sweater. Presentable. He did the time-honored test of breathing into his cupped palm.

Eric watched this display with interest and quirked an eyebrow in question. "Something you want to tell me, bro?"

"Nope." Riddick rushed from his office. He made a mental note to remind the temp receptionist not to send anyone back to their office suite without screening and announcing them. He'd get Lena to do it, so he didn't rattle her. Good thing Eric kept his office door open most of the time.

Riddick's heart thumped hard when he saw that it was indeed Khara standing in their waiting area. She was wearing a long, butter-yellow raincoat that was striking, like a ray of sunshine against her dark coloring. Proper, yes. Elegant, yes. Way more than pretty. He tried to sound casual with a polite, "Khara, hi."

Like he hadn't been thinking about her nonstop all damn morning since their text exchange about the afternoon's sightseeing plans. Like he hadn't dreamed of fucking her on the Metro in that sexy dress she wore last night. The bright smile she gave him in greeting made him feel a twinge inside.

"I'm sorry to visit unannounced. You said I could come by?"

"Yes, of course." Riddick looked around in dismay at the disordered seating area. Fought off the urge to tidy. Shit, she would think he was a slob. He wasn't, but she wouldn't be able to tell from the current state of his office. "I'm sorry. Were you waiting long? Our assistant's wife was in an accident this morning, and we're on our own today."

"Nothing serious, I hope?"

"Just a fender bender, fortunately, but Lena insisted on taking her to the doctor."

Khara nodded. "Good call. Is this yours?"

It took an effort to drag his gaze away from her face. She was gesturing toward a framed black-and-white photo of one of his smaller projects. The memorial conservatory nestled inside one of the city's historic hotels. "Uh, yes." *Chill, Riddick*, he told himself. He was jittery as a high schooler on his first date.

"It's beautiful. This one, as well?"

"Yes. All of these."

He watched her as she examined each of the five large photos thoughtfully. She was dressed in heather gray slacks and electric blue booties, a bold, patterned scarf at her neck. Pearls again. Sassy frames on her smart girl glasses. Her hair was braided up and looked like a crown. She looked delicious. Riddick had an almost overwhelming urge to muss her up with long, scorching kisses that would leave them both turned on and breathless. He'd noticed how full her lips were last night and had been thinking about them ever since.

"Your designs are mesmerizing. They have... an undeniable passion. Both weight and warmth. I admire how you've infused such personality and character into architecture. You make it dynamic and—oh!" She broke off, pressing a hand to her chest. "My apologies, I've interrupted you. I'm sure you don't want to hear me prattle on."

Oh, but he did. He could have spent hours listening to her talk about his work with that accent. Hell, he'd listen to her read a phone book. Riddick cleared his throat. "What brings you here? Would you like to come back to my office?"

Khara shook her head. "No, thank you. I can't stay long. I'm afraid I must postpone our plans for this afternoon. An urgent matter has arisen for the Queen, and it'll tie up the rest of the day."

He looked at her for a beat. Whatever perfume she was wearing was wrecking his concentration. It was earthy, carried hints of lemon, and it pleased him. "You could have just texted." Riddick winced inwardly at how abrupt the words sounded and softened his tone. "I mean, you didn't have to come all the way down here."

"True, but I wanted to tell you in person. And I was curious about your office. I hope you don't mind."

"Not at all." He lowered his voice. "You're welcome to come any time." He didn't mean for it to sound quite so suggestive but liked that something like the arousal he was feeling flared to life in her eyes. They stared at each other for a long, titillating moment. God, this woman and his reaction to her intrigued him.

Khara swallowed hard before she cleared her throat. "I can't say for certain how long this will last. I was very much looking forward to our outing."

"Me, too. Call me when you shake loose, and we'll make new plans."

"Alright. I'm sorry, the Queen—"

"Work stuff happens, Khara. I understand."

"I had every—*oh*!" She interrupted herself when she spied a bowl of colorful fruit perched on a side table. "Fruit instead of candy is a superb idea!"

Riddick found himself charmed by her enthusiasm. "We try to promote healthy choices here. Although we keep an emergency stash of chocolate around. We're not barbarians."

There was delight in her laughter. "Good strategy. May I? I missed lunch."

"Please."

"I love apples and I'm stealing this idea for my own office." Khara chose a shiny green apple and gave it a bite.

Before he could think better of it, Riddick used the pad of his thumb to wipe away the bit of apple juice that splashed near the corner of her mouth. He pulled back, but not before seeing how her pretty eyes widened in surprise. Not before a quick stab of desire had him longing to taste the sweetness of that apple right from her skin.

She didn't thank him. In fact, she seemed a little flustered. That blush rose in her cheeks again. God, he loved that.

"I—I must get going."

"I'll walk you out." She was so damn sweet. He grabbed a napkin from the holder for her, as well as an umbrella from the stand by the elevators.

A black SUV was waiting for her at the curb. Instead of kissing her there on the sidewalk like he wanted to, Riddick just thought about it and let her see it in his eyes. He could tell she felt it—she bit her lip, and he could see the pulse pounding in her neck. "See you soon Khara. Text me later if you get a chance."

He watched the car until it turned out of sight onto G Street. Whistling, he strode back to the elevator and punched the call button. If that crackling tension between them was anything to go by, they could scorch together.

"So," Eric started when Riddick returned. He'd been waiting for him by Lena's desk. "Elegant lady with the accent."

Smirking but saying nothing, Riddick grabbed an apple from the fruit bowl, tossed it into the air and caught it one-handed. *Superb idea*, she'd said.

"She the reason you're in such a good mood this morning? You got with some smokin' hot—"

Riddick whirled on his friend. "She's not like that. Don't talk about her that way."

"Easy, man." Eric put his hands up in mock surrender. "Just trying to put two and two together. Sorry I misread."

"We went out last night, yes. First date. Didn't even kiss."

Eric gave a low whistle. "She must be something special for you to jump down my throat to defend her honor. This defensive after just a first date? You might be in trouble."

Huh, he did kind of jump down his throat, didn't he? Riddick grunted, biting into his apple. "Nah. She's a diplomat, only here for a few weeks. Neither of us is interested in anything beyond that. One-time thing."

"You didn't say a word about your own, by the way." Eric trailed him back into his office.

"My own what?"

"Honor, Riddick. You defended hers but didn't defend yours."

Riddick snorted. "That's some outdated shit, man."

"Maybe."

"Definitely. Don't let Maya catch you saying that old-timey shit."

Eric shuddered at the thought. "With all the pregnancy hormones in the mix? She'd flay me." He paused at the doorway. "She is smokin' hot, though, bro."

"She is," Riddick agreed, then jutted an accusatory finger at him. "You say anything more than that and your block is getting knocked off."

"You can try. But noted. Well, as much as I'd love to stay here and watch you squirm like a fish on a hook, I gotta run or I'll be late to Holly's assembly."

"Tell her and Maya hi for me."

"Will do. See you tomorrow."

Riddick watched his friend go, then got back to work on the performance reviews. Chuckling to himself, he thought about how much things had changed. It was only a few short years ago that Eric was a confirmed bachelor. Now he was a happy, settled-down husband and father with a baby on the way, and Riddick loved that for him.

He and Eric met in college, where they'd commiserated over being older, non-traditional students, having both served in the military first. College wasn't in Riddick's original plans, but his mother insisted. If she was dying, she wanted to see him with a college degree first. Privately, he'd thought she was being melodramatic, but he would have done anything if it kept her from dwelling on how the breast cancer could kill her. So, he'd enrolled in the University of the District of Columbia and met Eric his second semester at an Architecture Club interest meeting.

The rest, as they say, was history.

They worked out together three times a week. Critical time that served as a combination of staff meeting, general brainstorming, and therapy session, all punctuated by vicious trash-talking. For all they bitched at each other, they were bonded as closely as brothers. Riddick's mother called Eric her other son. Hell, Eric met Maya and her daughter at his mother's "cancerversary" party.

They were opposites in many ways—Eric was short to his tall, light-complexioned to his dark. Eric hailed from a large family, while Riddick was an only child. They'd pledged the same fraternity. Supported each other through shitty relationships, painful breakups, then the death of Eric's father and grandfather in a terrible car accident. In the aftermath of the deadly crash, Eric struggled with depression in his grief. Riddick had refused to let Eric brush it aside as no big deal, even coming to blows over it. Eric told him years later that it might have saved his life.

Even though they'd gone to different grad schools, they remained close. Eric moved out west with his then-girlfriend and returned to the DC area after they broke up. They launched Riddick & Sloane that same year from their shockingly overpriced, run-down basement apartment in DuPont Circle. Riddick still couldn't eat pasta without remembering how they'd survived on packs of instant noodles and whatever odd jobs they could pick up, pouring every cent into their company to make it a success.

And now, years later, here they were—prosperous business owners with a strong work ethic and commitment to giving back to their community. He could not ask for a better friend and partner.

By the time he broke for lunch, Riddick needed a breather from his crowded thoughts.

Just before he jogged across Thirteenth Street to one of his favorite food trucks, an email came in from his mother, reminding him about their dinner next week. An indulgent smile tugged at Riddick's lips. He'd never once missed their bi-weekly dinner, but she needed something to complain about. She was a retired orthodontist who'd thrived on schedules for as long as he could remember. Since she'd moved into the active senior community the year before, she was busier than ever and happily so. The email also reminded him that this was their last dinner together before she left on her big cruise.

One of the junior architects leading a training session for interns startled when he slipped into the back of the conference room and took a seat. He waved off her raised eyebrow, indicating for her to continue the lesson. Although this cohort of five wouldn't be spending any substantive time with him on projects for another few months, Riddick was adamant about giving students regular access.

It mortified Riddick to find himself doodling again during the meeting. Frowning, he peered at what he'd drawn in his notebook. Nothing more than abstract swirls and shapes, but he didn't doodle anymore. He'd ruthlessly shed that habit years ago.

He looked up Lytua in a free moment to read the basics. Shook his head in amusement at the many pictures of Khara captioned incorrectly. That must be a true pain in the ass. Ignoring those, he focused on the accompanying text. Queen Lillianna was an attorney who'd served in Parliament prior to taking the throne. There was nothing substantial even on social media beyond the DC-based Lytuan Ambassador announcing that they were close to solidifying a new community partnership with the Howard University Hospital. That was posted weeks ago.

There was surprisingly little information about Lytua to be found. Was that by design or indicative of the island's level of comfort with tech? Then he remembered Khara saying they kept a low profile. Maybe there was good reason? It wasn't unheard of. Plenty of communities were insular and resisted being overrun by tourists.

Riddick thought of Khara's perceptive gaze on him when she asked what had drawn him to work with a youth in foster care. It was almost a relief that she'd only be here a short time. He got the feeling she wouldn't be hard to fall for. And with his childhood role models, he was not interested in falling for her or anybody.

When she woke the morning after their date and slipped her fingers between her thighs, Khara wasn't surprised to find herself soaking wet. She'd come out of a steamy dream where Riddick had taken her to bed and given it to her but good all night. Vivid dreams were a constant for her, and this was no exception. A lazy smile made its way over her face as she gave a huge, full-body stretch.

She'd masturbated while fantasizing about him right before falling asleep. Her favorite wand vibrator had her back arched in short order, and she drifted off into sexy, sexy imaginings. Apparently, her subconscious thought Riddick knew how to use those sculpted lips.

Khara was tingly, still turned on. If Riddick was in bed next to her now, she'd have pounced on him as soon as she woke up. Nothing she liked more than starting her day with bliss. A jolt of pleasure shot straight down to her core when she cupped her breast, tweaking her nipple. She indulged herself in another orgasm as she imagined those enormous hands of his all over her body. Instead of charging straight to the finish line, Khara took the time to tease—getting close and then backing off a few times until she burst with such magnitude she could scarcely breathe. She lay there lingering for a bit in a satisfied daze before all but springing out of bed. She'd never sprung out of bed a day in her life.

She'd just finished suiting up in workout clothes when her phone buzzed on the desk. Khara walked over to it and her stomach jumped when she saw Riddick's name on the display.

Riddick: Good morning, beautiful Khara. Have you had your coffee?

Khara: I have. Good morning to you. How long have you been up?

Riddick: Since 5. Didn't want to text too early, since that sounded like a deal-breaker.

Khara inserted a sleeping emoji and added a few zzzzz's for good measure:

Khara: Ha. You picked up on that, did you?

Riddick: I had a great time with you last night. Looking forward to seeing you this afternoon.

Khara squealed a little at that and heard Joanne call out, "*Avlah*?"
"I'm fine! Happy noise!"

Khara: I did as well. Will we be able to see much within such a short time frame?

Riddick: Depends. Do you want to see one or two things in-depth or more of an overview of several?

What a considerate thing to ask. Had anyone ever taken such care of her personally? Khara didn't think so. How refreshing.

Khara: I'll let the tour guide decide.

Khara let her legal mind take over and tried to poke holes in her own secret identity argument. The timing couldn't have been better. She didn't have as many social commitments and could easily explain away any absences. This could actually work.

Those feel-good sensations carried her through her first task of the day, even though it wasn't her favorite. Her mind wandered as she pushed through a brisk five-mile walk. She didn't complain when Renee, the Guard trainer, notched her pace up some. Renee traveled with them too and supervised their structured exercise. The smile stayed in place as she worked out with her team, even when Link admonished her to focus on her sparring.

She worked out with the Elites almost every day, where she'd learned practical skills like hand-to-hand and how to fall without knocking herself unconscious. Renee's goal had been to have her in good enough shape in the event she needed to do any running or evading. More than once, Khara had depended upon the endurance, agility, and flexibility she'd built over the years. While she'd never be anything close to a fitness buff, Khara kept working with the trainer throughout her treatment for breast cancer, adjusting as her strength and energy waxed and waned.

Jonnis Reed, one of the Elite Guard, insisted she learn at least some basic defensive moves based on her extensive martial arts background. She'd used those skills more than once, too.

After a long, hot shower and breakfast, Khara turned her attention to one of her favorite duties. "Let's see what the littles wish to know today."

She opened her public email and went to the folder "Kinder Q's". Every kindergartner in Lytua had her as a pen pal. A young constituent had once asked if the Queen would answer questions sent to her by her classmates, thus launching the Kinder Quest pen pal program a few years ago.

Questions came pouring in and Khara committed to answering three per day. So that she could get to everyone, she accepted questions throughout the first two weeks of each school year, then worked through them throughout the year. They came via email, video clips, letters, and once even by a paper airplane. Some questions were quite humorous, while others surprised her with their seriousness.

It was excellent practice of her diplomacy skills.

Khara was daydreaming about what she would wear on the afternoon's excursion, wishing the day would go by faster when things took a sudden turn. She'd been trying to settle a parliament committee dispute via video conference. Both sides were being intractable. That wasn't unusual. But one side invoking an obscure rule obligating all parties to remain in session until they'd reached a satisfactory agreement—that *was*.

It was an underhanded maneuver, and Khara suspected someone had done it just to inconvenience her. Then again, she was always suspicious whenever Senator Richardson was involved. She'd defeated him roundly in the election in spite of his nasty mudslinging. Since then, he never missed an opportunity to take a jab at her or make proceedings unnecessarily difficult. It was a constant irritation. He hadn't been this adversarial when they'd both been senators. She'd served a term right after law school before running.

Khara cursed under her breath. She was stuck and who knew for how long? These debates could last for days. When the realization that she'd have to cancel her sightseeing with Riddick set in, it took the wind right out of her sails. She adjourned the debate for a two-hour break. Both sides needed time to free up their calendars for the foreseeable future. After letting Joanne know, she asked to be taken to Riddick & Sloane.

Even after years of being embroiled in it, Khara had no tolerance for political grandstanding and machinations. Her role here was that of mediator, as she acted as a proxy for the interest of the public at large. It came with its own limitations. It was up to the two parties to hammer out an agreement they could both live with.

The bleak weather mirrored her mood.

As she was driven back to the hotel through the misting rain, Khara leaned back against the seat and closed her eyes. How tasty Riddick had looked dressed informally in a light sweater and dark trousers, his locs held back from his face with an elastic. He'd seemed pleased to see her. There were a couple of moments when it looked like he might want to kiss her. She wasn't sure if she would have let him. It was far too soon, but she still felt butterflies in her stomach at the thought. His fleeting touch near her mouth felt almost electric.

She could feel how hot her face was.

Khara was disappointed, but duty called. She'd been very much looking forward to spending more time with Riddick this afternoon. At least she'd had an easier time referring to the Queen as though she were a separate individual.

What would it take to get this committee matter settled as quickly as possible? Khara had a raincheck she was eager to cash in.

Chapter Sixteen

BACK AT THE HOTEL, before she dove back into round two of the parliament dispute, Khara dialed her best friend. She'd found her at home in Paris, where Yvanda and her husband were both university professors.

"How are you feeling? I can't believe you only have a few weeks to go. Wasn't it just yesterday you announced you were expecting this little jellybean?"

"I'm bored to tears waiting for this kid. And if Jamal asks me one more time how soon I think it will be, I don't know what I'll do. How many variations of 'not soon enough' are there?"

Khara could practically hear Yvanda rolling her eyes. She was exasperated, certainly, but probably enjoying the doting. Most of it, anyway. Jamal was a teddy bear with his boyish good looks, even though he was six-six with a naturally booming voice.

"Enough about us. What's up on your end? Parliament's going into session soon, isn't it?"

"Yes, I'm on travel now, but I'll be back home in time to open session next month. Not that I need a reason to call my bestie, especially with you about to pop, but I actually wanted to tell you something. Vanda... I met someone."

Yvanda's squeal was so enthusiastic it hurt Khara's ear. "Well, it's about time. *Spill!*"

"We went out last night and it was...." Khara gave a happy little sigh, touched her fingertips to the dreamy smile on her lips. "I thought maybe I just wanted to have a fling, but now I don't know. I don't want to muddle things up with sex, even though it would probably be amazing sex." She was babbling.

"Ha, well, that escalated quickly. What's he like?"

How to describe the yummy architect? "He's funny and smart, a gentleman—"

"That could be your cousin or an elderly neighbor, Khara. For pity's sake. *Spill.*"

Khara sighed and tried again, an unbidden grin curving her lips. "He's tall. Intense and quite sexy. Huge hands. Good dancer."

"Now we're talking! What else?"

"Muscles. Gorgeous smile. Smells delicious. But here's the best part, Vanda. He doesn't know who I am."

Yvanda gasped. "Shut the front door. Are you serious right now? Are you *sure*? How did you manage that?"

Khara's summary of how Riddick had mistaken her identity left Yvanda howling with laughter.

When she didn't say more, Yvanda prodded. "Khara, you're killing me here. My hormones are all over the place, and I feel like a blimp. I can barely fit through the bloody door frame these days. Let me live vicariously through you. Details, woman, *details*. I beg of you."

Describing their first date had Khara's belly fluttering in excitement again. Somehow, it was even more delightful as she told Yvanda. "Small problem. He doesn't like the Queen though."

"Oh? How do you figure?"

"He's had some unpleasant experiences with disreputable royals."

"Those lovely people again? I hate when that happens."

The sarcasm was hard to miss. Yvanda had grown up in Lytua, as well. She knew all about royals. "He's staunchly anti-monarchy. He worries the Queen is taking advantage of me. I can barely keep my stories straight. He thinks she's working Khara too hard. Or that I'm working Khara so hard she doesn't get to take breaks and enjoy down time. I'm working myself too hard? I keep wanting to defend her."

"Yourself. I mean Lillianna. Now *I'm* getting confused."

Hell, Khara was thoroughly confusing herself. "I don't know what I should feel when he.... Why on earth am I worried about what he thinks of the Queen?"

"Because it reflects on you, *chérie*. On Khara. *Merde*, you know what I mean. You don't want him to think you're a doormat."

"Yes. That's it precisely." Vanda was always able to pull her scattered thoughts into something cohesive. Part of why she'd made such an excellent campaign manager. "You'd tell me honestly if you thought I was exploiting Joanne, wouldn't you?

"Are you kidding? Of course I would! If you can't depend on your bestie to call you out on your bullshit, what good are they? He didn't see you in the press?"

"No, all the official publicity was done a couple of weeks ago. I was supposed to fly home last week, remember? You know how fickle Washington is. Interest has died down, and they think I'm gone. The press has moved on to the next bigwig coming into town. I had to do some fast thinking for why my picture is captioned as Queen Lillianna."

"Now this I've got to hear. What did you tell him?"

"The Queen and I favor each other and get mixed up in the press all the time. That the paparazzi has been sloppy in their haste to catch candids of the notoriously private and camera-shy Queen."

"Ooh, that's really good, Khara. Well done there."

"Lucky for me, he's even less of a fan of the paparazzi than of royals. Then I had the team remove the official portrait from the website and leave the ones where I'm in my traditional dress."

"You clever bunny. With the mask and headdress, he'll never be able to tell it's you. Unless he gets you close to naked, that is. Alas, I'm too rotund these days to even *look* at my Carnivale costume without crying."

"You'll be back in it soon enough. Maybe we can get you a matching baby carrier with sequins."

"Or feathers. I love that idea! Looks like the solution is simple here, *chérie*: just don't talk about the Queen. You're officially overthinking this. Like everything. You're brilliant at working through thorny issues. It's a trait that makes you a great Queen, as well as a phenomenal attorney, but you're not the Queen with this."

"Thank you. You're right, I know." Warmth bloomed in Khara's chest. "Vanda, you truly are the best friend a woman could ever have."

"You've been saying that since we were in grade seven."

"Still as true as it ever was. I'm so glad you were assigned to be my lab partner."

"Me, too, *chérie*. Better not let Riddick see any of the currency though."

Khara squeaked out a strangled gasp. "Mercy, I didn't even think of that." A stylized rendering of her countenance graced the front of all denominations of Lytuan bills. Panic started to claw at her insides. "This is preposterous. There's no way I can do this."

"Yes, you can. Just be yourself. Except not really. Okay, be a *version* of yourself. Khara is pretty wonderful all on her own. Your own. Gah, you know what I mean."

Khara smiled at the absurdity of the whole thing. She did tend to overthink things, so this was as good a time as any to try letting something play out.

Mentally exhausted after listening to the opposing sides bicker over the finer points of parliamentary procedure, Khara went straight from mediating to donning evening wear for the museum event. Like a superhero shedding her secret identity for a costume change. She hadn't eaten much of her dinner and was decidedly distracted during the speeches at the documentary premiere. Especially after a short text from Riddick. Just seeing his name on the phone screen put an uncontainable smile on her face.

Riddick: I'm glad you came by instead of texting. Hope she didn't work you too hard today.

As this was a private, press-free function, Khara wasn't overly concerned about exposure. Ending human trafficking was a cause she believed in and supported. She made a sizable donation to the organization hosting the event and was just leaving the reception when Speaker Crosby all but swooped in to greet her. Khara had seen her name on the program as a sponsor and had hoped to escape her notice, but no such luck. Her unmarried son wasn't with her, fortunately, but the woman still managed to work in another plug for what a catch he was. Khara demurred when the Speaker enthused that Rufus would be honored to show her around the city. That was *never* going to happen.

Back in her suite, Khara slipped off her gold polka dot stilettos in the foyer with a grateful sigh and carried them to the closet. She shimmied out of her long silk dress, already looking forward to getting into her pajamas, ordering room service, and having a nightcap.

Instead of preparing for the next day's continued mediation like she should have, Khara savored a glass of crisp Riesling along with the smooth harmonies of some of En Vogue's earlier hits. She lounged on one of the suite's luxurious sofas with her bare feet tucked up beneath her, nibbling on a fruit and cheese plate and gazing out at the city's twinkling lights. Her sleepy mind wandered, wondering what Riddick was up to. Was he in bed? Did he wear pajamas, or did he sleep nude? Had he thought of her today?

Thoughts of Riddick's gorgeous smile had preoccupied her all afternoon and evening. To say she wanted to see him again and enjoy every moment of him liking her was an understatement. She knew it couldn't last. At some point, she'd have to tell him the truth, and all bets might be off. Until that time came, though, she was going to wring out every drop of enjoyment she could.

Chapter Seventeen

RIDDICK JERKED AWAKE, COVERED in a fine sheen of sweat. It took him a moment of lying there in the darkness to catch his breath and slow his heart rate. Once he had, he padded to the ensuite bathroom and splashed some cool water on his cheeks, attempting to banish the nightmare.

These damn dreams rattled him, and he hated that. He didn't dream about his birth parents often, only whenever he felt stressed about something or had a lot on his mind. They always stirred up the lingering shame he felt over his childhood, even though he knew very well it was misplaced. Maddening.

He could still see the disgust on Evelyn's once-pretty face as she sneered at him the last time he'd seen her. They were in the courtroom vestibule. She'd grabbed his arm and given it a vicious squeeze. "Don't go thinking you're better than me, you little shit. We're the same. You'll always be gutter trash! Don't you dare look down on me."

He could still smell her sour breath.

It still cut.

Glaring at his own countenance in the mirror, Riddick could just make out hints of Evelyn and Jordan, or what they might have looked like if they'd recovered from the hard living and drug abuse that killed them. They'd come so close to taking him down with them. He hated when those memories intruded on his life. The pain had lessened over the years, but it wasn't his favorite thing to think about.

It was too early to get up, so he tried going back to bed. Sleep eluded him. After tossing and turning for longer than he should have, Riddick threw the covers back with a curse. He wasn't that kid anymore. He'd escaped his shitty parents. Barely, but he'd still gotten away.

Truly irritated now, Riddick threw on a pair of sweatpants and jogged downstairs. It was a rest day, but he needed movement and some fresh air. He'd sort it out while he ran.

Old Town Alexandria was a runner's paradise, and Riddick's thoughts churned as the city came to life around him. The rhythmic pounding of his feet on the riverside path soothed him some, as it usually did. He could feel the frown, and he ran until some of the tension dissipated. Tried to think of anything except his childhood, which didn't work. Even after a hard five-mile run at a punishing pace, Riddick was still edgy.

The light breeze coming off the Potomac chilled his sweat-soaked skin while he cooled down. He consciously willed his muscles to relax, calling on the mindfulness exercises he'd used in the past. Concentrated on his senses—the sharp tang of the river, the sunlight streaming through the bare branches of the trees, the early morning sounds of people starting to move about their day.

Riddick raised a hand in greeting to one of his neighbors as she rode by on a bicycle with her puppy in the front basket.

You're okay, he reminded himself, then went inside. *Not that foster kid anymore.*

He put on some Earth, Wind, and Fire while he was getting dressed in an attempt to lift his spirits. Before long, he was belting out the lyrics to "In the Stone." It buoyed him some, but he remained out of sorts all morning—griping about traffic, overly annoyed with a minor shipping delay, impatient with an intern. After overhearing the snarled curses when he jammed a finger in the paper drawer of his printer, Lena ordered him to go get a second cup of coffee and stay away until his mood had improved.

On a whim, Riddick texted his mother to ask, "You ever regret adopting me?"

The phone rang almost immediately. Dr. Parie Riddick was beside herself. "What kinda absurd question is that, Joshie? Never. Not for one moment."

It still choked him up to remember how devoted to him she had always been—right from the very beginning. "Even when I was a pain-in-the-ass teenager?"

"No!"

"Not even when Evelyn hurt you?" His voice dropped. He would never forget his outrage at finding out his birth mother had assaulted Parie, sending her to the hospital for several days. Terrified, Riddick flat-out refused when Child Protective Services tried to place him in another home on a temporary basis until they discharged her. He was determined to stay with Parie and was finally able to do so with the help of the social worker assigned to his case. He arranged it so that a temporary guardian spent those days at the hospital with him. It wasn't until years later that Riddick learned the social worker had been his biggest advocate, having argued passionately on his behalf during an emergency hearing on the matter.

"Not even then," Parie said. "What's bringing this on?"

That stupid dream. A jumbled mess of tangled and unidentifiable emotion twisted in his gut. "Just thinking." He loosened his grip some when he realized he was holding the phone too tight.

Their conversation, as it so often did, turned to Parie's upcoming around-the-world cruise. She reminded him again of their dinner date, that it was the last one before she headed out for nearly six months. He was almost as excited as she was for the big adventure.

Parie was a widow when she came into Riddick's life. She'd never remarried, but she was enjoying spending some time with a few dapper male residents at the active seniors' facility. *Good for her.* If anybody deserved a second chance at love, it was her. From what she'd told him, they were keeping things casual, so he hadn't been invited to meet any of the gentlemen yet. They sounded like decent fellows, but Riddick would still kick an old dude's ass if one of them did his Ma wrong.

"Seriously, Joshie, what's on your mind?"

He panicked a little when Khara's face popped into his mind. "Nothing, really. I, uh, gotta go. See you Friday."

Chapter Eighteen

"Hey. I was just thinking about you."

Riddick's voice in her ear still did something to her insides whenever Khara heard it. She could feel herself smiling at the phone. "Do you have a few minutes? I'm calling in my official capacity."

"Sure. What's up?"

"Allow me to offer congratulations. The Kingdom of Lytua would like to offer you the embassy project officially. The Queen asks how soon you'll be able to present a preliminary proposal. We have the budget information ready."

"Huh. About that. I was going to call today. I need to withdraw myself from consideration because of a conflict of interest."

Khara's heart sank. "Oh, no. I'm sorry to hear that. May I ask what's presenting a conflict?"

"I'm more interested in the Queen's assistant than taking on the project. I don't want there to be any ethics concerns."

Khara blinked, too stunned to say a word in response.

She was silent for so long that Riddick spoke up. "Khara? Did you hear me?"

"I... yes—but I'm not sure I—*what*?" It was three days after she canceled their date. They talked every night and texted often. She'd succeeded in getting the committee logjam cleared and their outing rescheduled. It had taken more coaching, navigating, negotiating, and patience than she realized she possessed. Then again, she was motivated—she'd really wanted to see Riddick again as soon as possible.

"Let me make this clearer. I'm turning down the project because I'd rather spend time with you. I can refer you to one of my former students. She does excellent work and is just starting out. This would be a perfect project to help her get established. I'll text you her contact information as soon as we're finished."

Khara was having difficulty getting her mind wrapped around this. Surely, he wasn't saying what it sounded like. "Wait. You're choosing to date over a lucrative professional project? That's—that's...."

"Potentially the best decision I've ever made."

Khara's breath caught.

"I like you, Khara, and I want to keep getting to know you better. I'm not foolish enough to throw away any kind of chance with you over money."

It was the sweetest thing anyone ever said to her. A goofy smile took over her face, and she hardly said two words during the rest of the conversation. She was still holding the phone receiver in her hand when Joanne breezed in after a brisk knock.

Seeing she was done with the call, Joanne smiled and started gathering the files from the conference room table. "I'll get the contract drawn up tomorrow for your review if that's alright. *Avlah?*" Joanne noticed she'd not moved. "*Avlah*, what's wrong?"

Khara blinked, her cheeks burning. She felt dazed. "He turned it down."

Joanne pursed her lips. "Well, we have some wiggle room in the budget if money's an issue."

Khara shook her head and laughed a little at the absurdity of it all. Had this just happened? "He turned it down because he says he wants to date me and doesn't want a conflict of interest."

Joanne brightened and gave an approving nod. "Smart man."

"No, he must be joking. Or delusional." When her phone dinged with a text message, Khara picked it up. It was from Riddick—the name and contact information for the referral, as promised. Her heart leaped when she read the second part he had written.

Riddick: What's a good time to pick you up? Where we're going is a couple of hours away and opens at 10.

Her hand trembled as she whispered, "He gave me a referral for one of his students, and he's asking what time to pick me up tomorrow."

"See? Not joking and not delusional. Just good taste and smart enough to know a gem when he sees her."

Khara warmed at the praise and thanked Joanne. Instead of texting him back, she called.

"You cannot be serious," she said when he answered.

Joanne quietly closed the door behind her as she left the room.

"I absolutely am. You have your referral. Now we can firm up our plans."

"But—"

"The subject is closed, Khara." His tone was low and resolute. It sounded like he was in a car. "I made my choice. Now, what time to pick you up? There'll be a bit of walking involved, so wear comfortable shoes and dress warmly."

They hung up after deciding they would get coffee when Riddick picked her up at half past eight. Khara hadn't a clue where they were going. Joshua Riddick had tilted her world on its axis.

He'd chosen *her*.

She'd already decided to come clean about her identity on Saturday, but now she hesitated. Since Riddick would no longer be involved with the Queen, there was no need to cut things short yet.

Here was a unique opportunity. She would be in the area for another few weeks. She could continue as the "Queen's assistant" in her off time for a while longer. Then she could just enjoy the company of the most fascinating man she'd ever met. The truth could wait for now while she maintained the fiction of things happening with the Queen. Better still, maybe she could delegate the embassy project to the current ambassador. It shouldn't be a complicated matter to exist solely as Khara with Riddick if she was careful.

After all, it wasn't as though they'd run into anyone who would recognize her. She hadn't yet.

Flicking on his turn signal, Riddick could feel himself grinning as he took his exit from the Beltway.

The conversation couldn't have gone better. By the time they'd hung up, he felt inordinately pleased with himself that he'd surprised Khara. Something told him she was probably impossible to catch off guard. Too observant and sharp.

He'd been overanalyzing things, he decided. They would have a few dates, maybe something more. Maybe not. Either way, nothing earth-shattering. He could do straightforward as long as he kept some distance. Easy.

Putting people before money was a lesson Parie taught him early. Bad things could happen in relationships when money got involved. Best not to go there. With the embassy project now off the table, he and Khara were free to do whatever they wanted. They could get on with things, whatever that ended up entailing.

Riddick used the car's wireless connection to send Dion a voice text reminding him that their study session at his office had moved up a half-hour. Then he placed a good-sized delivery order from Ben's Chili Bowl to coincide with their arrival. Riddick didn't even bother to ask about snacks anymore. The teen ate like he did manual labor all day. Watching him shovel in food made Riddick envious of the kid's metabolism.

Dion didn't really need Riddick to help him study, but his foster home was full of boisterous younger kids. It wasn't an environment conducive to quiet work and focus. Riddick made his office available as often as he could for Dion to get the peace he needed to do his best work. More than that, he got the opportunity to learn firsthand what it took to lead a successful professional life. Hopefully, through the behind-the-scenes access, he was growing accustomed to seeing people who looked like him as decision-makers. It wasn't enough just to tell him about it, Riddick believed. He needed to see it in action. He didn't sugarcoat or soft pedal anything—Riddick was honest about any frustrations or challenges he faced.

Dion had wandered around the office suite awestruck on his first visit, too afraid to say anything or even sit down. It wasn't until the third visit that he started asking questions. He was inquisitive and wanted to know how everything worked.

Riddick smiled to himself. That curiosity and thirst for knowledge reminded him very much of Khara.

These days Dion was utterly comfortable at Riddick & Sloane, leaving his belongings strewn about whenever he was there. Lena assured him this was trademarked teen behavior. He was at home lounging in the seating or kicking back on a pile of throw pillows on the accent rug. It made Riddick's soul happy.

A delivery guy laden with bags arrived at Riddick & Sloane soon after Riddick had gotten settled, loosened his tie, and rolled up his sleeves. Dion bounced through the door with his navy and yellow backpack stuffed to capacity as he was unpacking the cartons of food onto the table in his office. Within moments, the kid had kicked off his sneakers and slung his school bag into a corner with a thud. Dion grunted mostly one-word answers to Riddick's questions about his day while inhaling a mountain of half-smokes and chili.

He was distracted as Dion worked on his chemistry homework and a civics project. There were technical drawings to review and a board meeting next week he was supposed to be preparing for, but Khara was wreaking havoc on his concentration. How would he narrow down all the places he wanted to show her?

It took a few moments for him to realize Dion had stopped what he was doing and was giving him a strange look. "What?"

"What gives? Something's up with you."

"Nothing's up."

"Uh-huh." Dion crossed his arms and smirked. "Something's different. Is it a chick? It's a chick, isn't it?"

A jolt went through Riddick. *What could possibly have tipped him off to that?* "We've been over this. Women aren't poultry, Dee. Remember?"

"Right, right. It's a *lady*, isn't it?"

The singsong emphasis had Riddick snorting a laugh. Very little escaped the savvy, street-smart kid's notice. "Maybe."

Dion whooped. "Ooh, I knew it! Does she have a big—" He broke off when Riddick's eyebrows shot up. "Er, brain?"

Nice save, kid. "She's very smart, yes. Brilliant. But that's all I'm telling you until there's more to tell."

"Alright, then, playboy."

The nonchalance in his voice didn't fool him. Dion knew damn well Riddick wasn't a playboy of any sort, but Riddick recognized the ploy for what it was: a fishing expedition to get him to divulge further details. He didn't take the bait. "Okay, let's see some more work on this chemistry. *O prefieres practicar la conjugación de verbos?*"

Dion gave a dramatic groan. "I definitely do *not* wanna practice verb conjugation."

"*En español por favor.*"

With an accompanying eye roll, Dion huffed out, "*No quiero practicar la conjugación de verbos. Hoy o cualquier otro día.*"

He might bitch about it, but Dion's Spanish accent and pronunciation were excellent. Riddick let him off the hook for now, although just temporarily. There was a unit test scheduled for next week. The kid didn't know it yet, but Riddick had arranged for Dion to spend five weeks over the summer in a homestay immersion program in Costa Rica. A local art teacher would be providing private lessons too. Would he be able to hold out until the end of the school year to tell him about it all, as planned?

Satisfied Dion had his attention back on finishing his lab report, Riddick tried to keep his mooning over Khara to a minimum as he worked on his board meeting presentation.

Chapter Nineteen

A PUNCH IN THE gut couldn't have been more surprising than how fresh and appealing Khara was when she stepped off the elevator for their date. Swathed in a plaid poncho, jeans, and chestnut-colored knee boots, she cut quite a figure. Elegant, as Eric observed. That gorgeous smile was the kicker.

Riddick had texted from the lobby and didn't have to wait long for her to arrive. The man with her in the elevator didn't get out on the ground floor, only gave Khara a nod before the doors closed again. A ripple of curiosity went through Riddick. "Is that man with you? I've seen him before."

"One of my colleagues," Khara said. "Security. The Guard are very protective of me."

"I imagine so. You're a direct conduit to the Queen."

He'd left his car parked in the roundabout. She offered thanks when he held the door for her. She had to step up on the Audi's running board to get in. When he slid behind the wheel, she was peering around the vehicle's interior with huge eyes. "Did you drop something?"

"No, just thinking this is quite a large vehicle for just one person."

Riddick groaned dramatically as he fastened his seatbelt. "You wouldn't believe how hard it is to find something where my head isn't on the ceiling and my knees scrunched into my chest. Plenty with either or, though. I felt like Goldilocks."

"What will you do if you have tall children? Do you want children?"

"Someday. I'll have to cross that bridge when I get to it. You?"

"The same. Someday. Not anytime soon."

"Alright, then." Riddick retrieved his sunglasses from the cubby in the SUV's dash and slipped them on. "I know my audience. First stop: coffee."

As soon as they walked through the front door of Lot 38 on Second Street in Southeast, Khara closed her eyes and inhaled deeply. "It smells like heaven in here."

"They roast their own beans. This is one of my favorite hidden little gems."

Riddick watched Khara peruse the menu, then study the baked goods in their refrigerated case as though they held the meaning of life. When she had trouble deciding between a couple of delicious-looking options, he ordered one of each. He winked at her when she started to protest. "I still owe you for ruining your breakfast."

"When—? Oh, the morning we met!"

The coffeehouse was busy on a Saturday morning, but the wait went by quickly. Khara declared it worth every moment when she took her first sip of a caramello.

"Let's enjoy it here. We're not in a hurry."

Perched on stools at the window counter, they shared a fat blueberry muffin and a decadent chocolate pumpkin scone. She savored food, Riddick realized. It tickled him to watch the pleasure cross her face with the first bite of each sweet. Her lips were painted a soft, sexy pink today.

"I do love American breakfast pastries. So very decadent."

"What's breakfast like for you at home?"

"Typical Caribbean fare. Codfish, potatoes, none of the sweets common here. I do love a good pancake."

"Do you now?" Riddick sipped his mocha and filed that bit of information away for later.

When Khara stopped to read the historical marker at Canal Park on the way back to the car, she exclaimed, "Isn't urban gardening a wonder? How is this still so lush in the autumn?"

The three-block space was one of Riddick's favorite places in the city. "It stays green year-round. Underground cisterns collect the stormwater runoff. They reuse it for something like ninety percent of the irrigation, plus the summer fountain water and then the ice rink they build here in winter. This actually used to be a canal connecting the Anacostia River to the Potomac."

Khara was looking at him with wide eyes, nearly gawking. He heated under that impressed gaze and gave a self-conscious shrug. "I'm an architectural nerd. When I find cool stuff, I study it."

"The cisterns must be enormous."

"Eighty-thousand gallons."

Khara grinned and squeezed his forearm. "I love that you knew that off the top of your head! We've converted the tallest buildings in Augustus—that's Lytua's capital—to succulent roofs. The result of a recent island-wide push for greener initiatives. That's one of the things I'm here for."

Between her unexpected touch and the mirth dancing in her eyes, Riddick was glad to be full of recondite facts for once.

"So, where are we going?"

"You'll see when we get there."

"Very mysterious."

He laughed. "Don't worry, I think you'll like it."

They filled the drive with thought-provoking discussion interspersed with lots of laughter, the mellifluous vocals of John Legend in the background. Riddick remembered Khara saying he was one of her favorite artists on their first date. Her perfume was there again, that subtle citrus smell he remembered.

"I have a confession to make," Khara began as they cruised through the rolling hills of the Orange County countryside.

"Yeah? Go for it."

"I hope you won't think me impertinent, but when you first asked me to dinner, I thought I might want to have a fling with you." The words spilled out in a breathless rush.

Impertinent? Try enticing. It surprised him to find she was looking at him almost warily, like she was expecting some sort of blowback. It was the only time he'd seen her confidence falter. "I don't think you're impertinent for thinking about the same thing I did." Her use of past tense piqued his interest, though. "And what about now? You obviously changed your mind."

"You're more than fling-worthy, I assure you. It's been a long time for me, and I don't want to rush simply because I'll be in town only for a few weeks. I know we don't have endless time, but I would like to go slow."

"We can do that." Some of the tension eased from her features. He wondered at her. Had this been stressing her? Did she think he'd bail because she didn't want to jump into bed with him right away? Jesus, what kind of impatient assholes had she been dealing with? Rushing led to mistakes. Something told him Khara was damn well worth an investment of time.

"I may not be ready to get physical yet, but I believe it is important to discuss contraceptive concerns well ahead of time."

"Agreed. I always use condoms and get tested yearly. You?"

"I have an IUD. And regular medical checkups, as well. That's independent of if I'm involved with someone or not."

"Of course. Same. So, tell me, how is it that there's no ex-mister Therin in your history?"

She wrinkled her nose and made a harrumphing noise. "I was engaged a few years ago. Didn't work out."

"He must be a fool to have given you up. Truly an idiot."

Khara swiveled to face him in the car's interior. "How do you know I didn't kick *him* to the curb?"

"Did you?"

She made a face. "No."

"Then he must be a fool, like I said."

"My team, best friend, and sister all said essentially the same thing. The whole breakup was quite ugly and surreal."

Riddick's hands tightened on the steering wheel. He didn't like the thought of someone treating her unkindly. "I'm sorry. Sounds like it sucked."

"It was a nightmare. Abysmal timing. Such a busy time for me professionally, so much happening at once. There were signs that we wouldn't last, but it did hurt. I like to think he did me a favor. Getting let down horribly by someone you should be able to depend upon makes you re-prioritize things."

"I bet it did. Sorry, didn't mean to dredge up painful memories."

"No, please don't be. I haven't thought of him in a while. What was your last relationship like?"

"Not the greatest or healthiest. We both worked too much and had too little in common outside the, ah, the—"

"Bedroom?" There was a teasing lilt in her tone.

Riddick cleared his throat and shifted uncomfortably in the driver's seat. "Uh, yes."

"No need to dance around it. Sexual health is very important to us Lytuans. We talk about it openly, and you and I both know we've had previous lovers. Tell me about her. What was her name?"

"Her name is Shae. We dated for a few months. She's an art historian—highly respected, but honestly, we struggled to find things to talk about. Nothing salacious or dramatic in the breakup. We were wasting each other's time."

With no connection beyond the sexual, Riddick's interest fizzled. He could remember the exact moment when it happened. He was sitting across from Shae in a romantic restaurant, and she'd said something suggestive. She was all but spilling from a dress designed to seduce—and he thought—what the hell are you doing? Shae was successful and confident. Gorgeous.

And it bored Riddick out of his damn skull. He couldn't make it make sense.

He didn't have trouble finding company when he wanted it, though he didn't just go sticking his dick into any rando woman.

"Well... good sex shouldn't be a waste of time."

That quiet pronouncement surprised a laugh out of him. "You're right, it shouldn't. It wasn't. I was just... it wasn't enough." Damn, now *he* was flustered.

"Barboursville Vineyards," Khara read a giant weathered sign at an intersection when he slowed to turn down a gravel road. "Is this where we're going? I haven't been to a winery in ages! We don't have any in Lytua."

The delight in her voice made Riddick smile. "It's on the grounds of an eighteenth-century estate. I've reserved a tasting brunch and tour for us."

"Oh, that sounds splendid."

Brunch at the winery's remodeled Library 1821 was exquisite. Khara insisted on giving her compliments to the chef, and before long, she and the older Haitian gentleman were having an in-depth conversation about local sourcing, which led to an impromptu kitchen tour and a mini cooking lesson. He hadn't even known she spoke French, too.

Did *anyone* stand a chance against that earnestness and charming accent? Hearing her converse in two languages so effortlessly was kind of hot.

Riddick watched Khara light up with joy sampling a balsamic reduction glaze she'd just learned to prepare. He nearly groaned seeing her suck a dollop of the decadent sauce from her thumb as she approached where he was sitting. She was holding out a spoon.

"Here, try it." He accepted the taste she offered, even though he would have preferred to pull her down across his lap and kiss her senseless. "Delicious." The only way it could have been more so was if he'd drizzled it all over her body and was licking it off. *Down, boy, sheesh.*

Neither of them was a wine snob, but both enjoyed what they learned on the tour. Their guide was friendly and seemed genuinely thrilled to answer Khara's many questions about the winemaking process.

When Khara missed her footing going up the steep stairs on the tour, Riddick grabbed her around the waist and caught her up against him, preventing what could have been a nasty tumble. The motion pressed her back to his front for a moment, and her body was soft against his, with that curvy bottom of hers at just the right height to come into contact with his groin. He was reluctant to let her go but did so quickly before she saw what even that brief contact had stirred to life. Her gasp and breathy thanks did nothing to help his hard-on.

"Too much wine already?" Riddick teased. "Do I have to cut you off?"

The bright peal of her laugh floated back to him. "No. I'm not usually so clumsy."

After exploring the historic Landmark Ruins, they sat outside on the terrace in the crisp autumn air, laughing, talking, and playing lawn games, surrounded by the resplendent fall foliage of the Blue Ridge Mountains. Riddick was surprised to learn Khara had a competitive streak a mile wide. It matched his own. Between rounds of corn hole and croquet, the afternoon gave way to early evening. They were content even just to sit with their wine and house-made charcuterie, listening to the guitar trio that had set up on the back deck of the massive Wine Barn.

Before they knew it, the temperature was dropping, and the beginning of a spectacular sunset was underway.

When Khara reached for the poncho she'd shed as their ladder golf competition heated up, Riddick draped the baby-soft cashmere around her shoulders. Somehow, he managed to resist the urge to tilt her face up to his so he could brush his lips against hers. Everything about this day had been just right.

They decided to browse the vineyard's gift shop before starting the drive back to the city. By the time Riddick returned from buying a matching hoodie and hat for Dion, Khara had a cart filled to overflowing with merchandise. "What in the world?"

"Gifts for the rest of my team," Khara said. "I couldn't resist. Plus, two of their wives are pregnant." She chose tiny "Virginia is for Lovers" t-shirts for the babies, and bigger ones for the team's older children. "Let's get some wine to take back."

As the clerk rang up the purchases, Riddick sidled up to Khara to ask, "So, if I offered to pay for this, you'd say...?"

Khara gave a shake of her head and smiled. "I'd say no thank you. These are my people and I want to spoil them. It's a sweet thought, though."

They packed the boxes and bags into the car and set off. "This was a real treat, Riddick. I had a grand time. Although I bought more than I should have. Thank you."

This was a good choice. Khara consumed knowledge like she needed it to live. It was a refreshing change to have a more cerebral, creative-type date. So different from his usual haunts.

If they went to the winery again, Riddick decided he'd book them a stay at the nearby 1804 Inn. Maybe in one of the cottages for more privacy. The thought that they might only need one room by that point made the horndog within him rear its head. Some fascinating history, some eclectic music, thoughtful, scintillating conversation—those would be the ways to seduce a brilliant woman like Khara. And once he turned on her brain....

Riddick snapped his thoughts back from imagining firelight playing over the bare skin of her beautiful body—Jesus. He stole a look in her direction, but she'd reclined the passenger seat and her eyes were closed.

Khara nodded off on the way back to her hotel after they'd stopped for an early dinner. Something strange settled in Riddick's stomach at the sight of her relaxed face. He wanted to tuck the rogue curls that had escaped her headband back behind her ear but didn't. That was too familiar, too intimate. He rarely went for all-day dates, but this excursion left him wanting more. Not at all what he'd expected.

Riddick didn't consider himself especially romantic. Sure, he knew how to show a lady a good time, knew how to have an engaging conversation. The talks with Khara, though, were different. Much deeper, filled with a surprising amount of introspection.

She seemed to get him and his sense of humor. He would have examined that more closely if this had longer-term potential. Since she was only going to be in town for a few weeks, there was no need. They could have a lot of fun during that time. He was attracted to her, not looking for love or even a long-distance relationship. She was just as up for it as he was. So why not just relax and enjoy it?

Khara called ahead to request help with getting all the bags and boxes upstairs. Two Elites, Wyn Gregoire and Jonnis Reed, met them at the lobby entrance with a luggage cart. Both of them nodded to Riddick and offered friendly smiles.

"*Did you leave anything in the store, Avlah?*" The man asked when he saw the SUV's cargo area was chock-full. "*Thought you hated shopping.*"

"Oh, quiet you," Khara replied in English. "I have stuff for your wife in here." To the woman, she said, "For Trista and Kingston, too." To Riddick, she explained, "Her little girl and husband."

Riddick helped load the cart, then said his goodbyes. There was a moment of hesitation when it looked like he might kiss her, but he smiled and squeezed her hand instead. Khara's heart leaped to racing, even as she felt a brief pang of disappointment watching him climb back into his car. As she watched the dark, muscular SUV that was almost as sexy as he was turn a corner out of sight, she felt a frown crease her brow. Did he not want to kiss her? For that matter, why hadn't she kissed *him*? Wasn't it too soon? It was only their second date, she reminded herself. *Relax.*

As if reading her mind, Jonnis remarked, "I do believe Mr. Riddick may have wanted to kiss you there, *Avlah.*"

"Oh, he definitely thought about it," Wyn cosigned. "Game recognizes game."

Both Jonnis and Khara groaned at his flex. Everyone knew Wyn was mostly all talk. Even though he'd nearly messed it up beyond repair, he was happily married to the love of his life. He doted on his wife and would move heaven and earth for her. "Wasn't it your *game* that got Sam pregnant?" Jonnis asked.

"You're damn right it did. That's game of a whole different level."

All three of them laughed at that and went inside. Khara tried to ignore the secret longing that rolled through her.

Chapter Twenty

B ACK HOME THAT EVENING, Riddick gave in to the twitching of his fingers and got the art kit down from where he'd stashed it. He'd bought it on a lark a few years back thinking he might want to give drawing another try. He couldn't quite bring himself to do it. The mere sight of the tools evoked potent emotion in him at the time. He'd broken out in a sweat before he'd even finished setting it all up. Riddick had shoved everything back in the case with his heart hammering and forgotten about it until now.

No sweating this time, though, not even when the familiar scents hit him. Only relief that everything was still intact.

What the hell, he thought, then picked up a charcoal pencil.

There was just the slightest hesitation before he gave himself over to his creative instincts. The pull was powerful, like something wild yearning to break loose.

He'd forgotten that he always worked best when he didn't think about it too much, but instead let the medium decipher the tumultuous emotions jumbled inside. He let the urge flow out of him without any conscious thought. He wasn't certain what was compelling him. More than twenty years had passed since he'd drawn anything. And the last time....

His shitty childhood was something he didn't let himself think about often and with good reason. It was a rabbit hole of trauma and anguish. Without trying to direct any of it, Riddick let the heartache his memories stirred pour onto the page before him.

Jordan and Evelyn had often dumped him with the few friends or relatives who were still speaking to them so they could get high. They would pretend they were going to the car to get something and then take off, sometimes for days at a time. Whenever it happened, Riddick did his best to take up as little space as possible, keeping to himself and asking for nothing.

Why the hell was he thinking about this now? He hadn't thought of Cousin Vickie in ages. His memories of her were fuzzy, but he could still recall the kindness shining in her eyes when she looked at him. Smell the lilac hand soap she used. Vickie had been the one to make sure he got to school semi-regularly. She'd made him feel welcome in her home, even when his deadbeat parents disappeared for weeks on end.

An old, long-forgotten ache settled in the pit of his stomach as he remembered the barely-concealed resentment from Vickie's other children. She had several in the small, cramped duplex, and he was one more mouth to feed, one more burden on her shoulders. A rival for their overworked mother's precious, limited attention. How old had he been? Nine? Ten?

An observant teacher recognized his affinity for the visual arts and connected him with an artist who sometimes taught enrichment classes at the school. Now Riddick wondered who had paid for those classes. A scholarship, perhaps? He would never know. He'd been so proud to win a district-wide art contest, where the prize was a sizable gift certificate to an artists' supply store. He and Vickie alone had taken the bus across town to get there. Riddick could still remember the wonder in his heart as he meandered down every aisle before picking anything out. The place had seemed magical to him. He had painstakingly chosen materials and media he'd always wanted to try with trembling fingers. How his hands had shaken as he accepted the bags with his purchases.

The supplies had been his most prized possessions. After Riddick had caught one of the other kids destroying his sketchbook, he kept everything with him at all times. A couple of kids had tried to gang up on him to take it, but he fought back viciously and kept his mouth shut tight when Cousin Vickie demanded to know what happened.

Art class had been the one place he felt like he belonged. The one place where his raggedy, ill-fitting clothing hadn't mattered. Only the end result did. He'd learned from that first art teacher how to trust his talent and let his gift lead him where it wanted to take him. For a time, he had almost been happy. Vickie had known he was proud and made no attempt to force change upon him.

By then, Riddick had hardened his exterior into a solid "don't care" attitude. It was the only way to survive.

The falling out—when it had come—was utter devastation. He'd been awakened in the early hours of the morning by the screaming and sat there in the dark, wide-eyed and frightened. Then as Evelyn ruthlessly dragged Riddick down the stairs, Vickie ran after them in her nightgown, pleading with her to allow him to stay. He'd been shocked to see his mother ball her fist and strike the older woman in the face, knocking her to the floor. The sound of the blow had seemed to echo off the halls in the narrow corridor.

Riddick had tried to go to Vickie, but Evelyn wrenched him back so violently he stifled a cry of pain.

"He's *my* kid, not yours! He'll never be yours!"

Vickie had dabbed at her split lip and gotten unsteadily to her feet. "Please, at least let him take his art things."

The last thing Riddick remembered of the night was Vickie hugging him and crying desperately.

Overnight, his life had lapsed into a hell of uncertainty and precariousness again. Evelyn and Jordan had regularly beat the shit out of each other, and when he couldn't get out of the way fast enough or make himself disappear, him too. Food had been scarce. Stability even more so. Riddick hated every moment of their squalid existence.

Vickie had a heart attack shortly thereafter and died before the ambulance could get her to the hospital. Evelyn's cruelty had known no bounds, for she had gleefully told Riddick it was *his* fault, then laughed at his distress. She'd slapped him so hard his teeth rattled, and he tasted blood. Hurling insults at her son, she wrested the art supplies he'd been clutching to his chest and laughed even harder as she threw them down and stomped on them. Riddick had watched helplessly as his mother ground his precious instruments into powder. He'd learned an invaluable lesson that day. Not to get attached to anything or anyone. It was a weakness others could wield against him as a weapon.

Riddick closed his eyes for a heartbeat now, trying to banish the gnawing throb of grief. He would never raise a hand to a child.

While they had been squatting in an abandoned house, desperate for their next fix, his parents belatedly realized they could make money off his artistic talent. Once they had scrounged up some tattered materials, they came up with a grift. They put Riddick to work drawing caricatures of tourists at the beach's boardwalk while they pickpocketed the subjects. Riddick had hated every second of it and often dreamed of being anyplace but where he was.

The day his whole world crashed around him—Riddick had sensed it looming on the horizon. A knockdown drag-out fight had already taken place over the last stale donut, which had been the only food at the time. Jordan and Evelyn were both drunk and high—Riddick knew the signs. Their bloodshot eyes and unsteadiness told him it was going to be a bad day.

His painfully empty stomach had felt shriveled and curled in on itself, but he'd said nothing about it. Complaints only attracted unwanted attention. Just once, he would've liked to have made it through a whole day without drawing his parents' ire.

Jordan and Evelyn had grievously injured a would-be scam victim who fought back that day. It was what put Riddick on the radar of Child Protective Services. The sight of all the scam victim's blood sickened him, and he was too weak to run like he was supposed to when the police showed up. His legs wouldn't move. Seeing his grimy and malnourished state, the authorities removed him from his parents' custody and placed him in a foster home. It was the first of many.

Riddick had wanted nothing to do with art after that. His birth parents had corrupted the one thing that had brought him joy, and it had broken something deep inside him. He hated the part of himself they'd used to steal from people.

Now Riddick's hand ached from gripping the pencils too tightly, and he stopped abruptly, his heart knocking painfully against his ribcage. He blinked hard, sat back on his stool, and saw with a glance at his watch that he'd been drawing non-stop for over an hour. He hadn't moved from where he was sitting, at the high kitchen counter.

He'd had no plan, no idea what would come pouring out once he released the tight hold he kept on what was inside him. The energy had flowed unchecked. He was almost afraid to see the image that had taken shape on the page before him, but curiosity won out and he went ahead and looked anyway.

The backdrop of sinister, swirling chaos didn't surprise him in the least. It was so dark inside him when he let himself really look, too much a dismal morass for any significant light to penetrate. It was the face he'd drawn in the center of it that gave him pause.

Khara's face.

When she'd discovered the bowl of apples in his office.

Riddick leaned in to study the rendering critically. He'd captured her exuberance perfectly, right along with the keen intelligence and sly wit sparkling in her eyes.

Khara appeared to be holding the maelstrom at bay with her smile. He'd recalled every detail of her braids, the colorful scarf she wore, and that distracting, sexy coral color she'd painted on her lips that day. She radiated benevolence, almost as though she were counteracting the darkness just by existing.

Somewhere in the process, his bold, frenetic movements had given way to gentler, more careful, finer work. The curves and angles of her face were soft—delicate even—a stark contrast.

It was good work, but Riddick didn't like how raw it left him. He didn't quite know what to make of it. He ran a finger thoughtfully over the sensuous curve of Khara's full lower lip. How he'd wanted to sink his teeth into that lip tonight. Hell, all day, really. He'd just barely stopped himself from doing so.

Was this some sort of warning? A prediction?

With confusion fogging his mind, Riddick took care this time, packing the pencils and erasers away neatly instead of stuffing and jamming them back into the case. His eyes kept returning to Khara's face. The image needed a bit more shading, but he felt too wrung out.

What was this unfamiliar, hopeful feeling cropping up, making his chest tight? Riddick slammed the lid on that sentiment quickly.

Whatever his subconscious was trying to tell him... *no.* Absolutely not.

Other women had sensed the chasm in his soul, and a few had even made real attempts to bridge it, but here was a woman who was simply allowing him to be who he was. And all he could do was hope like hell his defenses were up to snuff. He had a nagging feeling he might need them.

Chapter Twenty-One

K HARA GLANCED UP FROM her laptop when she heard someone approach. She was answering a Kinder Quest letter asking if she could swim underwater. Shock painted her features when she saw the gorgeous flower arrangement Link was proffering. "For me? They're lovely. Who—?"

For a split second, Khara worried this might be an unwelcome gift from the Speaker's son she'd have to return. He was still emailing her. It might have been a mistake to acknowledge his apology, but it would have been rude not to. She was a lot of things, but rude wasn't one of them.

She regarded the vase Link sat down on the table next to her with a measure of suspicion. Damn, she did not have time for any shenanigans today. She'd never even met this man. Top marks for persistence, though.

She plucked the card out and broke into a huge smile when she read it.

Can't stop thinking about you.

—R

"They're from Riddick," Khara sighed. Relief and delight swept through her. Nothing trite like red roses from Riddick. It was a colorful bouquet of sunny yellow daisies, lilies in a deep hue of pink, and purple snapdragons. Khara sighed again, then laughed at herself and how often she'd been sighing over Riddick. She was... being *romanced*. The text she sent was brief.

Khara: The flowers are lovely. Thank you!

Riddick: You're welcome. Now maybe you'll be thinking about me, too.

Khara: I was already thinking about you.

Khara paused fleetingly, then added:
a lot.
Riddick's reply came right away.
Riddick: Good. See you this evening.

Khara: See you.
When Joanne arrived a few minutes later with the mail, Khara was still wearing a bemused smile.

She'd turned the new embassy project over to the Lytuan Ambassador and hadn't looked back. Since she and Riddick didn't talk about the Queen much, it had gotten easier to keep her two identities separate. It was a little like being a superhero with a secret identity.

Riddick shushed the snarky voice inside that piped up to tell him things like this were the exact *opposite* of keeping his distance. It was just flowers, for crying out loud, not a marriage proposal or anything.

Sending Khara the flowers was a simple thing, something he'd hoped would brighten the tough day he knew she had ahead of her. She'd lamented that the Queen had back-to-back meetings for most of the day, for the third day in a row. He liked the thought of her smiling and thinking of him every time she saw the flowers. As far as he was concerned, that was precisely what flowers were for. That was all.

"You look happy as a pig in slop," Lena observed from the doorway. "Your ten o'clock is here."

Startled, Riddick checked the wall clock. Had he really been sitting there at his desk imagining Khara thinking about him for fifteen minutes? He stood and gathered his notebook. It wasn't like he'd never sent a woman flowers before, even if it had been... years?

If he was being honest with himself, he just liked the thought of Khara thinking of him at all. He'd been wondering if he'd done the right thing by not kissing her after the winery. Hell, he was still wondering.

The question of who would deliver the flowers ended up being so hotly contested among the Elites that there was talk of Rock, Paper, Scissors being the only fair way to decide it. It was Link who'd won the squabble, and Jonnis, Cenn, Wyn, and Alene were eagerly waiting for him in the command center to report back on Khara's reaction to the flowers.

When Link recounted how touched she'd been, every one of them seemed chuffed. The five of them speculated about how things were progressing with Riddick and the Queen's impromptu romance while waiting for their briefing to begin. They'd never been in this situation before, and it made the atmosphere celebratory and fun. The Queen's fiancé had not been particularly affectionate or demonstrative and hadn't romanced her publicly, even after they were engaged.

"She's daydreaming." A wide grin lit Alene's face as she singsonged her observation.

Jonnis nodded in agreement. "I see her smiling all the time."

"I've never seen her like this. It's lovely."

"Should we worry?" Wyn wondered.

"What's happening?" Jaden asked when he came in a few minutes later and sat down.

"Mr. Riddick sent flowers to *Avlah* this morning." This tone of admiration came from Link. Despite being the youngest, he was the most thoughtful of them.

In the ensuing banter about sending their spouses flowers and other tokens of affection, Alene admitted to frequently clipping fresh flowers for her husband, Darius, from her garden. She and Quentin—their toddler—loved to do it together. The baby would often play in the grass while the family cat kept him company. Alene was a gifted gardener and kept all the office plants flourishing.

"Catch up, fellas," Cenn said. "I sent some to Marcus as soon as *Avlah's* showed up. He loves getting flowers."

"The good doctor does strike me as a hopeless romantic."

"He is. The twins are probably driving him nuts, so I arranged for a kid-friendly dinner to be delivered tonight, too."

"Good one. What husband wouldn't love that?"

"Cenn—" Link complained. "You're showing us up again."

Cenn's smirk took up almost her entire face. "You're still a newlywed for a few more weeks. You don't have this on lock? God knows we can tell how much you're missing Aria with all your moping around here."

Link's back stiffened. "I am not moping."

"*Totally* moping, man." She tossed one of her knives into the air and caught it with two fingers.

Wyn cut in, "Don't lump me in with them. I have macarons delivered daily to Sam. She's been craving them nonstop. Jesus, the tears when I couldn't find any in the middle of the night."

"I hope you've got a baker on speed dial." Alene could barely contain her laughter.

"Better. Some hidden in the freezer."

They all commended Wyn's ingeniousness. Everyone except Link had children and probably remembered the days of cravings from first- and secondhand experience.

"Still can't believe you got your wife pregnant while you were healing up," Jonnis said, shaking her head in disbelief. Good-natured laughter filled the room.

Jaden added, "That is major game, I must admit. It sounds like a romance novel or a news story." Putting on a newscaster's voice and cadence, he continued, "*Elite Guard critically injures himself helping to rescue the woman who's now his partner Link Trymble's wife when she almost dies at the hands of her abusive ex. Even a convalescence with broken ribs and bruised innards couldn't stand in the way of procreation for House Gregoire-Hennrick. Film at eleven.*"

The group roared.

"Hey, hey, now," Wyn joked. "It was the trying to prove to Sam that I was *nearly* ready to return to full duty that got her in the family way."

Cenn gave him a friendly elbow. "No matter how it happened, it's obvious you're both overjoyed. And we're all thrilled for you."

Jaden cocked his head, grinning as he soaked up the camaraderie. This was what it was all about. Come to think of it, it had been some time since he'd sent Aimee flowers. Macarons might not be such a bad idea, either. She was only a few months along with their second, but a sweet tooth came along with the morning sickness this time around. He pulled out his phone. Yes, he'd send her some flowers at work and ask his pastry chef brother to take her some macarons.

"What happens if *Avlah* marries Mr. Riddick, Jaden?" Wyn asked.

Still smiling, Jaden bobbled his phone. "I have no idea. I hadn't given that possibility any real thought. But we're getting ahead of things, aren't we? Whose turn is it to lead this briefing, anyway?"

The remainder of the day passed uneventfully, and it was early evening before Jaden had a chance to catch up with his family.

The flowers he'd had delivered had caused a stir at Aimee's school. She insisted half her staff would step on her to get to Jaden if he gave them any sort of encouragement, and the other half would keel over if he did one more romantic thing. Her administrative assistant told him years ago that if things didn't work out between the couple, she could be persuaded to leave her husband for him. Jaden flirted outrageously with the older woman, much to his wife's amusement and occasional consternation.

After speaking to his son and hearing all about what they were up to in his kindergarten class, Jaden settled in to talk to his wife. Unlike with Dorian, she was still having morning sickness at this stage. And afternoon and evening sickness, as well. The only thing that counteracted it was walking in the fresh air. He missed their strolls. Aimee was an elementary school principal and a walking biology lesson for her students, just as she was with their son. She'd only been sick the first few weeks with Dorian.

"What's really on your mind, my love? You're worried about something. Is *Avlah* alright?"

"She's falling in love," Jaden said.

Aimee gasped. "Really?"

"I think so. I've never seen her this... light."

"Jaden, that's wonderful! How lovely for her. Wait. It's not that smarmy politician's son you were telling me about, is it?"

"Oh, no. She hasn't given him the time of day."

"Then who is she in love with?"

"An architect. An American."

"Don't glower at her, honey. I can hear it in your voice."

"I'm not glowering. Just wary."

"It's your job to be wary, but...."

"But what?"

"Don't overburden her with the weight of your disapproval."

"It's not that I disapprove. The American architect is solid, showing to be a good match for her."

"That's high praise from you. But?"

Jaden was looking out the window at the city's West End neighborhood, missing home. "He doesn't know that she's actually the Queen. He thinks she's just an assistant, and I'm concerned about how this will turn out."

"Ah, I see. Good for her. Just be concerned about right now, my love."

"I can't protect her from this, Aimee."

"Maybe you don't need to. I know that doesn't sit well with you. Just let it unfold on its own. Is she happy?"

How to describe the state Khara was in these days? "She floats."

Aimee's wistful sigh came through the phone, loud and clear. "As a woman in love should. I still float for you. Be nice, Jaden."

Nearly seven years together. A great kid and another child on the way. A home. A life. Jaden still couldn't believe how lucky he was sometimes. "I'm always nice."

After he hung up, Jaden considered his wife's words. *Just let it unfold on its own.* He couldn't shake the slight sense of foreboding, but he'd do his best to try.

Chapter Twenty-Two

DINNER AT THE BISTRO restaurant was a styling and profiling event, and Parie always dressed to the nines. With her trim figure, coiffed silver pixie cut, and fashionable sequined cocktail dress of midnight blue, she was like a celebrity. There were determined matchmakers among his mother's circle. More than once, someone's single daughter or granddaughter would just *happen* to be visiting when Riddick was. He'd shared more than a few conspiratorial winks and apologetic nods. For his mother, he tolerated it without complaint.

As he always did, Riddick dressed up for dinner with his mother. They went to her favorite onsite restaurant in the senior community. There were several to choose from.

As she always did, Parie gushed over the flowers he'd bought her. He got two arrangements, one for the shelf outside her apartment door and one for her table inside. His favorite florist did spectacular work and loved having the license to be whimsical for Parie. She'd outdone herself this time with dramatic centerpieces of fluffy hydrangeas and brown-eyed Susans nestled among elegant raspberry foliage and ninebark. Sighing, she murmured something that went over his head about the texture marrying depth and movement. Watching Parie fuss with getting the vases situated brought a smile to his lips. It grew as he remembered Kimberly's enthusiastic fist pump upon hearing of Khara's delight with the arrangement she'd done for her. With a jubilant expression lighting her elf-like face, she whispered that she'd merely translated what she'd heard in

Riddick's voice into something unforgettable. Riddick didn't have a clue what that meant but Kimberly's artistry always dazzled, so there was that.

Riddick raised an "I'm-not-playing-with-you" eyebrow at Parie when she tried to leave her apartment without her cane. She didn't like using it, but her hip complained when she didn't. If he and her companion aide didn't stay on her about it, she'd conveniently forget it all the time.

For someone who had bemoaned the place being only for "boring old people", Parie had settled into her senior community well. She just about ran the place now and was involved in so many clubs and activities, she couldn't remember why she'd resisted moving. She was in the best shape of her life and flourishing. It was a hard sell that had taken the combined efforts of Riddick, Eric, Maya, *and* Holly.

There weren't any potential wives waiting to be met this evening, so he and Parie had a quiet dinner alone. Parie said she was pretty much finished packing, just needed to pick up a few more things. Taking an around-the-world cruise was her dream for as long as he could remember.

She was adamant about not letting him pay for the trip. She'd planned and saved for it for a long time. Little did she know that he'd already arranged for a multitude of surprises for her. She wouldn't know until she checked in that he'd paid for an upgrade to a suite for the duration of the trip and swapped her credit card out for his for her expenses. The biggest surprise was that he was sending her two favorite care companions to help keep things running smoothly. She only knew about the motorized scooter he'd insisted on purchasing for her. When she tried to raise a stink about it, he listened dutifully, then ignored her and made the arrangements for it to be waiting for her at the pier.

Parie was fiercely independent and had been looking forward to taking the six-month trip on her own for years. The companions were in their own suite and would only be as involved as Parie wanted them to be. Riddick knew his mother, knew she wouldn't want to "waste" his money, so she'd cave and allow the companions to help her. Their regular updates on how Parie was doing should be interesting. It was both brilliant and sneaky as hell. He'd been sitting on these surprises for months now. She was going to freak out when all was revealed. He couldn't wait to see how it all went.

They might have had a complicated relationship and history, but he'd walk through fire for her without a moment's hesitation. She deserved every treat he could give her and then some.

They had just ordered their coffee and dessert when Parie leaned in to ask, "So, who's the woman?"

"What woman?" Riddick tried, offering up his most winning smile.

"Joshie." She gave him the chastising tone. She wasn't immune to that smile, but she was close. "You've always been a private person, but I can read you like a book. There's a woman. You have a lightness I haven't seen in you before."

When her son's eyes met hers, she saw a smidgen of panic. Parie just let the moment breathe.

"She's different," he said, and her heart did a little dance for him.

"In what way?"

Riddick had much to say about how smart, funny and independent Khara was, how she knew her own mind and could dissect an argument like you wouldn't believe. Parie didn't miss how Riddick lit right up as he described her, more than she'd ever seen him do when he spoke of a woman he was dating.

"That's funny. You've been raving about this lady for five minutes and haven't once mentioned what she looks like." Interesting.

"I haven't?" That surprised him.

"No. Is she pretty?"

"Yes. Beautiful brown eyes, cute freckles, very smart. She carries herself in a way, Ma. Regal, almost. Even when we're casual. She knows what she's about."

The server arrived with their fruit tarts and coffee.

"Please tell me she's not one of those super-skinny supermodel types who never eats."

"No, Ma, she has *curves*."

Parie almost laughed. Her son's face had softened, and the way he said curves left no doubt about how he felt about them. Curves had always attracted him.

She let him change the subject back to the cruise but kept her eye on his mannerisms. He was a little antsy. Maybe he was meeting up with the mystery lady later. Parie smiled into her coffee cup. Her son was the pride of her life. It was delightful to see him taken with a woman. She would have to be something special to catch his interest this way. Joshie was not quite a player, but he didn't seem to be the least bit interested in settling down.

"I'm drawing again."

Startled by this quiet pronouncement, Parie looked over at him, her fork suspended in midair. "That's incredible. It's been a long time." She knew about the grift his parents had forced him to run, of course. Parie wasn't sure he'd ever forgiven himself. She hoped so but couldn't quite tell.

He'd put everything art-related away and turned his back on his gift. Hadn't used it since then, as far as she knew. She'd never tried to get him to take it up again. Drawing cost him too much on an emotional level. Or it had. Architecture seemed to be just close enough to fulfill his creative needs. Parie wondered if taking up drawing again was related to this new woman in his life. This Khara who was supposedly only going to be in town for a few weeks. Time would tell.

Parie squeezed her son's hand and told him she loved him to bits.

Back at her apartment, he wrapped her up in a big hug and told her he'd pick her up at nine sharp on Friday to drive her to the Baltimore Cruise Pier. Parie was still smiling over him when she got into bed. Her Joshie, she mused, all grown up. He'd arrived in her life like a kitten who'd gotten caught in a downpour, all claws and hisses and a shitty attitude. Puffing himself up to make sure the whole world knew he didn't need anyone to do anything for him. She'd never seen a child who needed love more. He kept it hidden well, but her Joshie still carried emotional scars. They ran deep and peeked out at unlikely times. How would this play out with this curvy woman with the beautiful eyes and freckles, she wondered. Time would tell on that, too.

Chapter Twenty-Three

RIDDICK AND KHARA WERE almost at the movie theater when a frantic text from Dion threw a wrench into their plans. Riddick explained, then got them headed in the new direction.

Swinging by his office to scoop up the forgotten calculus textbook shouldn't take long, leaving them just enough time to make it to the movie café and get their dinner ordered. Khara had never been to a movie theater that served meals and the very idea intrigued her. It would be cutting it close, but the completed midterm was tucked inside the book. Due tomorrow, of course.

Riddick retrieved the textbook from where it was sitting on the side table next to the couch as described and returned to the waiting area with it. He'd drop it off later in the evening. "Ready?"

"Look." Khara breathed as she moved toward the wide window behind Lena's desk. "I didn't even notice it was a full moon."

Lena was forever forgetting to close the blinds when she left for the day. An idea hit. "Here, come with me. You'll be able to see it better."

"Will we have time?"

"There's always time to appreciate a full moon."

Khara placed her hand in his when he held it out for her. They took the private elevator to the eighteenth floor. Riddick & Sloane hosted all types of events on the rooftop terrace and he and Eric had invested in comfortable, inviting furniture. It was one of Riddick's favorite places, although he spent little time here as of late. Glowing in the light of the full moon with the city lights as a twinkling backdrop, the Potomac looked almost like a photograph.

Charmed, Khara drifted to the railing to take in the breathtaking view. She stood transfixed. "So beautiful."

"Indeed," Riddick murmured in agreement, but he wasn't looking at the view.

He was looking at *her*.

Khara caught sight of greenery off to her side. "There's a garden up here on the roof?"

Then she was off. Riddick shared with her how Riddick & Sloane took part in a city-wide collective partnership where their community rooftop garden supported two nearby schools, one elementary and one middle. She was full of questions and didn't hesitate to get down on her knees to look closer.

Riddick admitted to only knowing the basics, but he loved digging in the dirt when the classes came. "I go where Lena points me."

"Oh, how is her wife?" Khara looked up from where she was elbow-deep in some of the bean plants. "After the accident?"

Riddick marveled at her. She had one hell of a memory.

"What?" Khara asked when he just looked at her.

With a shake of his head, he answered, "She's okay. It really was minor. I imagine Lena's hovering drove her up the wall."

He showed her the salsa and pizza gardens. She got a good laugh over how every year, they disappointed the new set of kindergartners by telling them that actual pizzas didn't grow in the garden, just the tomatoes, herbs and salad greens that would go into crafting a homemade pizza dinner. Riddick told her how the R&S employees clamored to dress up in toques and aprons with fake mustaches for the harvest pizza parties.

"You, too?" she teased.

"Oh, yeah. I'm the reigning champ on dough tossing. Honestly, I think the adults have more fun than the kids."

Khara insisted on the full tour and wanted to hear all about how the program worked, what the process was, how families were engaged, supply, production, scaling, and what other partnerships they participated in. Before they knew it, two hours passed, and he'd hardly been able to keep up with her. They'd laughed and speculated and batted ideas around, compared with similar programs in Lytua.

Only once he'd shown her everything and answered all her questions was she satisfied. Khara held up her dirt-covered hands. "Where can I take care of this?"

He took her down to the bathroom in his office and turned the water on for her. Without planning to do it, he squirted some liquid soap in his own hands, then rubbed at the dirt on hers. He slowed when he realized he was touching her and stroked a gentle thumb over one of her palms. The scent of her subtle perfume was in his nostrils again, tantalizing him.

"We've missed the movie," Khara said. She didn't sound sorry. Riddick thought this was time well spent. They wouldn't have had such a profound discussion at the theater.

"Worth it."

Khara was looking at him with curiosity shining in her eyes.

"I realize this might look like a lame set-up, but I assure you, it's not."

The side of her mouth quirked up. "Why would I think that?"

"I can see why it might look suspicious. Deserted building, full moon, beautiful view. Beautiful woman."

Khara dipped her head and looked up at him through her lashes. "Did you bring me here just to get me alone?"

"No." He was incapable of saying more as she took a step closer, and he couldn't take his eyes off her mouth again. He knew he wasn't being smooth, but damn, that sultry red had held his interest all night. He wanted to haul her up against him or back her into the wall and taste those lips. Were they as soft as they looked? He wanted to taste every damn part of her.

He liked her looking at him with open interest, liked how she wasn't being coquettish. That interest, that honesty, gave him an almost electric thrill. He'd seen how he'd pleased her with his words. Riddick didn't flatter and blow smoke to get women to like him. Khara was enjoying their dance of attraction as much as he was. At least he thought so.

Damn, he wanted to kiss her, but he suspected men probably came swooping right in and, truth be told, he wanted her to know he was different. He wanted to know her as a person first before getting physical. It shouldn't matter if she thought he was different, but Riddick couldn't deny that it did. This was a fine place to live for now, Riddick decided—with the anticipation building. He was going to kiss her soon. He knew it. She knew it. It wasn't a question of if but when. And if it was anything like the lead-up, it would be hot as hell. Well worth the wait.

Riddick eased a little closer to her, getting in her space. Her eyes widened, and those beautiful lips parted as she drew in a quick breath. He took his time reaching behind her to pull some paper towels out of the wall dispenser. God, she smelled good. She was blushing again. Affected by his nearness, just as he was by hers.

"We'd better get going," he told her in a low voice as he blotted her hands dry. Yes, he knew he was teasing her. Yes, he knew well that it was dangerous. This woman tested his control every time they were together. And fuck if he didn't like it.

"So, pizza then?" Khara ventured.

"Obviously. I know just the place."

Mario's Pizza House in the Ballston section of Arlington was doing a brisk business for a Thursday night. Khara didn't seem to care that she was way overdressed and dirty on top of it. She savored every bite of the square slice of cheesy, tangy goodness.

As they ate at one of the red picnic tables on the patio area, Riddick recounted the ways the area had changed over the years. He'd been coming to this spot since he was in high school, before developers knocked the sketchy hotel next door down. He and Parie had lived a few streets over. The area was ever-changing, with buildings being dropped to make way for newer, greener ones. But somehow, the essential neighborhood feeling remained.

"You know, Italian pizza is nothing like this, but I don't think I could ever choose between them."

"I know, right?" Khara shook her head, making her short, chocolate curls bounce. "If you ever come to Lytua, I'll take you to my favorite takeaway place, the Rainbow Diner. They make the most sublime conch fritters. Best on the island."

Until that moment, Riddick had given little thought to the fact that they lived in two different countries. What would that mean for them later on? He cut that line of thought off quickly. There wouldn't be a "later".

This was one of the best dates he'd ever been on. Maybe the very best.

Riddick pulled his attention back, reminding himself that it made no difference either way. He needed to get Dion's textbook dropped off before it got too late.

Chapter Twenty-Four

"IT'S AMBITIOUS."

The Intermediary's deceptively gentle voice sounded introspective but held a note of chastisement. The woman was certifiably brilliant, and once had a promising career in chemical engineering. She was a viper though, ruthless and deadly. Trina took a perverse sort of pleasure in knowing she'd helped her become that way.

She'd given her a week to prepare and travel, to establish a secure base of operations somewhere in the DC area. Then she made the call to discuss the next steps. The operatives Trina usually hired only received enough information to do the job she needed, never any context. At most, they'd be able to report a few disparate details that wouldn't lead anywhere. Trina had perfected her technique years ago. The Intermediary was the only exception to that.

The Intermediary would be the one to make the arrangements, keeping Trina one step removed with a side of plausible deniability. Perfect.

Trina had thought long and hard about the best way to bring about her desired outcome. The plan she'd carefully crafted was beautiful in its simplicity.

If her husband had been King like he should have been, everything would be different.

Sitting back in her desk chair, Trina closed her eyes and let the memories roll over her.

She didn't like to think about that fateful night of the election when she'd lost so much. Her husband's throne, her mother-in-law's respect, her shot at absolute power. The family had stood frozen and dumbfounded in their living room after the official results announcement. It hadn't even been close, as it had been when Corey ran against the previous Queen.

Corey had already made his concession speech, and now that woman—that *child*—was on the television giving a glowing victory speech. She was actually thanking her opponent. Trina's mother-in-law had downed Negroni after Negroni throughout the course of the evening and could barely stand. Now she looked at her with hatred brimming in her eyes—like *Trina* had somehow been the reason for the election's outcome. The slap came out of nowhere and stunned her.

"It was *his turn!*" The tiny woman had screeched, spittle flying, her face contorted with rage.

Only minutes before she keeled over from a fatal heart attack, Corey's mother had yelled at Trina about what a failure she was and listed several of her shortcomings as a wife. Trina had shrunk back in horror from the bitter words and looked frantically to Corey for help. Her husband—damn him—did nothing to defend her and instead sauntered over to the wet bar and poured himself another stiff drink. He was falling down drunk when emergency services arrived at their home. Cyrus had been clutching his grandmother's body and wailing inconsolably. It had been quite the tableau.

Watching the ambulance drive away, Trina didn't understand how they'd gotten there.

Victory had been within their grasp when that opportunist had come along and turned the public against them. The country had been taken in by her doe eyes and platitudes.

She and Corey were riding high as they entered the home stretch of the election season—one everyone deemed a mere formality. Sure, he'd said a few regrettable things, but nothing insurmountable. Corey had proven himself. No one had dared to enter the race against him. Trina was contentedly planning what she'd wear to his swearing-in and what colors she'd use when she redecorated the official residence.

Then a call came from a contact in the Clerk's office at the High Court to advise that Senator Khara Therin was now running. Trina distinctly remembered laughing. Senator Therin was a baby, young enough to be their daughter.

But it had turned out to be no laughing matter. The senator had come in *hot*, and they'd had to scramble to play defense. Instead of continuing the leisurely campaign they'd been running, Corey suddenly had to fight for it.

Trina quietly blackmailed a Guard with a gambling problem into spying for her, but there hadn't been anything untoward, no dirt to be leveraged, not even anything she could try to spin. Not a single fucking thing. It shouldn't have been possible.

The senator really was that earnest.

Planting anonymous stories in the press was an easy tactic Trina had employed to great success against other foes. Even those attempts went nowhere. Senator Therin was so popular that even rumors of egregious lapses in judgment with drugs and criminal activity weren't enough to break her candidacy. Not even the manufactured scandal of an affair.

Trina had even been behind a series of attempts to frighten her into quitting the race. Senator Therin turned out to be made of sterner stuff, though. The intimidation tactics had only strengthened her resolve, which Trina grudgingly respected. Worst of all, she didn't even have the decency to acknowledge the attacks publicly. It was positively infuriating.

Corey had always had a complicated relationship with alcohol, but he spiraled out of control after the election, leading to his being censured and embarrassed. He lost favor going after Lillianna the way he did while campaigning and, with his position weakened, barely hung onto his seat in the next election.

Trina had worked behind the scenes for years to solidify her husband's position and influence and campaigned hard to get him re-elected. From the shadows, she'd quietly removed obstacles, bribed some competitors, and threatened others. She quietly made things go away when necessary—problems, other candidates, evidence, witnesses. Trina felt no remorse about the killing she'd done for Corey's career. There was nothing she wouldn't do for her family.

As Corey descended deeper into alcoholism and lost interest in legislating, it had fallen to Trina to cover up his lapses and wrongdoings. Thankfully, she was excellent at cleaning up messes.

With a sigh, Trina drummed her fingers on her desk, ruminating on how she'd tried for *years* to rid her family of the usurper nuisance. Everything from thwarting her political agenda to attempting to eliminate her altogether and everything in between. Every one of the spies she'd tried to place within the Guard under the guise of "checks and balances" was somehow rejected as unsuitable. Almost as though they'd been sniffed out.

The first time Trina tried to kill Lillianna, the bitch had gotten supremely lucky. It had the unfortunate timing of coinciding with a failed coup attempt of the government she'd been a guest of, where the bitch had almost gotten herself killed mouthing off to the rebels. That would have made Trina's life exponentially easier. The official report of the incident was clear. Lillianna's quick thinking had saved lives during an intense hostage situation, including that of the assassin Trina had hired. Trina had sneered at the press's description that Lillianna, "Had the silver tongue of a statesman with far more experience".

Cyrus had been maudlin for days after news of the incident became widespread. She'd made the mistake of dismissing it and carried on with her plans to do away with the bothersome upstart. Trina wished she'd paid closer attention, although she wasn't positive it would have made much difference.

The bomb at Parliament would have done the trick if the bomber hadn't had a crisis of conscience and gotten cold feet. In trying to deactivate the bomb, the dumb bitch detonated it. While not the outcome Trina intended, her stupidity conveniently tied up loose ends she would have had to clean up later. It saved her the trouble of having someone deal with her after she'd assassinated the Queen. No need to look closer at the young woman hailed as a hero for her sacrifice. The drugs and gambling debt she'd racked up that made her vulnerable to Trina's machinations in the first place? Trina easily made those disappear. Keeping a straight face through it all was one of the hardest things Trina had ever done. A few whispered words in the right ear provided enough misdirection that no one could be sure the bomb had actually been intended for the Queen. Fortunately, she had easy access to the right people. One of the parliament chambers was now named after the bomber-turned-savior. The irony.

The fit Cyrus had in the aftermath of the attack left him almost catatonic. It caught Trina off guard, for she was usually much more attuned to his emotional state. Suffocating guilt pressed down on her as she sat next to his hospital bed day after day, where he mostly stared at the walls or ceiling with unseeing eyes. She'd mistaken his sadness after the coup attempt as loyalty to his father. But it turned out Cyrus had been harboring not merely a harmless infatuation with his former classmate but believed himself to be in love with her. Trina's shy, sweet son was beside himself at the thought of Lillianna being harmed.

Trina had been shattered. Was she to lose *everything* to Lillianna? Hadn't she taken enough from her?

Luckily for the new Queen, Trina's love for her son was greater than the hatred she had for Lillianna. Of course, it was. But how was she to balance the almost blinding desire for vengeance with wanting to give her son what he most desired?

The only reason Lillianna was currently still breathing was because of her son.

Cyrus had always been Trina's pride and joy. His stutter all but disappeared whenever he rhapsodized about Lillianna, which was often. It grated on her nerves to listen, but she feigned interest anyway.

If he ever found out his mother had plotted against the object of his affection, Cyrus would never forgive her. Trina couldn't bear the thought of him looking at her with anything less than complete adoration.

Trina opened her eyes and blinked away the memories. She stood. The plans were in motion now and this was going to work.

Of course, none of this would be necessary if Lillianna had just been reasonable and agreed to marry Cyrus and unite their families. Trina could still remember the flare of intense hatred she'd felt when Lillianna had recoiled at the suggestion. Oh, she'd tried to hide it, but it was there. The bitch thought she was too good for her boy.

Even years later, Trina would never forget the swell of anger that had nearly overwhelmed her common sense. How her hand had *itched* to slap that brief look of disdain from the Queen's face.

Her husband's humiliation had been heartrending, but her *child's*... that was a different matter altogether. That required an answer and action, even if it was years in the making.

A text came through on Trina's work phone. Her secretary letting her know her lunch appointment needed to reschedule. That was fine, as it gave Trina more time to review the union's proposed changes to the leave policy. She needed to get her draft response to legal soon, for the deadline was approaching fast.

As for the Queen, she was responsible for every misery in Trina's life. She'd rent her family irrevocably, and it was finally time for her to pay. She might have been the one to start it all, but Trina was certainly going to finish it. Her way.

Trina smiled to herself.

Tick tock, Lillianna. Tick tock.

Chapter Twenty-Five

R IDDICK COULDN'T IMAGINE HAVING this kind of outing with anyone other than Khara. Museums were one of her very favorite pastimes. She'd told him the National Museum of African American History and Culture was on her must-see list.

The heart-wrenching exhibits disturbed her, though she made no effort to conceal her tears and sorrow. He admired the strength it took to let herself be vulnerable. They didn't talk; there were no adequate words. Even after visiting several times before, Riddick still found it to be a powerful, transformative experience. Watching Khara soak it all in and mourn moved him.

He was not usually a hugger, but it was natural for the two of them to share an embrace upon exiting the first-floor historical exhibits. A poignant moment of human connection and solace after walking through so many years of atrocity. They held each other tight for a few moments, needing that closeness. When Riddick pulled back, the tears shimmering in her eyes gutted him.

He kept a comforting hand on her back as he led her to sit in the Contemplative Court. Riddick watched her from a nearby bench and gave her the space to process. The cascade from the cylindrical skylight fountain into the sparkling pool beneath it created a restorative and soothing atmosphere one desperately needed when feeling overwhelmed by the history of enslaved people. It was a place to recover emotionally.

Khara had her head tipped back and her eyes closed, as though absorbing the fountain's tranquility. If he'd had his sketchbook, Riddick would have tried to capture that serenity in her expression. So much character in her face. He felt compelled to draw all the time these days.

It was easier to keep Khara at a distance when he kept things superficial.

This was... not superficial, though.

They had an earnest discussion about the long-term effects of slavery over lunch in the museum's restaurant, Sweet Home Café. They taught American history in Lytuan schools, and it was interesting to hear thoughts about it from someone who hadn't grown up in the States.

When Khara returned from refilling her sweet tea, she asked, "How did it go dropping your mother off? Was she surprised?"

She remembered *everything* it seemed. It was a little daunting. "She cried buckets, of course. Then cursed a blue streak. Then cried some more. They'll treat her like a Queen."

"I bet it was a sight to see."

Riddick laughed. "Probably. I doubt there was a dry eye in the place."

His heart thumped seeing her lips curve into a wide smile. "You're an extra-ordinary son, Riddick."

Her praise felt good and warmed Riddick from the inside out. This woman had a way of making him feel on top of the world with a simple word or two. He thought again of how Parie grabbed him in a tight embrace before embarking and told him she wanted to meet this woman when she got back.

Riddick reminded her that Khara would be long gone, back home by the time she got back. The thought gave him a twinge. Parie merely gave him a knowing smile and said, "We'll see."

Sitting across from her now, Riddick was flummoxed. How was it he kept finding such deep things to do and talk about with Khara after such a short time? It felt instinctive, it wasn't a forced or stilted effort at all. She was interested in things other women hadn't been. Riddick didn't think he'd dated selfish women, just that in comparison, Khara seemed better attuned. Like with the R&S community outreach. He'd never talked to a woman about the programs in such extensive detail, which led him to question why other women had shown little interest when it was an important part of his life.

It wasn't that he was shallow. He didn't think he was, anyway, but it was curious how they kept falling into all these thought-provoking activities and animated discussions about things like social justice and giving back to the community. Had he ever had such a riveting discourse about taxes and healthcare inequities? He didn't think so. Hours slipped by when they talked, one melting into another. Honestly, the best part of his day lately was the time he got to spend chatting with her. They were doing things together he'd never done with any other woman. And he liked it. He couldn't quite put his finger on any one thing to explain why. Maybe because she wasn't from the area and, therefore, offered a unique perspective. Nothing wrong with that.

Relax, Riddick told himself. She was leaving in a few weeks. They were only enjoying friendly conversation and each other's company. Nothing alarming about that. He wasn't going to fall in love with her. With his shit childhood, he wasn't even the falling-in-love type.

Besides, Khara deserved to settle down with the Lytuan equivalent of a Ken doll who'd shower her with affection. Someone with a wholesome childhood and an ancestral home or some shit. She deserved a prince to sweep her off her feet, and Riddick for damn sure was nobody's prince.

He'd turned a little frosty at the end of their museum date, Khara mused later that day, leaving her to speculate on what was weighing on him—was it her or the somber experience of the museum itself? Khara continued to stare at her laptop screen with her chin resting in her hand, unable to concentrate on the task of sorting through the day's emails.

When she'd asked if everything was alright, he'd answered only that he was deep in thought. That may have been true, but Khara sensed that wasn't all. She wondered if he was aware of how expressive his face was. Was he having second thoughts about seeing her?

Khara chastised herself for jumping right to thinking the worst. Riddick wasn't the type to mince words. If he was having second thoughts, he would tell her. Wouldn't he? Yes, of course, he would. He was too direct to fake anything. Even though she believed that—Khara still felt a little off-kilter. Although truth be told, that wasn't so unusual these days. She felt off balance whenever she thought about Riddick.

Feeling a little unsteady and not caring for it, Khara closed the laptop and called Yvanda for some shoring up.

"Well, of course he did," was Yvanda's matter-of-fact response to Khara describing how Riddick turned down the project to date her. "You said he was smart. And don't forget, he's lucky you've even looked in his direction. How's everything else going? Is it what you were hoping for?"

Khara could practically hear her wiggling her eyebrows. "It's going well. He makes me feel.... We haven't kissed yet, but it's all I can think about."

"You said what, now? Wait, weren't you considering a fling?"

Khara blew out a breath and pulled a coil of hair from her face. "I thought I wanted to, but I like him liking me. It's silly."

"It's not silly. It makes perfect sense."

"I really like him, Vanda."

"Okay, time to get a look at this guy. Send me a picture!"

Khara scrolled through the photos on her phone she'd snapped while they were sightseeing. There was a particularly nice one that a friendly older lady offered to take of the two of them in front of the museum. It was a great candid, as she'd caught them before they were ready. Riddick's arm was around her waist, and they were both laughing at something he'd said. He looked quite dishy, even in just a casual henley and well-worn jeans. After they'd shed their jackets, she'd scarcely been able to keep her eyes off his bulging biceps. Khara sent the picture and a few seconds later heard Yvanda gasp, then exclaim, "Bitch, that picture almost put me into spontaneous labor."

Khara burst out laughing.

"If they try to induce me, just send me another picture of this man! Preferably shirtless, please, if you can somehow manage it. That smile, Khar!"

Well, at least she wasn't delusional—Riddick really was that hot.

"You sure you don't want to have a fling? He looks like he knows what to do with a woman."

He did but looks could be deceiving. Hadn't she already learned that lesson? *Stop fretting and keep it simple*, Khara told herself. She was dreaming about the man's skill in the bedroom almost every night. Although that wasn't exactly proof. More like aspirational thinking. If—in the unlikely event—Riddick was a terrible lover, she'd stop seeing him. Easy. "I think that was just what I needed to hear."

Chapter Twenty-Six

Even though Riddick told Dion several times he was coming and bringing Khara with him, Dion still looked relieved to see him. It hurt Riddick to his core, just as it did every single time. So many people had let the kid down in his young life that even the smallest of kept promises were monumental to him. Even after two years of building trust, Dion was still wary. Riddick didn't blame him or take it personally. Tried to, anyway. Because he got it. How long did it take him to trust his adoptive mother? Longer than two years, that was for damn sure.

Riddick had invited Khara to an art show where Dion had pieces on display. Dion attended a fine arts magnet school, and the show was being hosted by a trendy art gallery in the heart of downtown Arlington. Since parking could be scarce in the Pentagon City area of town, Riddick suggested the Metro.

Dion spotted them almost the moment they stepped into the brightly lit space and hurried over. He practically skidded to a stop in front of them, all but bouncing on the balls of his feet. "You came!"

"I told you I would." Riddick's first impulse was to hug that uncertainty in Dion's eyes away, but he held off, worried Dion might be considered uncool for it among his peers. He settled for squeezing his arm affectionately. "A man is only as good as his word, and I keep my promises. Khara, this is Dion Wilcox. Dion, Khara Therin."

Khara had been looking between the two of them, something clearly happening behind those pretty eyes, like she'd just pieced something vital together.

Dion, for his part, extended his hand promptly with a shy smile. Just like they'd practiced, he looked Khara in the eye and offered a firm handshake.

"It's a pleasure to meet you, Ms. Therin. Welcome and thank you for coming."

His polished greeting took Riddick by surprise. So he was making an effort, putting on his best manners. *Nailed it.*

"I'm so pleased to meet you at last, Dion." Khara's greeting was equally hearty. "Riddick has spoken so highly of your work, and I'm delighted to see it in person. I was quite intrigued by the picture."

Dion's brows knitted. "Picture? What picture?"

"Of *Adrift*. Riddick has it as the wallpaper on his phone."

The startled look in Dion's eyes sent a frisson of guilt through Riddick. Jeez, had he never told the kid what he thought of his work?

Dion was looking at him like he'd never seen him before. "You showed her—you have—you remember the *title*?"

"Of course. I thought it was some of your best work. Ma put it on the wall in her bedroom after you gave it to her."

"She did?"

"Well, what else would she have done with it?"

Dion dropped his gaze to his shoes with a shrug. "Dunno. Throw it away maybe?"

He said it lightly, but Riddick knew better. "Parie would *never*—"

Riddick broke off when Khara stepped a little closer and placed one hand on his shoulder and the other on Dion's. The tension he hadn't noticed gathering in his gut abruptly unwound at her touch. Flooded out of him like a tide. He'd been speaking more sharply than he intended.

Once Dion looked up, Khara gave him one of those luminous smiles that always seemed to make coherent thought fly right out of Riddick's head. "I feel like quite the VIP knowing one of the show's featured artists. Would you be kind enough to tell me about what you've submitted?"

It was just the right thing to do, for art was Dion's passion. He relished any opportunity to discuss it. Riddick hung back just a little as Dion led them to each of his pieces, observing. Dion was animated, with hardly a hint of his customary reticence with strangers. He answered Khara's questions with enthusiasm and pointed out the works of his classmates.

When Khara told him about an embarrassing pottery wheel mishap she'd had in a university class, Dion cackled. The easy way they interacted made Riddick want to dive for paper and a pencil to capture it. Dion bloomed under Khara's attention in a way he didn't with Riddick's. He was easier, more present, and had less nervous energy.

The kid was stunned to learn that one of his pieces had won the first-place award. A large blue ribbon pinned to the placard with the sculpture's title announced it. Khara was as happy for Dion as if she'd done the artwork herself.

Khara clapped with joy, then hugged Dion. "How splendid. Congratulations, Dion!"

Riddick no longer cared if it was cool or not. He pulled Dion to him and told him how proud he was of all his work, not just the prizewinner. Dion sniffed and took off to tell his teacher. It felt like he'd relaxed into the embrace for just a split second. Riddick thought he might have felt a tentative pat on his back and hoped he hadn't imagined it.

Khara's assessing gaze was on Riddick's face when he turned back to her, an unspoken question in the tilt of her head, the arch of her eyebrow. Almost like she'd understood something important about him. Instead of growing uncomfortable under the scrutiny, he found himself smiling at her. "Well, that was a surprise."

She touched his forearm and gave it a pat. "That was a truly lovely thing to say. About being proud of all his work."

Her approval meant more than it should have. What was up with that? Riddick cleared his throat and turned his attention back to Dion's prizewinning piece.

Khara had steered both Dion and him away from the stress and hurt of a vulnerable moment. Did she know? Or was it just her natural way to bring out the positive in others? It was something she seemed to do without conscious effort.

The roguish grin and double thumbs up Dion flashed Riddick when Khara's back was turned had him chuckling. *Subtle, Dee. Real Subtle.*

Chapter Twenty-Seven

AFTER SAYING GOODBYE AS the event wound down, Riddick and Khara waved to the school bus that would take the students back to their homes. They walked through misty drizzle the few blocks from the gallery to a restaurant called Matchbox. He could feel Khara studying his knitted brows as they went.

They opted for a cozy booth on the mezzanine level instead of sitting at one of the long high-top tables. The eatery had the look of a converted warehouse with its exposed ductwork and pipes. It was more modern than Riddick would have liked for a residential space, but the blond wood warmed the sleek steel fixtures, and the combination gave an almost Scandinavian feel to the open, minimalist floor plan.

Khara took her time perusing the featured menu of seasonal offerings, but he got the sense she was paying attention to more than the food choices. "Everything sounds delectable. What do you recommend?"

"I've only been here a few times, but I remember the shrimp and grits being fantastic."

"I'll try that then. Another culinary delight originating from the Low Country, I see. I really must visit this magical place."

Their gangly, bespectacled server was struck nearly speechless under the full power of Khara's irrepressible charm. Riddick shook his head in bemusement as the young man stammered that, yes, the table was made of reclaimed wood. The woman was damn near irresistible and soon they were hearing all about his major in college and copy-editing internship at a small publishing house. When the kid began to expound on his post-graduation aspirations, Riddick interrupted as politely as possible. At this rate, they'd die of thirst before he ran out of steam.

Once their orders were taken and they were alone again, Khara turned that perceptive gaze unto Riddick. That unfamiliar something clutched in his belly. She swirled the straw in her iced tea and regarded him. "You're subdued tonight. What's weighing on you?"

Riddick sat back against his side of the booth with a slight huff. He'd thought for sure he'd buttoned up his worry, although he should have known better. Khara didn't miss a trick. "You're pretty good at reading people."

"I'm a diplomat. I have to be. Would you like to talk about it?"

Riddick hesitated. Under ordinary circumstances, he never wanted to talk about this. It felt like having something small and delicate clenched in his fist and held tight to his chest. He could keep it tucked away forever, protected from the world, but it was Khara's empathy that made him want to unclench and have them examine whatever fragile thing was inside together. No attacking or judging, just the extending of an invitation. Riddick realized he wanted to talk about it with her. She was the difference. Before he could talk himself out of it, he said, "He still flinches if I move too fast. He's still surprised every time I show up, even though I've never missed a meet up, never even been late for one. He's so used to being disappointed it's like what I do doesn't even register."

Cocking her head some, Khara leveled her steady gaze at him. "It takes a long time to unlearn old habits, especially when we feel threatened. We must be reassured over and over. Dion likely feels threatened every time he sees you. You have the power to hurt him, to betray him—*you're* a threat."

These insightful observations of hers kept catching Riddick unawares. He looked at her in amazement. He sometimes needed the same reassurance from Parie. "Did I tell you Dion's history?"

"No. But I assumed, based on your work with youth in foster care, that he'd experienced it. That means trauma and heartache from the people who were supposed to protect and nurture him. Is this incorrect?"

His voice was a little hoarse when he told her, "No. You have it."

"You told me you were drawn to this work because you'd seen a lot. I saw a genuine connection between you and Dion. Him discovering you pay such careful attention to his art, I'm sure it meant the world to him. He may never be able to articulate how much. If you could have seen his face when you hugged him. Everything comes down to relationships, and those have to be built. I saw he kept an eye on you, almost like he was reassuring himself that you hadn't disappeared. Deep down, Dion knows he can trust you, but he may not trust that yet. If that makes sense."

Damn. It did. He drew in a long, deep breath and noticed once again how she didn't rush to fill the silence, but instead held the space for him. Khara didn't fear silence. She wielded it as skillfully as a surgeon with a scalpel. Even just gazing at him with compassion while he gathered his words made him want to spill his guts. She was probably an excellent diplomat. "I knew early on that I wasn't cut out to be a foster parent but put a lot of resources into making out-of-home placements successful. It's not just where kids sleep at night. It's access, people believing in them, plentiful opportunities to excel. Treating their success like a foregone conclusion. Fighting the stigma. Understanding that the shit you went through isn't how the rest of your life has to be. So many of them believe it's their fault. And that hurt and doubt never seems to go away completely. Life's dealt them such a shit hand, and it's just not fair. It's up to the rest of us to do something about it, to open the pathways."

Khara placed her hand over his and gave it a gentle squeeze. "You light up when you talk about it, you know.

"I'm passionate about making sure kids get their shot."

"That's heart work. Not something everyone can do."

"It is hard work."

"No, *heart* work, as in giving from the heart."

He'd said too much but didn't feel as caged or exposed as he thought he might. Khara had put her finger on it—relationships. It was unsettling how she understood something about him that no one else did, even without knowing the truth. She seemed sensitive to the moods of others, especially if they were in difficulty.

Khara read body language like an expert and proved herself to be remarkably in tune with those around her. Riddick imagined it was a skill the Queen valued. And if she didn't, she should. He'd witnessed her empathy in action during a recent day trip to Eastern Market, where he'd looked on in fascination as she distracted a toddler mid-tantrum. In between pulling faces for the delighted little girl, Khara offered her weary-looking dad an encouraging smile.

After taking her hand and kissing it, he thanked her for coming, for being so great with Dion, and for letting him vent. Even just that abbreviated bit of discussion helped. Some of the knot of tension he carried in his chest loosened.

He let her steer their dinner conversation into less emotionally fraught waters. It was as though she sensed his need to let the topic of Dion rest for now.

Chapter Twenty-Eight

T HE SLICE OF SIX-LAYER carrot cake they shared for dessert was good, but nowhere near as good as watching Khara savor it. Lord, that mouth of hers.... Riddick had never envied an eating utensil before, but seeing the enraptured expression on her face as she closed those succulent lips around the fork did something dangerous to his insides. Riddick almost moaned when she darted her tongue out to swipe at a smear of frosting on her upper lip.

"Oh, the pineapple makes this just divine." Khara was hooked after her first taste. He was hooked after her first taste, too. Riddick's imagination galloped away with him as he pictured her sucking a bite of cake from his fingers as he fed it to her. If they did that, they'd surely end up getting arrested.

It was nothing less than torture, but no way in hell was he going to look away. Riddick signed the credit card slip, then stood and held out a hand to help her up from the booth. "You up for a walk? There's a shopping area a few blocks away."

"Sure."

Pentagon City metro station was right in front of the restaurant; they'd double back after. Wandering around Pentagon Row, peering at the colorful fall displays of the outdoor mall's upscale stores was more fun than Riddick would have thought. They stopped to observe a cooking class through the window of Sur la Table and tried to guess what they were preparing. Whatever it was, there were lots of herbs involved.

"That couple there—that looks like a first date gone wrong."

Riddick didn't see anything that pointed to that. All he saw was a young man and woman performing different tasks. He was squinting at a recipe card and the woman was meticulously stripping a giant sprig of rosemary. "Huh. What makes you think they're not just an old married couple?"

Her curls danced as she shook her head. "They're awkward and stiff. Having trouble negotiating the space, see? An old married couple knows how to move together in a small area. Like them." She pointed with her chin at another couple on the other side of the kitchen classroom.

She was right. Riddick saw right away the two older gentlemen were navigating more smoothly. One placed a steadying hand on his partner's back as he guided himself around to reach for something. They didn't seem to mind being close to one another physically. Looking back at the first couple, little telltale signs jumped out at Riddick. The man and woman kept bumping into each other and her back was ramrod straight, her shoulders tense. The man was gesturing with his hands—maybe talking too much. He couldn't unsee their disconnect, like a trainwreck in slow motion.

The older couple faced each other while speaking, attending fully to the conversation. They were working together, even as they were doing separate things. "That's fascinating. What can you tell about the other couples?"

Khara's witty and insightful observations were probably on the mark.

The sky opened up without warning when they were three blocks from the Metro. Riddick grabbed Khara's hand and ran. Khara shrieked with laughter as the chilly rain turned into a deluge that drenched them.

Riddick pulled her into the alcove of a shop's doorway at the ground level of a tall office building. Neither of them had an umbrella.

"We'll have to wait it out. Here." He opened his jacket as an invitation to share his warmth. It was quieter here, away from the bustling street.

Grateful, Khara stepped close, and he enfolded her. "Ahh," she sighed. "Thank you. You smell good. How long do you think it'll last?"

"Forever, I hope. I like where I am."

Khara laughed and looked up at him. "Me, too."

Riddick wiped some of the droplets from her cheek. She flattened her palms on his chest, looking up at him with longing. Hell, he was probably looking at *her* with longing. "What are you thinking so hard about?"

Decision made, Khara cupped his neck and brought his mouth down to hers.

He let her lead the kiss, take as much as she wanted from him. It was a slow, thorough kiss that had Riddick bunching the back of her dress in an effort to control himself. The rain-soaked material clung to her skin.

When she pulled back, she gave a soft moan as she bit her lower lip. "I've been wanting to do that."

"Why didn't you?"

"I was too nervous."

"Damn," Riddick breathed, then took her face and pulled her back into his own kiss, this one hotter, deeper. He leaned her against the door and kissed her breathless, as he'd been wanting to for days. When he had to come up for air, he touched his forehead to hers. "I wanted you the moment I saw you."

"Is that right?"

"Please tell me this isn't one-sided."

She brushed her nose against his and smiled. "It's not one-sided, Riddick. I've wanted you, too."

"Thank God." He took them under again, lost the battle to keep his hands off her. Smoothing his hands down to her hips, Riddick pulled her closer, up against his body. They fit perfectly together.

They stayed in the alcove kissing for some time. It was intimate, sweet. A perfect first foray, cocooned there from the hushed sounds of the rain and passing traffic. Riddick was pretty sure he could have stayed there indefinitely with Khara's soft, curvy body up against his. He was in no hurry to leave, especially when she rested her face against his chest with a breathy little sigh. Her skin was chilled, though, and he didn't want her catching a cold.

Riddick glanced over his shoulder to where a sliver of the street was visible between the buildings. "It stopped raining. We'd better get going while we can."

Chapter Twenty-Nine

HE WAS CLEARLY NOT thinking straight.

It was the only plausible explanation Riddick could come up with.

He berated himself all the way home. There had been a lot of mutual attraction in those searing kisses and no pressing reason to stop when he had. Why'd he call it off then, instead of inviting Khara home to spend the night with him? Under any other circumstances, he would have been all about it. He would have taken Khara to bed and brought every bit of his A-game. When she left his bed in the morning, she'd be on shaky legs and the most satisfied she'd ever been. And looking forward to coming back.

Hmm, he thought, picturing a sleepy, satisfied Khara naked in his bed. Slippery wet from all the pleasure he would have given her. Eager to take him again and again. His dick hardened in response, eliciting a heartfelt curse.

Riddick's mind was full of questions. Would his advances have been welcome? Why the hell was he feeling uncertain? It wasn't like him to second guess himself. He was usually quite decisive when there was something—or someone—he wanted. What caused him to hesitate, then, where he wouldn't have before? Was it because she was from overseas? And dammit, why did it please him so much that she'd kissed him anyway, despite her nervousness?

At least he hadn't forgotten his damn car this time.

It was still on his mind later as he lay in bed, trying to figure it all out. Riddick wasn't used to the kind of interactions he was having with her, and it was throwing him off-balance. There was something about Khara that made him want to handle her with care. She wasn't fragile, that wasn't it. She was cautious. A woman that vivacious must have guys hitting on her all the time. Probably obnoxious ones with no business thinking they were anywhere *close* to her league. Or folks who might want to use her to get to the Queen. That would be tiresome. Hell, he'd be cautious, too.

It was just a hunch, but he suspected Khara might need to feel in control. That was fine by him. She'd asked for slow. He was more than happy to give her the reins and enjoy the ride. A woman in full sexual bloom taking charge was something he appreciated the hell out of. Was there anything sexier? The image of Khara riding him, her bountiful breasts filling his hands while she took what she wanted... damn.

Oh, he could most definitely give her the space for that. No doubt.

Now he was hard again.

Sleep continued to elude him as he fantasized about her.

Khara was too busy reliving their steamy kisses to do anything so mundane as sleep. She couldn't stop smiling, couldn't stop thinking about how amazing Riddick's lips had felt on hers. Somehow soft and firm at the same time.

As far as kisses went—first or otherwise—that was off the charts.

Heavens, that man could *kiss*.

She'd been wracked with nerves, standing there encircled in his arms, surrounded by his warmth and magnificent scent, but he made it easy for her. She liked that he'd let her make the first move. Liked that he'd been restrained, had deliberately waited for her invitation before going deeper. And *oh*, the way he'd used his tongue to tease her so skillfully should be illegal. Previous kisses had never gotten her so riled.

That sexy man had set her senses alight, left her weak and muzzy-headed and feeling like she was melting into a puddle. Gracious, the way he looked at her and held her. Even just remembering the feel of his hard, muscled body against her own made her squirm. She'd badly wanted to unbutton his shirt so she could slide her hands along his naked skin and trace those impressive pecs.

She'd had a fanciful thought. Decorum be damned. Being trapped between the door and the hard heat of him—well, that was enough to make a woman wanton. How hot would it be if Riddick took her right there, in public?

Not hot enough to get arrested for. Face disgrace for. Some fantasies were better left as fantasies. Khara let Riddick lead her away but knew she'd be revisiting this scenario in her imagination later.

His gaze on her face felt like a caress on the Metro as they stood facing one another. He'd turned her on so much it was a wonder there wasn't steam rising from her wet clothes.

Khara sighed the whole ride home to the hotel and could have sworn she heard Jonnis' soft chuckle from the front seat. They'd felt secluded, but it was highly unlikely that the Elites would have let her fully out of their sight. They must have been nearby. Likely shielding her from public view by redirecting any passersby. The Elites were the souls of discretion; anything she did was held in the strictest confidence. No need to feel embarrassed about them knowing what she'd been doing.

What a night.

Dion was sweet and it had done something to her ovaries seeing Riddick bursting with pride in him. She was glad Riddick had trusted her enough to open up a bit at the restaurant, for she'd heard the sorrow, the rejection beneath his words. There was an intriguing depth to Riddick that wasn't immediately obvious. It was overshadowed by his larger-than-life presence, and one could easily be taken in by the good looks alone. She'd seen how other women's eyes followed him when the two of them were out. Who could blame them? Whenever she looked at him, everything female in her shivered with awareness.

Khara couldn't wait to see him again.

Chapter Thirty

S HE'D JUST FINISHED UP a video conference with a group of students in a grade eight civics class when her personal cell phone vibrated with the pattern she'd assigned to Riddick. Khara's heart lifted as she answered. That all-hands meeting she was heading to would simply have to wait for a moment. Khara grinned at this surprising new attitude in herself, for up until recently, she'd been almost fanatical about punctuality. "Well, hello there."

"Good afternoon to the best Queen's assistant around. Hope your day is treating you well."

Merely hearing the low timbre of his voice sent excitement flitting through Khara. "It's exponentially better now. Yours?" Who on Earth was this brazen woman who flirted so effortlessly nowadays?

"Same. I only have a minute," Riddick rushed out. "I've got a trade association cocktail mixer thing tonight I forgot all about. You want to be my plus-one? I promise we'll just put in an appearance, then get out of there and do something fun."

They hadn't made any plans for the evening, so Khara was a tiny bit confused. She'd intended to have an early dinner and a bubble bath and had already told the Elites she'd be staying in for the night. None of them would gripe about being pressed into service after all, but it gave Khara a moment of pause. Deciding she'd make it up to them with a night off soon, Khara replied, "That sounds marvelous."

Someone called his name in the background, and Riddick told her he'd text the address and see her there. The rest of the afternoon passed in a flurry of nonstop activity to where Khara had to leap into the shower and rush through her ablutions to make it on time.

Riddick was waiting for her at the elevator, looking dashing in his navy pin-stripe suit. He'd coordinated it with a dusty pink shirt, and a bold tie and pocket square combo. Khara gulped. She adored how he always looked so polished and powerful. She'd known tall men who used their height to try to intimidate people. He towered over nearly everyone, but he exuded only strength and competence. She felt safe with him. "Sorry to cut it so close. The Queen had a late call—"

There was warmth in his gaze that made Khara's stomach feel fluttery. "No worries. You look lovely. Thanks for coming." He guided her inside with a hand at the small of her back.

She wanted to ask questions, but there simply wasn't time, as a petite woman with gold beads adorning her cap of short silver locs took the podium and introduced herself as the association's president. She launched right into a brief welcome and began with an abbreviated biography for each of the honorees.

The space had soaring ceilings and was filled to the brim with men and women in festive attire. Cocktail dresses in every conceivable color and material abounded. Most of the men wore dark suits, although a few flaunted the fashion rules by donning collared shirts instead. Candlelit centerpieces on the high-top tables glinted off sequins and cast a warm glow on the gauzy fabric draped along the walls. Fairy lights and striking floral arrangements around the room lent an air of quiet sophistication.

Khara thanked the server for the glass of champagne and opened the program a bubbly hostess had given her in the lobby. She made eye contact ever so briefly with Jonnis and Link, who were on the other side of the room, posing as a couple. When she heard Riddick's name announced, she almost choked. He gave her a nonchalant shrug.

"It's nothing," he mouthed.

Of course, it wasn't "nothing". It was prestigious, a peer-nominated award for Riddick & Sloane's philanthropic work. Khara listened to what the nominating committee put in their submission packet, how R&S baked their innovative community engagement programming into everything they did. She looked at Riddick in astonishment, her heart swelling with pride. Clapped enthusiastically when the room erupted into applause for him. The committee would announce its decision in four weeks once the voting concluded.

Riddick's smile was sheepish as he acknowledged the praise. "Eric usually does these things, but he's out of town. We'll just stay for a bit, then—"

The arrival of a group of fellow architects offering congratulations interrupted them. Riddick was gracious as he accepted, but Khara saw that the edges of his smile were forced. Nonplussed, he looked like he'd rather be anywhere but here. To give him a bit of space, she asked him to hold her glass and excused herself to the restroom.

There were photographers present, but for once, she wasn't too concerned. She didn't think she was immediately recognizable in the low lighting—she was dressed differently and not appearing in any of her regalia. Really, she looked like any other woman at the event. Khara angled her body away from the crowd a bit just in case. It had taken a little time, but it seemed she was finally getting used to this.

Her heart almost stopped when she heard someone call out from behind her, "*Avlah!*"

Khara turned to see an acquaintance she'd made weeks ago beckoning toward her with a frantic wave of her hand. A second woman, perhaps her friend, following close behind. A ribbon of panic wound its way through her chest. *Valscht*, what were the chances?

The two women descended upon her; wide excited smiles were plastered on their faces. "I thought that was you!"

"Hello, Dr. Huffman. Good evening." Khara saw Riddick was still being fussed over, his back to her. If he happened to look over, all he would see was her talking to two other guests. Nothing suspicious about that. "How are things with your research project?"

"My stars, if I'd known you were going to be here, I would have had them introduce you. Quick, let me—"

"No!" Khara put her hand on the woman's forearm when she tried to head off toward the association president. "That won't be necessary, I mean. I'm, ah, incognito tonight. I wouldn't want to take any of the spotlight away from the nominees. You understand."

Dr. Huffman lowered her voice to a conspiratorial whisper. "Of course, of course. My lips are sealed." She mimed turning a lock over her lips and throwing away the key. Her companion did the same.

Leaning in closer, Khara offered her a grateful smile. "I just know I can trust you." Dr. Huffman didn't seem like the type to run to the press, but a little flattery couldn't hurt.

The anthropologist nodded so hard she probably rattled her eyeballs. Khara breathed a sigh of relief, for her secret was still safe.

Goddammit, Riddick thought as he watched Khara go. If only she'd arrived a few minutes earlier or later. He'd explain once they left.

If it hadn't been for Lena's reminder first thing that morning, Riddick would have missed the event he'd RSVP'd to weeks ago altogether. There it was, blocked off on his calendar; he just hadn't bothered to look. Since he couldn't very well get out of it, he figured he'd make the best of things and called Khara in between meetings to invite her. He'd stayed light on the details and apologized for the short notice. Just before the program started, she'd bustled into the airy loft event space in an amethyst-colored slipdress that had heads turning and his tongue almost lolling.

Riddick did his best to pay attention to the conversation with his industry colleagues, asking after their projects, their families. A partner at a firm across town had recently become a grandma for the first time to her daughter's set of twins. Another woman had been on a sabbatical in Fiji until the week before. He was ready to bounce. Maybe another twenty minutes for good form, then he and Khara could—

"Josh," a booming voice sounded behind him, setting his teeth on edge. "When are you going to give up that little business of yours and come make some real money with us?"

Riddick's stomach tensed. No matter how many times he corrected him, the man insisted on calling him by his first name. Not only that, but the shortened version, too, as though they were old buddies. It wasn't a slip-up. It was a pathetic power play that made him look like a grade-A asshole. As if Riddick needed another reason to reject his offer. Thankfully, Khara was still in the ladies' room. The knot of people around him scattered.

"Adrian," Riddick said. He wasn't about to let this tool ruin his night. "I'm doing well. Thanks for asking. Still not interested in working for someone else." Adrian Designs often won top honors for their sleek, futuristic work. Riddick didn't care about honors, never had. That never seemed to resonate with people like Adrian, who were in it for the glory. It had incensed him when Riddick declined his ostentatious job offer. He brought up the standing offer every time they were in each other's company. It was a shtick he never grew tired of. How was he still salty?

Sasha Adrian didn't say it outright but seemed to think doing work that supported the community somehow was something to be looked down upon. Never missed a chance to take a crack at him about it. "As I've said before, do what you're passionate about and the money will follow." Why did he assume he was hurting for money? He wasn't.

"You'd make more money if you didn't give so much away, am I right?"

"Maybe. But children need us to invest in them."

Khara appeared at his side just then, a vision with her curls swept back from her face in a way that emphasized the beauty of her eyes. "Yes, they do." she agreed, accepting her champagne flute back from Riddick with thanks.

The short, older man got a good look at Khara wearing the hell out of that dress and coughed, his face reddening. She looked like a damn bombshell. *Yeah, choke on it, asshole*, Riddick thought. He did his best to be congenial when he introduced them.

"Well, now, aren't you just a huge upgrade from the girls Riddick usually dates?" Adrian gave a condescending, braying sort of laugh, but Khara narrowed her eyes. She pulled her hand from his too-tight grasp.

"I'd assume Riddick's taste in *women* is as impeccable as his taste in everything else. Except perhaps some acquaintances. Excuse us." Khara downed her champagne. "Shall we get out of here?"

She shoved her empty flute into Adrian's hand and left them both standing there with their jaws hanging open as she strode toward the exit. Riddick shook off his amazement and went after her. Found her seething by the elevator bank.

"My apologies for overstepping." Khara spoke without looking at him. "I can't stand that type. Scoring petty points by wrapping insults in compliments. I wasn't going to let him insult you, me, or your previous girlfriends or dates. That was just unbelievably rude." Her voice shook with the derision threading her words.

Riddick followed her into the elevator and hardly let the door close behind them before taking her in his arms and kissing the daylights out of her. Her handbag slipped from her fingers onto the floor with a thunk. She didn't seem to care. The dress was halter-style, dipping low in the back, allowing him to spread his hands over smooth, naked skin.

"I hope I haven't complicated things for you." Their lips were a mere centimeter apart. He swore he could still feel their heat.

She was complicating his *life*, but she had complicated nothing with Sasha Adrian. "That was seriously hot, Khara."

"You think so?"

"The word 'comeuppance' springs to mind. You being gorgeous while serving it up was just a bonus." He retrieved her handbag.

"If that gets me kisses like that, I believe I may tell people off at random. Are you going to tell me what that was about?"

Riddick gave a snort. "Ego."

Khara sucked in a breath when the elevator doors slid open again and an elegant older woman in sky-high heels stepped inside. The newcomer stopped short when she spotted Khara.

An awkward silence persisted, where the two women seemed to be having an entire conversation with their eyes.

Puzzled, Riddick asked, "You two ladies know each other?"

"Ah, yes. Riddick, this is Dr. Amelia Huffman. We met at a dinner a few weeks ago. She's doing a fascinating research project on Black sexuality and economics."

"That does sound fascinating. Nice to meet you."

Before anyone could say anything more, Dr. Huffman whipped out her phone. "I'm so sorry, I have to. Do you mind? I promise I won't post it."

Khara nodded, then smiled in a way he'd never seen before as she snapped her picture. Almost a practiced, camera-ready shifting. It was a subtle change in her posture, how she held her head. Her smile wasn't fully genuine, but it wasn't quite insincere either. Rehearsed maybe.

"Thank you so much," the woman gushed, then nearly stumbled off the elevator when it dinged at the lobby and the doors whooshed open.

"That was weird." Authentic Khara was back, but her demeanor had stiffened the tiniest bit.

"She thought I was the Queen. It was easier to go with it."

"I figured. Well." Riddick brought her hand to his lips. "I see Khara Therin for who she really is."

A flicker of something crossed her face but was gone before he could decipher it. "You do. And that is both lovely and refreshing."

"*You* are both lovely and refreshing."

Her smile up at him was a sweet one, just a little shy. Riddick did his best to ignore how much he liked seeing it.

Chapter Thirty-One

TRINA TAPPED HER FOOT impatiently and looked at her watch again for what felt like the millionth time. They were late for this call, a disrespect she would never have tolerated in any other part of her life. It had already been a shit day all around, and she was behind schedule. Budget season was upon the department, and that always meant managing bureaucratic bullshit. The tedium exhausted her, but it was unavoidable and necessary. The men and women who served under her deserved her best effort. She gritted her teeth and tried to take a bit of solace in the fact that the fall from grace she'd meticulously engineered for Lillianna was close.

At present, the Queen was more popular than ever, having somehow come away from every obstacle Trina threw in her path smelling like a goddamn rose. It was alright for now, though, for it served her purposes. The higher up Lillianna was, the farther she had to fall.

Even at the bombing, Lillianna had been so wildly brave and foolhardy that she was lauded for her heroism. Which she downplayed, of course, and gave all credit to the Guard and first responders who'd dealt with the emergency. Trina had been on the scene that day and witnessed firsthand the Queen's taking charge of the chaos, her flat-out refusal to be evacuated until all the Parliament members were safe.

Rumor had it the tall female Elite with the no-bullshit demeanor and endless supply of throwing knives had been incensed over her reckless actions. Trina wondered at the time if there was a way she could exploit that knowledge but ultimately decided against it. The Elites, as Lillianna nauseatingly referred to them, were loyal to a fault.

The only hitch in the current plan was Trina's guilt that a Guard was going to have to be killed. It was a necessary component to orchestrating Lillianna's downfall, but it didn't sit well with her. She'd deliberated for weeks about which Elite Guard would be the unlucky one. It was torturous to think about, as they'd done nothing wrong, and Trina felt a kinship with them. Lillianna was easy—she deserved every bit of scorn and hatred Trina heaped upon her.

While she regretted that a good public servant was going to be sacrificed, she'd find a way to make peace with that after the deed was done.

Trina might have relished the opportunity to pit her skill against Cenn's at an earlier point in her life, but middle age had settled upon her like an unwelcome house guest and largely robbed her of the speed and agility she'd taken such pride in. She still trained regularly, though it got harder and harder every year, and she had to berate her sparring partners into actually fighting like they meant it. They saw her as an unassuming non-threat. Cenn Driscoll wouldn't take it easy on her. God, how refreshing that would be.

At thirty-seven minutes past the appointed time, the burner phone vibrated in her hand. Galled, Trina made sure the voice-altering app was running before answering. "Well?" Trepidation was making her stomach roil. "You're late. Is it done?"

"Uh, not yet. We hit a snag," came the apprehensive-sounding response, "there's a man with her, like all the time."

"Yes, her security team is always with her. You'll have to get creative in separating them. I already told you that." Annoyance was buzzing through her. Trina glanced at her watch again.

"Don't think this is security."

"Why not?"

"From their body language, it looks like maybe they're *together*."

Why did the fool whisper "together" like it was a swear word? He was fine with criminal activity, but quailed over *that*? Unbelievable. Trina pinched the bridge of her nose to stave off the headache. "You must be mistaken. She's not involved with anyone. Never mind, it doesn't matter. I didn't hire you to think or speculate. Just do the job I hired you for or I'll find someone else who can."

"We took a picture," the other dimwit protested. "I'll send it now."

A blurry picture came through the text app. Trina couldn't make out anything helpful, even squinting. "What is this supposed to be? I can't see anything in this shitty picture. Get a better one, then we'll talk."

A few hours later, Trina was looking at the face of a man she didn't recognize and wondering if the dumbasses might have been right. He was tall, wearing sunglasses and a good suit, standing close to the Queen in the texted picture. Too close to be one of her Guard, even an Elite one. The Queen was smiling, her posture relaxed. She seemed to be laughing.

Who the hell was this?

She was cheating on her son, while he'd been nothing but faithful? The nerve. Well, to be fair, Lillianna didn't know Cyrus was pining for her. But still.

The Queen was pretty enough, Trina supposed as she took a hard look at her face. Eventually, this would be her daughter-in-law, after all. The mother of her future grandchildren. She could be a little charitable. Trina would just have to keep a close eye on her parenting when the time came to ensure she was doing it right.

It took a few deep breaths for Trina to calm down enough to make the call. The goons were ready with assurances that they could still do the job, even with some dude in the picture.

"We'll find a way. Don't you worry. We could, ah, use a bit more cash, though. We're running low."

These amateurs. Trina closed her eyes and sighed, pinching the bridge of her nose again. She reminded herself that they were decoys, only in the picture for misdirection. It was why she hadn't sent more valuable operatives for this piece. "These advances are coming out of your back-end fee. You understand that don't you? Are you eating at five-star restaurants for every meal? Jesus."

"Well, if you don't wanna pay, we can always just go to the police. Or the FBI. Bet they'd love to hear all about you, *Boss*."

Trina's eye started to twitch. Greedy, bloodsucking opportunists. This belligerence was getting out of hand. Didn't these idiots know who they were dealing with? "Fine." she snarled, then clicked off the phone and resisted the urge to pitch it across the room.

The would-be kidnappers kept needing money to lie low, for supplies, for transportation. She wouldn't recover the money she was paying the fools, but it would be worth it. Their first attempt to snatch the Queen had been a bust, over before it even began. The two of them had been run off—foiled by attentive Guards. Despite being fed good intel, they hadn't made it anywhere close to the Queen, probably hadn't even made it as a footnote into her daily security briefing. When Trina got wind of that, she'd instructed them to stand down until the heat was off. If they tightened security around Lillianna, they'd never be able to grab her. Everything hinged on them doing so. They were running out of time.

Even knowing the Intermediary was working behind the scenes to execute the other parts of the plan, Trina couldn't help but worry.

It's going to work.

With all the recon she was doing, the Intermediary would surely have known about the man, although she might not have thought it was an important detail to tell Trina. She hadn't shared any of the whys or hows with the Intermediary, just the basics of what was to be done. If she asked about it, she'd alert her that this was more than a regular assignment, and she didn't want to give her that kind of leverage.

A man could complicate things some. Or maybe this wasn't a big deal at all. "I'll come see for myself." Trina whispered. A glance at her watch told her it was too late to catch a flight out of Lytua tonight, but she could make arrangements to fly to Washington, DC the next morning. Right after she transferred the requested additional funds to the lackeys.

Footsteps sounded in the foyer, alarming her. Trina looked at the clock; her husband was home from work. Cursing, she secreted the burner phone away. She'd made sure she was alone before making the call but had forgotten he would be home early tonight. Trina chastised herself and schooled her face. She'd come so far, and she couldn't afford to be sloppy now.

Chapter Thirty-Two

P ARIE RIDDICK FELT LIKE she'd died and gone to heaven.

That rascal outdid himself with all the surprises. Flowers and a fruit tray were waiting in the suite. The sealed gold foil envelope he'd given her contained a letter explaining what to expect, like the premium wi-fi and unlimited drinks packages, along with an unnamed sum of money on her cruise account. Knowing Joshie, she figured it numbered in the tens of thousands. She should want for nothing and enjoy every moment.

He'd written just a few sentences about how much her taking a chance on him meant to him. He wanted to give back to her a fraction of what she had given him.

The last line read, "You never stopped looking for me."

The letter was now tear-stained and a little wrinkled.

She'd tried to refuse the gifts at the terminal, but Joshie put his foot down and wasn't having it.

You deserve this and more, so stop bitching and let me spoil you.

Really, what could she say to that? And that was *before* she'd learned about the companions.

Parie tried to send Joshie a short missive every night. He'd told her a few tidbits about this new woman he was seeing, and she did her best to read between the lines. It tickled her that things seemed to be going well. That kid had always been so guarded with his heart. Not prying was an exercise in restraint. It was one of the hardest things she'd ever done to not bombard him with questions. She wanted to know everything about Khara, about what kinds of dates the two of them were going on. Parie admonished herself to have patience. She had a gut feeling this might turn serious. If it did, Joshie would tell her only when he was good and ready and not a moment before. The stubborn rascal.

Parie and her care companions, Dina and Meredith, spent hours dissecting every email, scouring for clues, and trying to decode each word. From what they could deduce, Khara was funny and sweet, but with a sassy side that kept Joshie on his toes. It sounded as though they laughed a lot together. He was lighthearted in his descriptions of her and the things they did together.

Afternoon tea was a custom Parie took to immediately. The conscious slowing down encouraged her to really reflect and, unsurprisingly, she spent a great deal of time deep in thought about what her son was up to.

What would it be like for Joshie to be in love? She knew there was a tender heart beating beneath his handsome, polished exterior. Was Khara the one who might break through to it? Maybe waltz right past all his defenses? The thought of a woman being able to keep up with Riddick and give him what-for made her chuckle.

Truthfully, it sounded as though he could be half in love with her already. He hadn't answered her oh-so-casual question of if he'd kissed her yet. Parie took that to mean yes, and that it must have been something. With luck, it would be like the fireworks she'd felt with her Emmanuel, rest his soul. Parie wrapped her hands around her teacup and let the heat seep into her fingers. Oh, Joshie, her heart. Trying to temper her imagination wasn't working worth shit. There was just no stopping the anticipation that started winding through her every time she saw Khara's name mentioned in the emails. She was practically jumping for joy. More than just reading about Khara, Parie was delighted at how relaxed and enthusiastic Joshie was coming across.

This was all fascinating new territory she'd never been in before. Her Joshie was wonderful, with many incredible qualities. Well, now, Parie wondered, if he fell in love, would he still be "her" Joshie? She felt a bittersweet tug in her heart at the thought. She'd joyfully relinquish her claim for a partner who made him truly happy. All she'd ever wanted for him was happiness, whatever that looked like. She harbored some concern that he'd be confused by unfamiliar feelings, that they might cause him to panic. Those tricky emotional scars certainly had real potential to trip him up. And that was the thing about scars—they could give the illusion that the deep wounds that caused them no longer hurt. Sometimes that couldn't be farther from the truth.

If Khara was the one for him, could he trust her with his pain, his truth? Could he let her love *him*? Now those were some serious questions to noodle on.

The cruise director reminded guests over the PA system that the luau deck party was about to get underway. Parie perched her floppy white sun hat on her head and stood. She'd have to trust that her Joshie could sort things out with Khara for himself.

Chapter Thirty-Three

KHARA CAUGHT RIDDICK ON his cell when he was getting ready to leave his office. "I had a change of plans for tomorrow. Nothing major, but I need to do a bit of work for it tonight. It won't take long. Would you mind terribly if we meet after?"

"Is it something you can do from anywhere?"

"Yes, I just need my laptop and my phone."

"How about you come over and work while I make us dinner? We can watch a movie after, maybe make out a little in front of the fire. Have a nice quiet night in."

The thought of making out in front of a fire made Khara feel a little toasty inside. It was the first time he'd invited her to his home. "You wouldn't mind?"

"Not at all. Give me an hour."

Riddick set her up at his dining room table, where he could keep an eye on her from the kitchen. He'd already opened a Viognier from their winery trip to let it breathe and warm some. He poured them both a glass and set a crudite platter down for her, then got busy chopping. He wasn't a gourmet cook by any stretch of the imagination, but Parie had seen to it that he knew his way around the kitchen and had a few go-to recipes in his back pocket. It had only taken a quick spin through the supermarket to pick up what he needed. He cooked and surreptitiously watched Khara work.

It was interesting to see her process. She focused intensely in bursts and used some sort of visual timer to break up her screen time. When she stood and stretched at regular intervals, Riddick tried not to get caught looking at the masterpiece that was her body. Up on her toes, with her arms stretched over her head as she looked toward the ceiling, it afforded him an unobstructed view. Full breasts straining at her blouse, long limbs despite being on the short side. A tiny sliver of golden skin at her waist. That delicious curve of her ass made his hands actually itch.

She made three phone calls, all in Lytuan. He could only make out a few words, but it was easy enough to read her body language. Two business, one personal. When he refilled her wineglass, he stopped to give her a brief shoulder massage. The groan of relief she let out as he worked his thumbs into the kinks and knots turned him on so much, he wanted to tear her clothes off. Take her right there on the table. With her hair twisted up, it exposed a beauty mark at the juncture of her neck and shoulder he hadn't noticed before. He wanted to bite it. He settled for kissing the top of her head and returning to his prep.

"Let me know when you're about fifteen minutes from done and I'll get everything finished."

He busied himself with setting the table and getting dessert ready. Her hair was different every time he saw her—he dug the variety.

Riddick remembered cooking for other women on occasion, but this felt different. There was an unfamiliar pull here to care for Khara. He pondered that for a moment, and decided that nope, he was not ready to look any closer at that just yet. *Stay in your lane, bro*, he told himself. Again.

Chapter Thirty-Four

KHARA COULD FEEL RIDDICK'S eyes on her as she worked, and the knowledge that he was watching her made her skin prickle with excitement. She'd been a little self-conscious at first, but he made it easy. In no time, she was elbow-deep in the presentation she'd need to give to the parliament committee on tourism in the morning. Riddick was at ease in the kitchen—he glided around the well-designed space, with no wasted movement. He knew what he was doing.

His home was lovely—a spacious end-unit townhouse with many tall windows and an awe-inspiring view of the Potomac River. Old Town Alexandria was a darling neighborhood full of quirk and charm. It was a place she would have chosen to live. The brief tour he'd given her revealed guest bedrooms, an office, and a theater set-up in the basement. Dark, masculine furniture, but not stuffy. Khara fought back a shiver seeing the massive bed in the master bedroom.

Khara ran her hand along the polished banister. "This is amazing. It suits you perfectly. You must have looked forever to find just the right place."

"It took me forever for the work to be finished. I designed this community."

She thought of the character in the buildings. While she knew intellectually that this was what he did for a living, it was almost intimate to be in a space that started in his imagination. "Is that why it suits you so well?" Her eyes were sparkling.

"I design homes as though I were going to live there. With details I would want in my own home. Is this design good enough for my mother? Then it might be ready to show to clients. We have a team of incredible interior designers on staff."

He kept tabs on her and stayed connected, which was unexpected. He'd asked considerate questions when she arrived—would soft music be okay, or did she need silence? What kind of music would she like to hear? Did she need a notepad or other supplies? Would he be a visual distraction if he was in the kitchen? Take all the time you need, he told her. He could finish dinner in a snap whenever she was done. Wearing a black and white hounds-tooth apron, he'd tossed a matching dishtowel over one broad shoulder. He'd rolled his dress shirt up to his elbows, exposing powerful-looking forearms.

He looked sexy as all hell. Every time he turned his back to her, her concentration suffered because she kept stealing looks at his backside.

Khara had a brief call with Joanne, then Cenn, and called Yvanda to see how she was feeling.

"*He's making me dinner at his house,*" she answered when Yvanda asked how things were going with the hot American. "*I had to do some work. He's kept me in wine and cheese and is waiting patiently for me to finish.*"

Khara was glad Riddick didn't speak Lytuan, so she could speak in front of him in her mother tongue. He'd asked her how to say phrases and objects, but she felt safe talking this way. At most, he might get a few words.

"*Valscht, Khar. You might need to marry this man. He sounds like a dream.*"

"*There's a roaring fire, some sort of dessert baking that smells delicious, Chopin in the background. Oh, and he's wearing an apron.*"

"*Now you're just showing off—oof!*"

"*Are you okay? Is it the baby?*"

"*I swear, this kid and I are only tolerating each other at this point. Merde, valscht, shit, I'm ready to have my body to myself again.*"

"*You want me to try to get that shirtless pic for you tonight?*"

"*Girl, if you get that man shirtless tonight, you'd better not be thinking about me at all.*"

She had to go in search of him when she'd reached the fifteen-minutes-out mark. She found him dozing on the couch, a football game on mute on the television. And didn't he just look divine? She took a moment to admire him as he slept. Riddick was quite good-looking. Best, he wore those good looks lightly. Everything about him attracted her. He was funny and smart, generous. And quite a good kisser. It tempted Khara to crawl into his lap and wake him with kisses. Would he think her too forward? Would it lead to the fling she wasn't quite sure she was ready for? What would it be like to feel him on top of her?

He must have sensed her, for he roused himself and stood, reached out, and snagged her hand. "Sorry about that. Long day. You just about ready?"

Khara nodded. She could smell his woodsy scent. Her resolve was weakening.

"Great. I'll get started."

What followed defied description. Riddick served up fajitas with all the fixins, including homemade salsa and tortillas. The tortilla press fascinated Khara, and she insisted he show her how to use it. He'd marinated a flank steak and didn't blink when she asked for her portion to be well-done. He plated everything beautifully, and it was oh, so delicious. The steak was so flavorful and tender that Khara moaned with the first bite.

Khara stuffed herself without apology but made room for a sliver of apple cake. "Did you make this, too?"

"You said you loved apples."

Good gracious. He'd remembered that off-hand comment in his office? Khara gulped.

Since Riddick cleaned up as he prepared the meal, there weren't many dishes. Khara insisted on helping with what remained, and the kitchen was restored and set to rights in no time. They laughed and teased throughout the process—Khara had never laughed so much in previous relationships. Then again, she'd never spent this kind of unstructured downtime, either. She was surprisingly at ease and felt no need to plan or censor what she said.

With full bellies, the two of them sat close together on the couch and made it through half of a movie before they were kissing. Khara started it. The man had wooed her with his culinary prowess. She thrilled at the feel of Riddick's muscular thighs beneath her when he swept her into his lap. A whiff of his spicy scent made her pulse increase.

Their making out was subtle, fun, and hot. This man knew how to kiss a woman, how to read her cues, how to make her feel beautiful. His kisses were exploratory, some gentle, some less so. He nipped, sucked, and made her feel sexy under his undivided attention. His hands felt huge on her neck and face, in her hair, and on her hips. There was power there, but his touch was gentle. Like he was cherishing her, almost.

Not much in the way of risqué touches and yet he wound her up right proper. He brushed his lips over the sensitive skin under her earlobes. Trailed soft, sweet kisses along her jaw that had her taking his face in her hands and pulling his mouth back to hers.

They were both breathing hard when they stopped before things got too steamy. Riddick was looking at her in a way that made her feel irresistible. She'd never felt so... desired, so savored.

"I like kissing you, Riddick. I like how you kiss me, like you're wholly in the moment and enjoying yourself and making sure I am, as well. But there's another layer there, too, like energy barely restrained. Maybe not quite tension."

"Oh, it's tension. The good kind."

The unadulterated lust in his eyes excited her even more. Her face and neck felt hot, and she knew she was blushing again. Maybe he wouldn't notice. Of course, he would notice. He noticed everything. "I should get back," she said.

"Yes," he agreed. Neither of them moved.

"Riddick."

"Yes, beautiful Khara?" He traced a gentle fingertip over where the blush had spread across her chest, making goosebumps break out.

"We have unbelievable chemistry."

He chuckled, nodded, then nuzzled her neck. "We do. When you're ready, we'll see how deep it goes. Until then, kissing is just fine, because I like kissing you too. You control the timing."

Giving her that control had her feeling treasured, catered to. She wasn't altogether sure what to think or say to that.

Chapter Thirty-Five

RIDDICK STOOD WITH HER in his arms, chuckling again when she gave a panicked gasp and clung to his neck. He'd never drop her. It was just a few steps to the front door, where he set her on her feet, sure to let her slide down the length of his body. In their bare feet, she was tiny next to him.

Riddick wanted to lift her so that her legs went around him as he sank his cock inside her. He could take her up against the wall or door easily, kissing her all the while. Would she like being taken that way? He didn't dare ask now. If that question left his lips, he was a goner, no matter the answer. While he did want to find out more about what she liked and wanted, his beleaguered self-control couldn't handle any more temptation tonight. He plucked her coat from where it was hanging on a hook in the entryway and helped her into it.

"Where's your mother this week?"

Riddick liked that Khara always remembered his mother and took a genuine interest in her big adventure. He told her the latest from the email she'd just sent him from Patagonia. The dramatic landscape and antics of the Magellanic penguins delighted Parie. She was heading out to the Pacific Rim now.

Earlier in the day, he'd received Parie's postcard from Panama. It had taken some time for it to wend its way from Central America.

I've always told you that you don't need a woman to live a complete life. I'm so very proud of the life you live. In my eyes, you'll never find a woman worthy of you, of all that you are.

I'm happy to be wrong.

Riddick had stood in his foyer, reading his mother's words again and then a third time. She'd printed them on the opposite side of a card that pictured a tranquil beach with water in an otherworldly shade of blue-green. He instinctively knew Parie would love Khara.

Why did that make his chest feel like it was burning?

Now they held hands as he walked her to the waiting car, where he nodded at the driver. He kissed her one last time but made it almost chaste.

This day might have started strangely, but he liked how it was concluding. There had been a voicemail from his ex waiting for him on his desk line that morning, inviting him over. Riddick knew what "over" entailed. A few weeks ago, he would have been glad to take Shae up on her offer. He must have talked her up.

He didn't even consider calling her back. For once, his dick didn't even respond. Riddick had hit delete and sent Khara a text instead.

A broad grin came over his face as he watched the car pull off to return Khara to the hotel. Oh, yeah. This had been much better.

Khara smiled all the way back to the hotel. A contented sigh escaped her. Was she falling for Riddick? No, certainly not. She couldn't be. She wouldn't. Love wasn't meant for her. This was a one-time thing with no possibility of heartbreak. Her stomach clenched at the thought of telling him who she really was. The subtle note of derision in his voice whenever he spoke of the Queen made her heart squeeze every time she heard it.

Her phone pinged with an incoming text message as she was slipping into bed. It was from Riddick.

Riddick: Sweet dreams, beautiful Khara. I'll be dreaming of how good you taste.

Khara gave a muffled squeal at his suggestive words, then called out a pre-emptive, "I'm fine!" before the Guard came crashing in. She flopped back in bed with the phone clutched to her chest, a goofy grin spread wide on her face. It was like being in high school again, mooning over a crush.

Khara: You taste pretty good yourself. Dinner really was delicious. Thank you for that and for giving me the space to finish work.

Riddick: Anytime, beautiful. You make a soft noise in the back of your throat when we kiss that drives me wild.

And just like that, all thoughts of sleep vanished. Khara's nipples hardened into aching points again as she remembered the feel of his mouth on hers, how he seemed to be everywhere at once, how he let her take control, then how he took control, how his tongue felt playing with hers. How his hard body felt against hers when he lay down and pulled her up on top of him. She rubbed her thighs together, squirming at the memory of how he'd cupped her hips in those gigantic hands of his while his mouth slanted over hers. Feeling his hardened cock against her was a naughty delight. He'd left her wanting more. Panting for it. Again.

Khara: I won't get to sleep with you telling me things like that, sir.

Riddick: LOL. Is that good or bad?

Khara wondered if she dared admit how much she was attracted to him. She chewed on it for a moment, then decided not to overthink it and just go with it.

Khara: You drive me wild every time you kiss me.

Riddick: (makes mental note to kiss Khara more) Good luck with your thing tomorrow. Hope the Queen appreciates your hard work.

Khara felt the tiniest flicker of guilt about hiding her identity, but then it was gone. She didn't know how this was going to play out, but she was determined to enjoy every moment she could.

Chapter Thirty-Six

TRINA WAS INCENSED WHEN she saw the idiots seemed to have the right of it. She watched in sheer disbelief from a corner in the upscale hotel lobby, where she'd been staked out all day. Dressed to blend in, she was just another wealthy professional on holiday. She'd booked a room under a false name so that no one would get suspicious of her lingering. It seemed unlikely the Guard would recognize her out of context, but she'd worn a wig and oversized glasses just to be sure.

She'd tested the waters when she checked in with a casual observation. "There seems to be quite a bit of extra security. Do we have a celebrity guest staying with us?"

The front desk clerk said nothing, just offered a placid, polite smile. Of course, she'd never divulge the name of a guest, especially one as VIP as Queen Lillianna. She was well-trained and gave away nothing. Sanctimonious bitch.

Trina was sitting next to a gigantic planter, pretending to read a bestselling biography, when a ripple of activity changed the ambiance. The Queen arrived without fanfare, breezing through the lobby with the same tall man she'd seen in the picture. They weren't touching, but their body language gave them away. He walked her to the elevator, then squeezed both her hands and gave her a quick kiss at the corner of her mouth.

Trina was so overwrought she could scarcely see through the rage. This was her son's woman. What was she doing with someone else? It was unseemly. She took no notice of the man leaving once Lillianna stepped into the elevator.

Things moved quickly from then.

Seething, Trina waited for the security to fall back, then hurried out of the lobby and back to her actual hotel. It was in a much less glamorous neighborhood. She arranged a call with the two flunkies who kept botching this.

So, the stuck-up slut who thought she was too good for everything and everyone, was cozied up to some American. An *American*. When she could have *her* son. It was too wild to be believed. Trina poured herself a drink with shaking hands and downed it in a single swallow, ignoring the burn in her throat.

Enraged, Trina shrieked and hurled her glass against the wall. The shattering sound was more satisfying than it should have been. She stared at the whiskey splashed on the wall and carpet. She'd have to pay for that. Another thing that was *her* fault. Trina took a deep breath and pulled herself together.

The American man didn't matter.

She went over the plan again. The Intermediary would make sure one of the Elite Guard was killed in the line of duty after the goons kidnapped Lillianna. The public adored the Guard, and it would be an outrage to lose one. Especially once it came to light that Lillianna had organized her own kidnapping in order to embezzle the ransom money that would have been paid for her safe return. Trina had the incriminating evidence ready to plant and would tip off the press as soon as it was in place. The Queen would be disgraced. Parliament would impeach her. Strip her of her title and power. Lillianna would be arrested and put on trial. Maybe even jailed. Trina smiled at that. Oh, what a glorious day that would be.

Then, when she was at her lowest, Trina would offer her redemption through marriage to her son. She'd be desperate to regain the public's favor. An alliance with a powerful political family could go a long way toward that. Cyrus would have a willing Lillianna to play with for a while. She wouldn't be recoiling from shit then.

On the back end, the Intermediary would take care of the goons.

Corey would step into the power vacuum and be elected King.

By the time Lillianna pushed out a kid for her son, Trina would have found a suitable replacement to comfort Cyrus after Trina disposed of her. Someone she could bend to her will. Trina was living for the day when she got to choke the life from her body. Or perhaps she would slit her throat instead and watch her bleed out. Either way, she wanted Lillianna to know it was her.

Everyone in her family would get what they wanted. What they deserved.

The peal of her personalized ringtone dragged Trina from her revenge fantasy and changed her entire demeanor. She took care to smother any residual anger before she answered his call. It was a talent she'd gotten quite good at over the years. "Corey, sweetie, hi." He thought she was on a shopping trip with her younger sister.

"Hi, baby. Having fun? I still can't believe you managed to pull your sister away from the lab."

A stab of guilt pricked at Trina's heart. She'd asked Bella to cover for her so she could go on a quick trip for early New Year's gift shopping. "She thinks they're close to a breakthrough, but you know how it is. They may be ready to start clinical trials late next year."

"That's great. She must be so excited."

Trina made a mental note to take Bella on an *actual* trip. She and her team had been hard at work for years on a fast-acting, short-term sedative. They were developing it for emergency use with aggressive psychiatric patients.

Muffled voices sounded in the background. "I've got to get back to my committee meeting. I just wanted to hear your voice."

Trina's mood was vastly improved by the time they hung up. She did her best to clean up the mess she'd made before requesting housekeeping come vacuum. The wall and carpet were just going to have to smell like liquor for a while.

When her secretary called a little while later, Trina swore before answering. She'd forgotten to clear her damn calendar. Fabiola had called all day, leaving increasingly frantic messages. Trina affected a pitiful tone of voice and told her she wasn't feeling well and wouldn't be in the next day. Fabiola could take care of the apologies and rescheduling.

Trina made another note to send her secretary a token of some sort to show her appreciation. A spa day, perhaps.

One last thing to do before heading back to Lytua in the morning. She needed to get in contact with the Intermediary to see where she was in her part of things.

Chapter Thirty-Seven

"So, you've heard of Thanksgiving, right?"

"I'm familiar with it, of course. Turkey, buckle shoes, big gathering."

"That's all you know about Thanksgiving?"

"Well, it *is* an American holiday."

"Ah, right. It's next week. It kinda snuck up on me this year, but my Ma and I usually spend it with Eric's family. If you're still in town, would you like to come with me?"

Lytuans might not celebrate Thanksgiving, but even Khara knew that this was a *Big Deal*. There was no way she was going to miss this.

They were back at his house after a mellow afternoon strolling hand-in-hand and people-watching at National Harbor. They'd taken the water taxi both ways and kissed at the top of the Capital Wheel with a phenomenal view of the city from one hundred feet above. Another near-perfect jaunt. Their plans for the next day would begin with some culinary exploration at the Union Market gourmet food hall. An author they both admired was giving a talk at Politics and Prose that evening.

It was far too easy to get caught up in her romance and forget that there was a schedule to keep. Khara was supposed to be heading to New York to accept a citation from the United Nations and attend a conference. The original plan was to stay there for a few days. Perhaps she could squeeze the return trip in earlier than expected? She needed to talk to Joanne to see about moving her schedule around.

Time was growing short. Khara was due to return home in just over a week. Appointments were already packed into her schedule there. She was behind on work but couldn't seem to find any sense of urgency. All she wanted to do was spend time with Riddick. Even knowing Joanne might kill her, she told him, "I'd love to. Let me see what I can move around." She must get it together.

The smile Riddick beamed at her made her feel slightly gooey inside. "How do you say that in Lytuan?"

"Thanksgiving? It doesn't translate. We would just say *Thanksgiving*."

"Well, it sounds sexy in your accent."

"Thanksgiving?" She laughed, gilding the word with some extra accent. "What if I told you I find your American accent sexy?"

Riddick's forehead wrinkled with a frown. "You do?"

Khara nodded. "You say my name a little differently than it's actually pronounced, but I like it."

"I've been saying your name wrong? Shit, I'm sorry. That's not cool at all." Riddick pulled her to sit on his lap.

"Not wrong, just different. The Lytuan pronunciation is car-ah, like driving a car, with just a tiny roll on the r. You change that first 'a' sound a bit."

He said it, heard the subtle difference, and asked her to repeat it. He corrected himself when he tried it again. "Names are important. I'm sorry I was mispronouncing yours. I like the way you say my name. Your accent with it is... delicious. You roll the r with your tongue the tiniest bit. I love it."

"So, you like the way my tongue moves with your name."

"I like the way your tongue moves, period. Hell, I dream about it."

And she'd thought *she* was being cheeky. His lowered voice shot heat through to her core again. The notion that he was dreaming about her? *Whew.*

It was when she was falling asleep that night that Khara realized something. She was having so much fun out of bed she kept forgetting she was supposed to be getting Riddick *into* bed. Was she subconsciously shying away from intimacy? Khara snuggled deeper into the covers, deciding that was a thought for another day. Every day they spent together made it that much harder to tell him the truth about who she was.

If she was getting fed up with her, Joanne didn't let on.

With Joanne working some scheduling magic, Khara could shorten her time in New York City so she could be back in DC for Thanksgiving. Joanne seemed quite pleased by this turn of events, judging by her bemused smile. Something about the mischievous edge to it prompted Khara to ask if she'd been lightening her days.

Khara preferred having her days jam-packed and front-loaded with any meetings. That left her, more often than not, exhausted by the evening, but feeling accomplished. A worthwhile trade-off as far as she was concerned. As she thought about the last week, Khara realized she was nowhere near as tired because her schedule showed meetings spaced further out from one another, allowing her time to regroup. And freed-up evenings occurred more frequently than not.

Joanne affected an innocent expression when Khara asked her about it over tea in the conference room. "Me? Manipulate your schedule so you can have something left in the tank when you go out with that fine-looking American? I don't know what you mean."

She couldn't help it. Khara burst into delighted laughter. Joanne was not a joker by nature, so her playful teasing was a novelty. The only time Khara saw her at complete ease was when her two adult sons visited from overseas.

The thought of Joanne having a hand in facilitating her romance made Khara feel even more fortunate to have her. Khara and Riddick had enjoyed a myriad of adventures from the Aquatic Gardens in Kenilworth to a trivia contest and everything in between. No one would have believed it—the Queen of Lytua laughing so hard while trying to roller skate she thought she'd pee her pants. The Harriet Tubman Underground Railroad Visitor Center was a recent highlight. They'd visited a couple of independent bookstores for lectures. She could have stayed in the stacks at Mahogany Books and Sankofa for days.

She'd asked Riddick to show her things off the beaten path. He delivered. What new experiences would the big holiday get-together bring?

Fortified with steamy kisses that had her melting like a Popsicle in July, Khara told Riddick she'd see him on Tuesday and then flew up to New York. Several years had passed since she'd last been to the United Nations. The Assembly Hall was just as majestic as she remembered, and Khara was humbled to accept the Human Rights Council's award for public service delivery innovation in women's empowerment on behalf of the Kingdom of Lytua. The coinciding summit on ecological tourism kept her engaged, and the fascinating topics gave her a great deal to think about. While Lytua purposely kept a low profile when it came to tourism, Khara wanted to consider opportunities for sustainable growth.

Khara couldn't shake the feeling that she was being watched. No one was showing an inordinate amount of interest in her, but an unsettled feeling persisted. She was but one world leader in a room of many, but it felt almost like someone with ill intent was studying her. The Elites had trained her to never dismiss her intuition, but a surreptitious sweep of the hall and lobby turned up nothing unusual.

There were familiar faces, other elected leaders and officials she'd come to know over the years in attendance. When a Prime Minister she was friendly with invited her to dinner, Khara declined. She was eager to get packed and be on her way first thing in the morning.

Her memory hadn't exaggerated how opulent the Waldorf-Astoria was. Even so, she was up and ready to get back to DC early the next morning. It surprised both Joanne and the Elites. She laughed good-naturedly when she walked in on Wyn and Link in the sitting area, waiting for her. They were her early birds, speaking in hushed tones so they wouldn't disturb her. Khara was dressed, packed, and stood raring to go, all before a single cup of coffee.

Link quipped that they'd better check the weather because hell must have frozen over. It startled Khara to realize she'd been so absorbed in her courtship she'd neglected her social relationships with the Elites. Abashed, she resolved to take some time to do just that and sat.

She would always have a soft spot for Wyn, as he was the newest Elite, and she remembered vividly what it was like when she was a newbie. The missteps, that burning need to prove herself. The self-imposed pressure to be worthy of the confidence placed in her. When Wyn came on board a few years ago, he replaced Alene's husband, Darius. He'd resigned from the team when the two of them got together after finally realizing they were in love. Khara thought fondly of their cheerful boy, Quentin. She missed his infectious chortling and cherubic little smile. She'd set up some quality Q time when they got back home.

"How's Sam feeling these days?" Khara asked.

Wyn's huge smile threatened to take over his face. He gave her a pregnancy update; it was their first child, and he and his wife were thrilled. Sam was relieved to have just moved out of the morning sickness phase. Furthermore, she was pleased as could be that she was showing at last.

"Look at her little baby bump! And she's growing her hair out," Khara observed when Wyn showed her a recent picture on his phone. "She looks terrific. You two are so stinking cute together."

"Aren't they?" Link cosigned with a laugh.

Khara rolled her eyes as she turned to him. "As if you and Aria aren't just as cute. Someone could get a cavity with all the sweetness around here."

"You are adding to it, you know."

Khara couldn't stop the grin or her blushing. Link had gotten married a few months ago and, even though he didn't say as much, was missing the new wife he'd left at home. No, wait, it was close to a year now since their wedding. The time was flying. What had started as a marriage of convenience took them both by surprise when sincere feelings developed. One minute they were spouses in name only and then madly in love the next. Khara couldn't have been happier for them when she officiated over the renewing of their vows, even as the tiniest sliver of envy wedged itself in her heart.

Khara had heard of the horrors of Thanksgiving travel and could appreciate how it only mildly inconvenienced her on a private jet. She had to wait onboard for longer than usual to be cleared by customs, but she worked and texted in the meantime. It gave her a little pocket of time to catch up on some of her email correspondence.

The Speaker's son seemed to have gotten the hint. There was nothing from him this time. She'd ignored his lunch invitations, suspecting they were nowhere as innocuous as he made them sound.

Her attention drifted as she pondered her answer to the loaded Kinder Q, *What was hard on your first day?*

If she was being honest, everything was hard. It was a day full of discovery and little fires that needed to be put out. Khara could still remember how her knees and hands shook when she arrived at the Queen's office suites. Things had moved at lightning speed from the moment she decided to enter the race. The transition of power took every available brain cell. It all seemed very real now. Now that she'd sworn the oath that properly installed her as Lillianna, Queen of the Kingdom of Lytua.

She'd really done it.

Back then, she poised at an open door—figurative *and* literal—almost afraid to go inside. After a fortifying deep breath, Khara stepped over the threshold into the Queen's office. *Her* office, she corrected herself as someone closed the door behind her. It was a surreal feeling. She looked around the room in wonder, turning in a circle to take everything in at once. Though she wasn't normally superstitious, she'd held off going in until after she'd taken her oath.

According to Joanne, there was room in the budget to redecorate, but at that moment, Khara couldn't imagine changing a single thing. The space's design was magnificent, with soaring ceilings and plenty of sunshine spilling in through enormous windows. There were new office items sitting untouched in their packaging. Khara approached the desk and pulled out the comfortable-looking chair. She unwrapped the plastic around it and sat down with a heartfelt sigh. This was the real throne, where the actual work of running Lytua would take place.

"Nearly done." Link's voice interrupted her reminiscing, returning her attention to the present.

In retrospect, that first "getting started" part hadn't been too difficult. She still cringed when she thought about how awkward it all was. Khara replied that getting to a new team where everyone was already close was hard. It took time for them to mesh as a new unit, and it couldn't be forced. She urged Jessie to ask many questions and get to know the people on the team when she comes in as the new person.

As soon as Dulles air traffic control cleared them, Khara went straight to Riddick's office. From there, they would be heading to the grocery store, then his house to prepare a side dish to take to Thanksgiving dinner. It was late in the day when she arrived; Lena and the rest of the staff had long since gone home. Riddick drew Khara into his lap to greet her with long, intoxicating kisses that made her feel almost dizzy and told her he'd missed her.

Khara jumped about a foot when Eric knocked and popped his head in to introduce himself formally. She tried to spring off Riddick's lap, but he held her there and nibbled her earlobe. "We're just kissing. And I know the owners."

Eric Sloane reminded her of a bulldog—short and barrel-chested, with light skin and a bald head. He tried to assure her she didn't need to bring anything. Khara wouldn't hear of it. She was after the authentic experience, squabbling family members, undercooked or dried-out turkey, lumpy mashed potatoes and all. The description made both men roar with laughter.

Since she'd never cooked any of the traditional dishes, Khara asked Riddick if he would choose something for her to try. He assured her he had the perfect thing.

Chapter Thirty-Eight

K HARA PEERED AT THE short list of ingredients and wrinkled her nose. "What is this, again?"

"Green bean casserole," Riddick told her with a proud smile. "My go-to."

"I mean no offense, but this—" Khara poked a finger at the pink sticky note. "This sounds dreadful. Canned green beans? Condensed soup?"

"It's a Thanksgiving tradition. A quick and easy one."

Khara laughed, then sobered. "Oh, you're serious. But... you can cook. I still dream of those fajitas."

"Yeah?"

"The homemade tortillas put it over the top. How about an alternative?"

Riddick agreed that he'd try a Lytuan special occasion dish with chicken and rice and watched in fascination as it came together. Khara wasn't the best cook, but she did alright. She explained it was a popular dish to serve for New Year's Eve in Lytua. They weren't big on Christmas, but New Year's was a blowout celebration occasion.

She hoped that the simple ingredients would appeal, then worried if she should have tried something more complex. Then she remembered Riddick was going to take canned veg baked in reconstituted soup. Her dish already exceeded expectations.

Thanksgiving Day dawned crisp and cloudless. Choosing to err on the side of caution and dress more formally than expected, Khara wore a dupioni dress with a full, pleated skirt in a bold magenta floral. She was being invited into someone's home on an important holiday and meeting Riddick's closest friends. It was a great honor, and she wanted to make a good first impression. Khara fell back on an old trick she'd learned in a public speaking course at university to combat nerves; she went without underwear. The tactic had always proven to be an excellent distraction, and she hoped this would be no different. She'd quizzed Riddick for details about the Sloane Family and tried to keep them all straight. It was the same as studying a briefing file. Khara laughed at herself when she considered asking the Elites to prepare one for her. *No shortcuts*, she scolded herself.

Clutching the festive chicken and rice dish in one hand and a hostess gift of a pretty glass cheese plate in the other, Khara tried to calm her racing heart as Riddick rang the Sloanes' doorbell. They were just people, for crying out loud. She hadn't been this anxious meeting with the Queen of England. Riddick pressed a kiss to her forehead and offered a reassuring smile. Her nervousness must be showing. *Get it together, woman.*

When the door opened, relatives swept them up into the Sloane household amid excited chatter and greetings. Twenty-nine people were in attendance from all over the country and eager to meet her. In no time, she was sitting at the big kitchen island with a glass of wine and in deep conversation with Maya Sloane and a host of her female family members. Riddick and Eric disappeared outside to tend to the turkey smoking and frying prep.

Maya muttered, "Please don't let them start a fire like last year."

Khara's eyebrows shot up as she pressed a hand over her heart. "You had a fire? My goodness, how awful!"

"Two actually." Maya's daughter, Holly, didn't even look up from her phone while delivering the deadpan comment.

"One dog knocked over a candle on the dining room table at almost the same time the other knocked over the turkey fryer. While everyone was dealing with the fire outside, the tablecloth caught on fire and took the entire table up in flames with it." Maya cast her eyes heavenward with a gusty sigh. "The suppressant chemicals from the fire extinguisher got everywhere and smelled terrible. We ended up ordering Thai and eating on the screened-in porch. It was something like thirty degrees, mind you."

Khara bit down on her lip to keep from bursting into giggles. "Funny, Riddick did not mention this escapade at all. I'm sorry, I shouldn't laugh, but the image—"

"It is funny. *Now*. The damage was minimal, all things considered. Thank goodness no one was hurt. But I'll be lording it over Riddick and Eric for the rest of their lives. Damn turkey fryer."

"To be fair, though," Maya's mother put in. "I was responsible for the flaming turkey that set the trash bin on fire the year before. It was a reflex to run and throw the pan out."

"Which is why I had the damn thing catered this year. Couldn't talk those two out of turkeys, though. Even with dire warnings that I didn't want the Fire Department here again for the third year in a row. Talk about embarrassing."

The Sloanes lived on a cul-de-sac in the quaint DC suburb of Falls Church, in a beautiful brick home filled with so much love, it was almost visible. There were groups of people everywhere, some playing cards or video games, babies crying, pets and children of all ages running through every room. A knot of elders was engaged in a trash-talking game of dominoes. A karaoke battle royale was taking place in the background.

Maya was tall and willowy, just starting to show with baby number two. She'd lucked out, she said—the scheduling gods smiled on her as she had the day off. A radiation oncologist, Maya usually worked on holidays or was on call at the very least. When she did, they'd just celebrate on a different day.

Khara downplayed the travel part of her visit to Maya when she asked, reporting only that it wasn't too bad. They talked some about Khara's homeland. None of the women were familiar with Lytua. Riddick boasted to everyone that Khara worked for the Queen. She felt a twinge of guilt for misleading everyone. Then she thought about how she would never have had this opportunity if she'd corrected Riddick's initial mistake. Packing that away for examination at a later time, Khara decided to just let herself enjoy the day without any self-recrimination.

During a lull in the conversation, Khara turned to Maya. "Thank you for what you do. I am a breast cancer survivor, and my care team was amazing. They made all the difference."

Maya smiled at her and gave her burgeoning belly a rub. "Many times, we come in at the end of the journey, but I love what I do. How long?"

"I'm four years cancer-free. Triple Negative Breast Cancer. I was just twenty-eight when I was diagnosed."

Tossing her long box braids over her shoulder, Maya lifted her wineglass of sparkling cider. "That's one of the harshest chemo regimens out there."

"Don't I know it. That was a hard five months."

"You're well now?"

Khara nodded. "I am. I have a family history and have been getting routine mammos for years. Early detection and universal health coverage saved my life."

"I'm so glad you're well. Sadly, health care is far from universal here. It's a constant fight, with Black women having the worst outcomes as a group. It's outrageous. I'd love to see what universal is like up close. I imagine things move faster without the red tape. Or I would hope so, anyway."

"Yes. From that first abnormal mammo, I had the ultrasound and biopsy the same day and started chemo less than a week later. We have a much smaller populace, though, and that plays a part. Please come visit anytime—I'll make sure you have all the access you'd like."

"I might take you up on that. I plan to take a longer break after this kiddo is born."

At this, Khara lit up. "Come and bring Holly and the baby with you. Two of my... team's wives are pregnant now. There were several babies born to the team in the last few years. So much fun."

"It's always nice to see someone else close to their team. I love mine."

"The Elites keep me—keep all of us, that is—on top of things."

Khara realized with a start that she hadn't been fretting about keeping her port scar covered of late. She couldn't remember a time when it hadn't been an ongoing concern.

Chapter Thirty-Nine

RIDDICK AND ERIC DIDN'T trust the tending of the turkey frying and smoking equipment to others and they knew better than to leave it unattended.

Holly wandered out to the backyard and gave a dramatic, angst-laden huff. Riddick gave the teen a one-armed hug and asked how eighth grade was going. In typical teen fashion, she shrugged her answer.

"Bored with the women already?"

The girl shrugged again, already deep into a text conversation with her friends. "You know how it is when my mom gets started talking about work. Now they're talking about when Khara had breast cancer."

Riddick froze. "Say what, now?"

"That's what she said."

Riddick exchanged glances with Eric. "Go on, I've got this," Eric assured him, nodding toward the turkeys.

Maya and Khara were still talking when he came inside. "Holly may have misheard, but says you're talking about when Khara had cancer?"

"Yes," Khara confirmed. "It's been a while, though."

He didn't expect to have learned everything about her already, but this knowledge threw Riddick for a loop. Frowning, he grabbed a beer from the cooler and refilled Khara's wine glass. Held out a hand to her. "Tell me while we take a walk?"

Khara started giving him the condensed version while they walked down the winding path to the fire pit at the edge of the Sloanes' property. The radiologist discovered the tumor early at a routine mammogram. Even with the hell of heavy-duty chemo, a lumpectomy surgery, and thirty rounds of rads, she'd been one of the lucky ones.

They sat hip-to-hip in the fireside love seat, sipping their drinks while she told him. Riddick listened with rapt attention, his brow furrowed in what seemed to be consternation.

"You were so young. Isn't that unusual?"

"My mother had breast cancer when she was quite young, so my sister and I were getting scanned regularly since our twenties. Most breast cancers don't have a genetic component, though. But you know what I found most upsetting? They never tell you the oddball things that come with cancer treatment, like brain fog or losing your nails, or that the sensation doesn't come back in the breast. I mean, the other one is fine, but still."

They were silent for a few moments, each absorbed in their thoughts. Then Riddick said, "My mother had breast cancer years ago. It's why I chaptered out of the Army. To come home and take care of her. She doesn't have any other family and no way I was letting anyone else do it."

Khara placed her hand over his and gave it a little squeeze. "I'm so sorry. That must have been awful for you both. Where were you stationed at the time?"

She was comforting *him*? When she'd had her own journey? That tweaked something deep within Riddick. "Seattle. I was overseas when I found out, though. They got me home pretty quick. I hired a nurse for post-surgery and radiation burn care. Ma didn't want me to fuss with changing her bandages and stuff, so I took care of everything else." He gave her a thoughtful look. "Who took care of you when you were kicking cancer's ass?"

A shadow passed over her features. "Well, I was newly engaged when they diagnosed me. He couldn't hack it, though."

"He hired a nurse, too?"

Khara made a face. "No, the whole cancer thing was too much for him. He broke it off around halfway through chemo."

Riddick shot up straight on the seat cushion, jostling her some. "Wait. Your fiancé broke up with you while you were fighting fucking *cancer*?"

"It was a lot to ask of anyone."

"Fuck that. It is, but he should have been by your side every step of the way."

"He was at first. It took a toll. Better to have found out then, though. It could have been even more disastrous than it was."

"Even so. What a shitbag," Riddick spat. "You just don't do shit like that."

"Oh, he got over me pretty quickly. Good riddance. I still run into him occasionally."

"What's that like?"

"Quite uncomfortable for him. Gratifying for me. I refuse to make it easy for him." Khara held her wineglass up to the firelight and twisted the stem to make the liquid sparkle.

"Living well as the best revenge, huh?"

"Oh, absolutely. Petty as it sounds."

Riddick shook his head. "It doesn't sound petty. It sounds like just desserts. You living your best life when you run into an ex who fucked you over? That's classic poetic justice. I hope you looked and felt like a million bucks whenever you saw his triflin' ass. Good for you."

That made Khara laugh. "Could you have gone back? To the Rangers?" She asked.

"Maybe. I wasn't interested in leaving Ma alone again after that. Her getting sick changed my priorities. Realized I wasn't actually invincible and didn't want to leave her alone in the world if I got killed in combat."

"It's sweet how close you are to her. I miss that with my mother."

They sat in companionable silence for a few minutes before heading back to the house. Riddick put an arm around her as they walked up the path and tucked her into his side some. The sound of hearty laughter drifted from the house, carried along by voices singing along to the lively old school music. Khara paused and soaked up the loving atmosphere glowing in the windows. She let the merry scene fill her heart.

"I was sick—so, so sick—for an entire year. Just fighting so hard for extra time. For my family and friends, for myself. For doing, seeing, eating, visiting, experiencing things that are important to me. I received a gift that wasn't given to every woman who fought alongside me. It changed me, changed my priorities, too. Life is for savoring. I won't squander it."

Riddick squeezed her and placed a lingering kiss on her cheek. "Here's to savoring, then, beautiful Khara."

"To savoring."

They scandalized a couple of teenagers who caught them kissing. A mash-up of exaggerated gagging and kissing noises floated over until they laughingly broke apart and went inside.

"Well," Maya started as she plopped onto the couch next to Riddick and threw her feet up on the ottoman. "She is lovely. What the hell is she doing with you?"

Riddick grinned at his friend, not offended in the least.

"I've gotta ask about her skin care regimen. I'd kill for that glow. I didn't peg you for a long-distance relationship kind of guy."

"Me either, but I'd be an idiot not to at least try."

"I'll drink to that." They clinked glasses.

"I feel like I know her from somewhere, but I can't put my finger on it. It'll come to me."

There was a yell and a crash from somewhere deep inside the house. Maya closed her eyes and sighed, "As long as nothing's on fire...."

Remembering the previous year's Thanksgiving catastrophes, they both broke out laughing. Riddick looked over at Khara, who was being coached in how to play Spades by some of Eric's nieces and nephews. Or were they cousins? She was wearing an intense look of concentration, as though the game was a high-stakes international negotiation. There was that competitive streak again. She really was something.

Chapter Forty

B Y THE TIME RIDDICK dropped Khara off, he was ready to declare victory. It was the best Thanksgiving ever. They usually said goodnight in the hotel lobby, but this time, Khara asked if he'd walk her up to her room.

"I'm really glad you came. You looked like you had fun."

Her smile was brilliant. "I did. Your friends are wonderful. Thank you for sharing them with me."

What Riddick hadn't said at dinner was that he was thankful for the chance to get to know Khara. It felt too private to share in front of everyone. He wished he'd been able to say something clever like she had.

For new friends and new reasons to smile.

She was a diplomat, he reminded himself. Her entire career revolved around wordsmithing.

Spending all day in her company, seeing how easily she slipped into conversation and bantering with his friends and their family had felt like she'd always been there. *She's leaving*, he reminded himself. *Don't get attached. You're supposed to be just staying in the present.* Why did he have such a hard time doing that with her?

There were two people stationed at either end of the hallway of the twenty-second floor. Khara gave them each a wave when they nodded to her. Riddick assumed they were security.

It should have been a simple goodnight kiss. Hot, yes, but simple. Riddick was about to leave after the sweet kiss they shared in the doorway when Khara stepped back a little into her room, a silent invitation in the tilt of her head. A continuation of the flirtation they'd been engaged in all day. Her expressive amber eyes were bright, and she was looking at him like she wanted at least a more thorough kiss. That he could do.

Riddick moved with deliberate slowness, not wanting to spook her, not wanting to misread how much she was asking for. He followed her and closed the door behind him with a soft snick. A little gasp escaped her when he turned them to put her back to the door. He got in her space, his fingers nimble as he unfastened the clip from her hair and set it down on the nearby table. Before her thick curls had even finished falling around her face, he'd thrust his fingers into them and had his mouth swooping down on hers again. This was different from all their previous kisses. More urgent, less controlled. Desire was sparking between them with undeniable insistence. He felt her hands at his waist, on his back.

Riddick leaned into her more than he had before, kissed his way down her throat and over her collarbone to trace his lips over the very top of her breast. Lingering there, he smiled at the accelerated thumping of her heart before trailing gentle kisses up to her ear. Her puffs of breath heated the base of his neck. He braced his hands on the wall by her shoulders, caging her against him. He knew he couldn't have her right here, right now, but, Lord, the desire was there, immediate.

They both needed this—*something*—some sort of relief.

With as badly as he wanted her, Riddick had to ask himself—could he give to her while taking nothing for himself? He was hard as concrete. What he sensed in the arch of her body against his was tempting. Was she as turned on as he was? She clung to his shirt as he kissed up one side of her neck and down the other. He wanted to rip her dress open and carry her to bed. *Fuck it,* he thought, then went for it.

With his lips close to her ear, he commanded in a low voice, "Spread your legs for me, Khara. I want to touch you. Will you let me make you feel good?"

Khara widened her stance in answer, surprising him. Maybe even herself, too. "Please touch me."

Her voice held just the hint of a quaver. Riddick made a sound deep in his throat. Even more possessive, unrestrained lust sprang to life in him. He leaned back to take in how disheveled she was, her hair mussed from his hands, her lips swollen and inviting. Her arousal was right there at the surface—she wasn't trying to hide it or play hard to get. No shame, only open need. *Please touch me.* Jesus. So sexy.

His fingers grazed the ridged line of her scar. "Your port?"

She nodded and inhaled sharply when he traced the inside curve of her breast. Riddick felt a devilish satisfaction when her skin broke out in goosebumps. "Which breast has sensation?"

Khara swallowed hard before she could answer and, when she did, her voice was hoarse. "The left."

"I'll remember that."

He drew her dress up with a careful slowness that had both their hearts pounding in anticipation. Khara rose into his touch when he pinched that left nipple right through her clothes. When his questing fingers found her folds naked and slick, Riddick groaned in appreciation and eased his body still closer to hers. Christ almighty, she'd been bare under this dress all day?

Just the thought of that was hot, but it was encountering the tender skin of her most intimate area for the first time that was almost more than he was ready for.

Khara was wet for him. Nothing could have pleased him more.

Mine, he thought, even as he recognized how irrational it was. He wanted inside that secret, needy place that was a mirror image of his own desire. Riddick admonished himself to focus; he was supposed to be giving to her. Her breath hitched as he gave the hair covering her sex a gentle tug.

All while watching her face, he explored her using his fingertips, his knuckles, his words. She was so responsive her pleasure was easy to read. He changed his angle, the pressure, his motion, based on her reaction until her eyes flew wide. Hips jerking, she gasped. Riddick continued the teasing circles on her clit, his knuckles brushing her sensitive flesh. When he could sense the release building up inside her, he eased a finger inside her slippery heat to stroke and tease and search for that perfect angle.

"Don't stop," she panted. *"God."*

When Khara went up on her toes with her hips undulating, he followed and didn't let up. A flush crept up her chest and neck—heralding her release. Then she was there.

Khara tensed and tightened, her whole body going rigid. She held his gaze as she went over, clutching his sweater in her fists, crying out and giving a soft moan. Riddick enjoyed watching the pleasure consume her, how her lips parted, how she shook. How she unraveled. He'd never seen anything more beautiful.

She took a while to come back to herself. He waited until then to slide his finger from her heat and let the front of her pretty dress fall back into place. Not the slightest hint of embarrassment on her face. God*damn*. She'd gushed into his hand. He sucked her cream from where it coated his fingers and kept his gaze on hers as he drawled, "Delicious."

Her eyes grew wide. Imagining her thoughts to be as X-rated as his, Riddick told her in that same low voice, "That was... thank you for that."

Khara's voice was husky, too. "You're thanking *me*?"

"Yes. You let me touch you. I got to watch you come. That's a good night, by any definition."

Khara reached for the front of his pants, but he stayed her hand with his own and shook his head. He'd go off like a rocket if she put her hands on him. "This is enough."

"I want to touch you, as well."

"And I want you to touch me. Another time. This was for you. It was damn satisfying seeing you come." He couldn't interpret the long look she gave him. "What?"

"You're unlike anyone I've ever dated."

He watched her, knowing he was looking at her with naked lust. Didn't bother trying to hide it. She should be well aware of his potent attraction to her. He was imagining stripping her naked, going to his knees before her, getting his mouth where he'd just had his fingers. Bringing her off even harder. Hell, she could keep the dress *on*. He wanted more of that sweetness. He wanted *all* her sweetness, everything she had to offer. With difficulty, Riddick managed to get himself under control. It wasn't time yet.

"I've never done anything like that before." Her words were lazy, almost a drawl.

He kissed her again, made it long and deep. "Neither have I."

"I don't think I've ever even really kissed in public."

"How come?"

She thought about it for a moment. "No one's ever made me forget myself, as you do."

Ah, shit, Riddick thought. The lilt of her sexy island accent was more pronounced than usual. Like a cat that had lapped up every last bit of cream, she sounded satisfied and dreamy. "I'd better get out of here." *Before I embarrass myself by begging.* "I'll see you tomorrow night."

Going down in the elevator, Riddick brought his fingertips to his nose to get another hit of Khara's intoxicating scent. *Mmm, heavenly.* He hadn't planned on touching her so intimately, but he sure wasn't sorry.

Chapter Forty-One

SLEEP WAS A LONG time coming for Khara, even after the busy day of activity. How could she sleep with the image of the desire, approval, and satisfaction burning in Riddick's eyes? With knowing the only thing holding him back was her say-so? If she'd given the word, he'd have made love to her with almost more intensity than she could handle. She was certain of it. It was a heady feeling to be in charge of how the physical part of their relationship unfolded. Just thinking about it made her shiver.

Khara had felt a flutter down in her belly as Riddick's gaze roamed her face. It made her feel nervous in the best possible way. Him remembering and asking about her breast? That had moved something unexpected in her.

He'd made her feel good alright. *So* good. Like he'd taken her apart piece by piece. Khara couldn't help but let out a dreamy sigh, remembering how he'd coaxed that incredible orgasm from deep within her. Goodness, his fingertips skimming up the inside of her bare thigh felt electric. She'd just about lost her mind with that one hand working magic between her legs. It was beyond titillating to watch the muscles in his forearm work as he touched her.

That wasn't the touch of a terrible or selfish lover. That was the touch of a man who would be relentless in his pursuit of her pleasure. Her fulfillment. One who would never leave her unsatisfied.

Khara wasn't sure how she'd been brave enough to hold his gaze while climaxing. Doing so had sent a sharp thrill of excitement and fear racing through her body. It was daring for her and, oh, so sexy. Watching him watch her come turned her on so. The sexual tension was unbearable.

She'd worried her knees might give out. There'd been a tempting moment when she wanted him to take her right there, right where she stood. She had never been this reckless or needy. Not by half. It might have been silly, but she'd felt compelled to point out that she didn't regularly get felt up against a hotel room door.

Should she feel embarrassed? Khara didn't think so.

Why hadn't she just grabbed him by the sweater and pushed him onto the couch or her bed and taken him? She'd felt how hard he was. Khara sighed again, this time in confused exasperation. She needed to sort out if her hesitation stemmed from simply being nervous or if she wasn't ready. Those were two very, very different things.

Not to mention that she was still concealing her identity. Khara flopped back into her pillows with a grimace.

How had this gotten so tangled? One minute she was contemplating a fling and the next she was being invited to Thanksgiving dinner.

And what a dinner it had been—a loud, hilarious, delicious, and messy affair. So many conversations happening at once made it difficult to keep up, but Khara loved every minute. Her dish was well-received, even though the younger children flat-out refused to try it. She'd spent enough time around children to know it wasn't a personal slight.

Khara volunteered to help clear the table but was shooed away and told that was the children's job. Maya told her their cleaning company would be by in the early morning to do the cleanup. "Hella expensive," Maya confided, "and worth every penny to not have to supervise it myself or stop the elders from trying to do it. A few years of that had me ready to call the whole thing off. I just can't even. Turns out more and more people were outsourcing the hard work."

Khara agreed wholeheartedly, for she'd been doing the same for years.

Holiday get-togethers for Khara were a fraction of the size of the Sloanes'. She was already planning to host a New Year's Eve dinner with the Elites and their families.

Saying goodbye to Riddick's friends had been harder than she'd anticipated. Khara felt like she'd gained several new friends. When Maya hugged her and told her she hoped to see her at next year's dinner, regret twisted in her heart.

She had to find a way to tell him. She wouldn't be able to face his friends this way again. Obscuring the truth was starting to feel distasteful. Smarmy, even.

With an angry hiss, Khara turned on her side and punched her pillow into a more comfortable shape.

She shouldn't have told him so much about her cancer battle, exposed herself that way. Yet he'd been so incredibly thoughtful, supportive. It touched Khara how Riddick was so angry on her behalf. Even in the short time she'd known him, she could not imagine him leaving his fiancée the way Gary had left her when she needed him most. She'd been so vulnerable. The whole situation had crushed her, but she'd had a large support system to help her get through that and the rest of her cancer treatment.

That hellish year in her life was something she tried not to think about too often. She was a great big ball of stress when the mammogram and oncologist check-in visit time rolled around, though.

Why had she been so open about the cancer? Surely, it would have been wiser to keep her mouth shut. Surely, she should have held something back?

Because he asked.

That wasn't why. Or, at least, not the only reason. Most people—even folks she knew well—were eager to behave as though cancer had not changed her on a fundamental level. As though things could ever go back to the way they were before. Riddick had listened with uncommon patience and compassion in a way only other survivors had. He seemed to understand how life-altering the disease had been.

This marvelous man was somehow burrowing his way into her heart. It was the last thing she'd expected to happen. And she had no defense against it.

Everything he said and did made her wonder how things might have unfolded had they met under different circumstances.

Even knowing it was only a matter of time before her whole double identity scheme came crashing down and left her heartbroken, she selfishly wanted to put it off just a tiny bit longer. She didn't want that welcoming warmth in his eyes to give way to cold detachment. Betrayal.

She wanted those molten kisses that stirred her right down to her core. More of the caresses that ignited her senses and made her forget herself. She craved Riddick in a way she didn't recognize, and she wasn't in a hurry to deny herself more of his touch.

Khara had never been so happy. Or so miserable.

Chapter Forty-Two

WITH NO APPOINTMENTS ON her calendar for the day after Thanksgiving, Khara had nothing to do but dither over what she would wear out that evening. She was edgy and nervy as she tried to concentrate on narrowing down choices, but her mind just wouldn't stay on the task.

Khara stopped her pacing in the middle of the suite's lavish walk-in closet, finally admitting to herself that this task was simply beyond her capacity. It was time to call in the big guns. Resigned, she plopped down on the velvet chaise and pulled out her phone to dial the expert. There was no time for pleasantries.

"Vanda, I'm having a legitimate wardrobe-related emergency."

"Ooh, *chérie*, let me guess! You need lingerie."

Khara stammered into the receiver. "How the devil did you figure that out?"

"You told me you met a hot guy with huge hands who you might sorta want to have a fling with. Although you're doing it wrong since you haven't gotten naked yet. Eventually, you were going to get to the point where you needed sexier underwear than the granny panties."

"Hey! I do not wear granny panties." Absently sliding the toes of one foot over the other, Khara frowned when she spotted a chip in the burgundy nail polish. She needed to have her pedicure redone. "Often," she amended.

"You forget we were roommates at university? I told you then and I'm telling you now, sexy underwear makes a difference, even if nobody else sees it. *Vraiment*. Trust me on this."

Khara felt a flutter deep in her belly as she remembered just how perfectly sexy Riddick had looked licking the taste of her from his fingers and calling her delicious. Heavens, she hadn't been able to look away from his tongue. "That's why I'm calling. We're going to the theater tonight and... well, can you help me or not?"

"Of course. Where are you again?"

"Washington, DC."

"Ooh, there's a great shop called Cherry Blossom Intimates nearby. I visited several times while stationed there. Jamal was *very* appreciative."

"I bet. It needs to be simple, though. I don't know what I'm doing with this stuff. I'm already nervous enough. Don't want to be cute and end up poking myself in the eye."

Yvanda snorted a laugh. "They'll take care of you and get you what you need. No more than you can handle, promise. You'll get the hang of this fling thing yet! Although I think it's pretty safe to say you left that territory behind some time ago, no?"

Khara sat quietly for a long time. In the way of good friends, Yvanda gave her the space to think. "What if he doesn't want anything to do with me after he learns the truth?"

"That would suck, and it is a possibility. But maybe he'll forgive you and you can move beyond it. Have you thought about that? You won't know until you tell him. Everything else is pure conjecture. I've never known you to back away from a confrontation, Khar."

"I know. I just wish there was more time."

Once they hung up, Khara straightened her shoulders, then went in search of her assistant.

Joanne swiveled from her desk to face her, pulling off her reading glasses and slipping them into her pocket.

Faced with Joanne's expectant expression, heat crept up the back of Khara's neck. She bit her lip and clasped her fingers together to keep from fidgeting. This wasn't something she'd ever needed before.

But remembering the sensation of Riddick's admiring, sensuous gaze on her last night? She wanted that again—for him to look at her like she was the most desirable woman in the world. Like she was driving him wild.

She cleared her throat. "I need a dress. A knockout dress. And there's an intimates boutique I'd like to visit."

Joanne didn't even blink. She gave Khara a small, knowing smile, almost proud. "Very well. I'll see to it and inform the Elites."

Examining herself in front of the three-way mirror, Khara could not deny that she felt different. Bolder. She'd made a new playlist full of sexy songs to boost her confidence and entitled it Swagger Mix. It surrounded her as she took some extra time to pamper herself properly in preparation. The wrap dress was a fiery red, adorned with a line of flirty ruffles down the edge of the front panel and at the hem that swished around her knees. It had a plunging V-neck that was just this side of racy and hugged her curves like it was a second skin. Khara smoothed her hands down over her hips as she turned this way and that to view every angle. She'd worried that she might feel self-conscious, but she couldn't remember a time she'd ever felt sexier. Once dressed, she snapped a selfie and sent it to Yvanda with the caption:

You were right. I do feel different. I will tell him tonight.

Yvanda sent a heart-eyed emoji blowing kisses in response.

Yvanda: In that dress, he won't remember a single word you say. Seriously, good luck, and let me know how it goes.

Khara: I will. Thanks, Vanda.

Yvanda: Now, go get it, girl. Looking like that can get a woman pregnant!

She was nowhere near ready to have kids, but Khara laughed so hard at that description she needed to touch up her makeup.

When she opened the door to Riddick's knock, his mouth dropped open. He looked her up and down, and she could feel the blush and tingle all over, her whole body growing hot. His gaze lingered on her heels and legs. She filed that tidbit away.

"Uh, wow," he said, and the smile she gave him was luminous. His gobsmacked expression was worth every bit of annoyance at being fussed over by the personal shoppers.

She could feel the heat of Riddick's gaze on her body as she turned from him to get her coat. Now, this was an excellent start. Once she'd given voice to the truth, she'd feel even better. Khara took a fortifying breath and straightened her spine, firm in her determination that she could and *would* do this. It was beyond time.

By the time they'd left their outerwear at the coat check and finished a pre-show cocktail, Khara was heading toward nervous breakdown territory. She'd chickened out on making her confession several times already—in the car, walking from the parking garage. The words continued to feel lodged in the back of her throat.

When Riddick leaned in to speak directly into her ear, Khara caught a whiff of his woodsy scent and her resolve weakened yet again. The whisper-soft caress of his lips against her earlobe curled her toes and threatened to melt her panties. "You look... ravishing tonight. Think we'll get thrown out of here if I kiss the hell out of you the way I want to?"

Khara had to shove the growing sense of panic down as she chanced a look up into Riddick's face. His thumb brushing over hers was making it hard to think straight. She berated herself for waiting too long in this undertaking. Now there really was no best time to come clean. It was now or never though, even in public and in the middle of a date. Even with her heart feeling as though it would pound right out of her chest. She pulled in an unsteady breath. "Riddick, I have to tell you something," she rushed out.

She'd just opened her mouth to spill the whole sordid truth when the urgent message pattern vibrated her smartwatch. Khara could barely tear her gaze away from the curiosity alight in those eyes. "Ah, excuse me. I need to take this."

Wyn's text message was brief:

Wyn: Ambassador Momo heading your way. Think fast.

A gasp escaped before Khara could stop it and the blood drained from her face.

"Khara, what is it? Are you alright?" Riddick put a steadying hand under her elbow, alarm hardening his handsome features.

"I—I...." Khara swung her head around to her left and, sure enough, there was the Ambassador waving and giving her a sunny smile as she approached across the crowded lobby of the Kennedy Center. Oh, *no*. She felt a little light-headed.

"You look like you've seen a ghost. What's going on?" The note of worry in his voice made her feel sick to her stomach.

Ambassador Momo had her young daughter in tow, who was bouncing with excitement at seeing the Queen again. There wasn't time to explain or escape. Khara did the only thing she could think of—she took a couple of small steps forward and offered the Ambassador the traditional Lytuan greeting of a hand placed over her heart and a small bow. The Ambassador skidded to a stop in her shock and hastened to return it. She should have been the one to perform it first since Khara outranked her.

"*Avlah*, what—?"

Speaking in rapid Lytuan, Khara urged, "*Please don't refer to me as the Queen, just call me Khara.*"

The Ambassador quailed at the unorthodox request. "*I could never—*"

"*I'll explain later. Please.*"

"*As you wish... Khara?*" Her given name sounded unnatural and came out sounding like a question. They weren't close, but they were friendly. The woman's gaze slid to Riddick standing nearby. She must be burning with curiosity, although she would never be so indelicate as to ask.

Her daughter hadn't heard the exchange but was scandalized by her mother's perceived lapse in decorum. "*Mama!*" She gave Khara the greeting.

Amused uncertainty laced Riddick's voice as he looked between them all. "Do I—?"

"No, no, that's only done if you are Lytuan," Khara assured him. "Riddick, this is the Lytuan Ambassador to the States, Patricia Momo and her daughter, Julianna."

"Ladies, a pleasure."

"Likewise, sir. Well, we'd better get inside and find our seats. Maybe the Queen could cut you loose for lunch tomorrow? We need to catch up."

Julianna giggled at her side, twirling in place to make her pleated pink skirt billow. "Mama, why are you being silly? The Queen—"

"Come along, now, little one," Patricia cut her off. "Have a good night, you two. Call me tomorrow so we can chat."

"Bye, *Avlah*!" Julianna called.

Khara's heart was pounding so hard she could scarcely take a breath.

Riddick harrumphed. "By 'catch up', does she mean pump you for information about the Queen?"

"More than likely." Oh, she had a great deal of explaining to do. Khara looked down as he entwined his fingers with hers.

"I'm sorry you can't just have a day or night totally to yourself. Seems like the Queen is never that far off. How does it not wear on you?"

There it was again, the faint disapproval mingled with the concern. It was sweet and yet frustrating, as well. "It's alright, truly." Despite her best efforts to turn his opinion of the Queen—*her*—around, he simply wouldn't be swayed. How could she tell him it was *her* he didn't care for? Would he find the lies more distasteful than her true identity? The thought of Riddick looking at her with mistrust made her chest feel heavy.

"So, what were you going to tell me? It sounded like it might be important."

"Just that... I had a very fine time with the Sloanes yesterday." She'd lost her nerve entirely.

The brilliant grin lit his face and made her stomach clench.

How would she ever adequately explain that the Queen he thought was taking advantage of her was *her*?

Chapter Forty-Three

RIDDICK HAD A DIFFICULT time concentrating on the elaborate production of *Porgy and Bess*. Especially after an amusing run-in with Sasha Adrian. What were the chances? For once, Adrian only nodded at him and quick-stepped to another part of the lobby. He'd cut his eyes at Khara and cringed, surely remembering her polite verbal smackdown the previous week. Riddick hadn't been able to hold in the chuckle. It was almost as entertaining as meeting the Lytuan Ambassador.

All he'd been able to think about all day was how Khara clasped his fingers, how she looked and sounded when she'd orgasmed for him the night before. That hitch in her breath right before she fell. When he'd gotten to sleep after lying awake for hours thinking about her, it was all dreams of her.

He'd gotten zero work done today.

He'd only just gotten himself under control by the time he arrived to pick her up. Then she'd gone and dressed like she was trying to give him a heart attack. Not for the first time, Riddick thought the Queen must be quite confident in her own appeal if she'd have a woman as beautiful as Khara around.

Sitting across from her at dinner challenged him in a way nothing else ever had. He did his best to make polite conversation while trying to keep his eyes off her breasts and his mind off unwrapping the stoplight-red dress from her with his teeth. The skinny, leopard-print high heels were almost more than he could bear. He liked the pretty toes he saw peeking out through the peep-toe opening, polished the same shade as her dress. Riddick liked when women took care of their feet, but polished nails in sexy shoes had never affected him the way Khara's did. It was her, the entire package.

They were planning to watch a movie at his house, and Riddick spent most of the drive there trying to figure out how he was going to keep his hands to himself. Maybe if he kept something in his hands, like a glass or a bowl of popcorn. They were pulling into his garage when Riddick said, "You've been quiet tonight. Everything okay?"

Khara watched as he put the car in park and turned off the ignition. The garage door rumbled closed behind them. "I hardly got any work done today."

"Why's that?"

Khara turned to face him in the intimate space of the car. "I was too busy thinking about how hard I came for you last night."

"Shit, me too." Riddick huffed out on a laugh. "It's all I've been able to think about. Stay right there."

He jogged around the front of the car to open her door. He all but lifted her out and had his mouth on hers the moment he did. After closing the door with one hand, he tried to guide them toward the door to the house. Realized right away they weren't going to make it before he needed to feel her. "Let me touch you again?"

"Please, yes."

Thank God—he couldn't wait another second to touch her. He leaned her back against the car, unbuttoned her hounds-tooth coat, and eased it open to allow him access. These damn dresses were going to be the death of him. She'd *slayed*. Riddick felt her nipple harden under his palm when he squeezed her breasts.

It was erotic as shit to discover her panties already damp when he slid his fingers into the waistband. Getting her off fully clothed? Yes, please, and thank you. Now that he knew what to do to give her pleasure, he slowed down and prolonged it. While the rolling of her hips urged him for more, harder, faster, he teased her instead of taking her straight to climax. It was cold in the garage, making her heat more pronounced. She was tight and hot, pure perfection.

"Do you want this, Khara?"

"You to make me come? Yes!"

"Because I can stop any time." he teased.

"Not if you know what's good for you."

Sassy. Funny. So fucking sexy. "I'll give you what you want, beautiful Khara." He stopped teasing her and drew the pad of his fingertip up and down over her g-spot with the exact rhythm and pressure he now knew she liked all while circling her clit with his thumb. It was fucking gratifying to see her dissolve into a moan as she came for him. She slumped back against the car, weak-kneed. Wheezed something in Lytuan.

Still panting, Khara cupped his cheek and looked right into his eyes. "Take me to bed, Riddick. I want to make love with you tonight."

He would have liked to say something seductive, but his wits had deserted him the moment his fingers came in contact with her heated skin. He could only grit out, "Are you sure?"

When she nodded, he grabbed her hand and tugged her through the garage's connecting door. His mouth was on hers again before it closed behind them. They dropped their coats as they moved into the living room, bumping into a floor lamp, kicking off their shoes. Khara pushed him onto the sofa and climbed right into his lap to straddle his thighs.

He liked her take-charge attitude. She was a little bossy, as he'd suspected. Before he could even get his tie off, she was already unbuttoning his shirt, pulling it wide. God, she was going to be a wildcat in bed, bring him to his knees.

She gave his exposed chest and abs an appreciative once-over before flashing him a crooked smile. "Nice. That early morning gym time pays off."

Riddick's laugh was rich and low. "Glad you approve." He was running his hand up over her thighs and stopped dead in his tracks when his fingers came across a garter belt. An honest-to-God, old-school garter belt holding up her stockings. Sweet. Jesus. His cock was doing its best to break free from his pants. He didn't think it could get any harder.

Sliding his hands into the short curls at the nape of her neck, he trailed nibbling kisses along her throat, nipped her under her chin. He was determined to slow them down a little, or else he might blow in his pants. His fingers moved of their own accord, slipping down into her panties again. Khara moaned. Her hips bucked when he stroked the welcoming dew there on her outer lips.

"Give me one more, Khara," he murmured against the pulse point in her throat. She smelled incredible. "One more before I take you to my bed and we have the best damn night of our lives." With that, he sank a deft finger deep inside her slick channel, giving his own groan when she contracted around him. Her hold on his shoulders tightened, and she kissed him again. Hungry this time. She broke off with a gasp when he curled his finger forward to stroke over the spot that made her squirm.

She whimpered his name and dropped her head to his shoulder.

"Look at me," he commanded in a ragged whisper. He loved the desire he saw burning in the depths of those gorgeous eyes when she did. "I want to take you slow, Khara, but I don't think I can. I want you too damned much."

"We can go slow the second time."

"Deal." Jesus. This woman. He turned his full attention to bringing her to completion.

The scent of her arousal hung heavy in the air, fueling his own need. Within minutes, she was coming in his hand, quivering, crying out without censure as she rode his fingers. They maintained eye contact as the spasms rocked her. It was satisfying as hell watching the release overtake her and leave her weak. Breathless, flushed, and aroused. For *him*.

"Beautiful," he told her as she panted and squeezed him. She was going to feel like heaven coming all over his cock. He couldn't wait to feel it. Riddick flipped her onto her back and shed his open dress shirt before she had a chance to recover. No way in hell was "slow" even in the realm of possibility anymore.

Hell, he wasn't sure he'd last long enough to taste her. His cock was throbbing with the need to get inside her. "You're so sexy when you come."

Unknotting the tie holding her dress closed had his hands shaking some. Riddick loosened it, revealing the filmy black chemise she wore beneath it. *Jesus*, he thought. He'd expected a treasure, but this was next level. The lace of her bra was just visible—also red, for fuck's sake. Was she trying to kill him? He glanced up to see Khara watching his face. A touch of nerves there, he saw. She was biting a lip swollen by their kisses. "I like this," he told her as he skimmed his fingers over the lace at the top of her stocking, the satin skin of her thigh. "I like all of this."

She let out a breath and relaxed a fraction.

"Do you feel sexy wearing it?"

"Yes. Very."

"Good. You are. I've been turned way the hell on all night. I couldn't stop staring at you. These luscious curves could make a man lose his mind."

Then he was kissing his way down to the fragrant curve of her breasts. He slid his fingers inside her bra to tease her already taut nipple with gentle pinching and twisting. She was wonderfully responsive, arching into his touch, then sighing when he sucked the sensitive bud into his mouth, right through the material.

Seeing her disheveled and aroused this way again was the best aphrodisiac in the world. Her face flushed with her excitement and release, too. He knew she disliked being light-skinned enough to blush, but he loved that she couldn't hide how his touch affected her. Would she even try? Hmm, he'd have to test that.

His reaction to her undergarments had Khara sending silent thanks for Yvanda's guidance.

Good Lord, Khara wanted this man. Lost in the sensation, she could only concentrate on how badly she wanted Riddick naked and inside her. *Needed* it. She might have babbled like an undignified dork, telling him she was ready. Oh, how she wished she'd said something clever or beguiling, but he'd reduced her to a pile of mush. If he could do this to her fully clothed, with just his fingers, how would she ever survive his mouth on her? The thought made her tingle all over with excitement.

Deep, drugging kisses had Khara responding to Riddick on a chemical level. Giddiness overwhelmed her. And why shouldn't she spend the night with him? They were single. It didn't matter that she wasn't in love. She'd never wanted anyone like this. But then a guilty thought flitted through her desire-addled brain.

She hadn't told him the truth yet.

Maybe she could tell him another time, even though he might very well break it off when she did. Or tell him now and hope that he'd still want her? Khara's thoughts scrambled with his lips all over her neck and chest, his locs soft and tantalizing against her heated skin. One of his hands was under her dress, palming her ass.

Her hormones were screaming at top volume—yes, to bed, *to bed*! But her sense of integrity insisted she pump her brakes. As much as she tried to tell herself this was harmless, casual fun, she knew deep down that it wasn't. It mattered.

Riddick didn't know who she was, and this was not the time to tell him.

Her hormones tried to assert themselves again, entreating her to make love to Riddick *right now* and to hell with everything else. Dammit, couldn't she be just a little unscrupulous for once in her life? She wanted this so much.

No, of course not. Not while she was lying to him. She respected him too much.

"Wait," she whispered.

Riddick sat back from her, concern etched on his handsome face. "What's wrong?"

"I...." She touched his cheek, surprised to feel tears welling in her eyes again. "Riddick, I like you very much."

His hold on her tightened a little. "And what about that makes you cry, sweetheart? What am I doing wrong?"

Khara shook her head and took a deep breath. "It's not that. I, ah—" She still couldn't make herself say it. "I'll be going home soon. Maybe we shouldn't start something we can't finish."

"Lytua has an airport, right?"

"A small one, yes."

"You still have your cell phone?"

"Yes."

"An unlimited texting plan?"

"Yes."

"Email?"

She giggled and sniffed. "Of course."

"Snail mail address?"

"Snail mail?"

"Good old-fashioned written correspondence that comes to an actual mail-box."

"Ah, yes, I have a snail mail address."

"Seems to me we're starting something we can finish, then. Just maybe not right here, right now. Sex between us isn't going to be the endpoint, Khara. No pressure."

Riddick got his shirt back on and stood. His cock was complaining mightily, but he'd deal with that later. He took a deep breath and tried not to think about how he'd turned his bed down at the last minute before leaving to meet her. Just in case the sizzling hot attraction between them did more than simmer. The image of her there in his bed—under him, weak from all the pleasure he would have given her—was enough to make him doubt his fortitude.

Khara sat up and pulled her dress closed at the neck with nervous hands. "I feel a little greedy."

"For enjoying pleasure freely given? Please don't."

"I'm not a tease."

"Of course not. I didn't think you were. You can change your mind, no matter how far along we are."

"You're not angry?"

Now he shook his head. "If you're not ready, then there's a reason. I'm not going to pout like a horny college student. Physical connection is one thing, but the rest? Worth waiting for. I can wait to make love to a woman I care about. We go at your pace. You're in control here on the timing. Case closed."

Khara looked at him for a long moment. "You're not like anyone I've ever dated before."

"You keep saying that."

He admired that she didn't apologize for calling a halt. No need for that. He wanted her to want him without hesitation. "We'd better get going."

She turned confused eyes to him, her brow furrowed. "That was abrupt."

"I know we're supposed to watch a movie, but, Khara, if I don't get you out of here, I'm going to try to change your mind, and I don't want to be that guy."

"Do I have no active part to play?"

Riddick groaned and scooped her coat and purse off the floor. "Please stop talking."

"What if I don't want to?" she teased.

"Have mercy on me, woman. Please. Your voice, your accent...." He shook his head again.

Khara raised an eyebrow, stopped herself from saying more, then gave him a flirtatious smile.

Riddick's cock twitched again. For the first time in his adult life, Riddick worried about his control. A big part of him wanted to say, "fuck it" and do whatever he could to convince her to stay the night. He'd never needed to talk a woman into bed. Alarmed, he thrust her belongings into her hands and yanked the front door open. He needed to get them out of here.

Her hands were shaking as she re-tied and straightened her dress. She gave him an amused look. "You parked in the garage."

Shit. Now Riddick could feel his own face flushing hot. He closed the door and headed toward the garage, but her voice stopped him again.

"Riddick?"

He turned back and his gut clenched, seeing her standing there looking downright edible.

"Your shoes?"

Fuck, fuck, *fuck,* he thought as he came back, did his best not to notice how good she smelled. It took every ounce of willpower he possessed to not take her in his arms again. He stuffed his feet into the closest pair of shoes and cursed when he saw they were his house shoes. He kicked them off and stepped into some casual slip-ons, tried not to even look at her.

Chapter Forty-Four

THE DRIVE TO HER hotel was a silent one. Riddick waved the valet off and caught Khara's arm when she made to dash out of the car. "Wait." When she turned to him, he said, "I'm not rejecting you. I want to be clear on that."

"No? I know I said I wasn't ready, but you told me to be quiet and practically threw me out of your house."

Damn. "I apologize—I didn't handle that with nearly as much care as I could have. Should have. Let me explain. With you smelling as delicious as you do and looking good enough to eat, we had to leave. I wanted to strip you naked and take you right there on the couch."

Khara's eyes widened.

"Your voice, your accent, are extremely sexy to me. I was afraid I'd try to convince you to spend the night with me. I want to feel you under me, make no mistake about that, but I never want to talk you into something. We both need to want it. No hesitation. When you've reached the point that you want me so much, you feel like you need to have me? Like you can't wait another single moment? Then we're in business."

Khara unbuckled her seat belt and looked at him for a long, charged moment before leaning in close. "I understand, Riddick." She continued in Lytuan, adding a little extra accent, *"You don't want us to have regrets. We're going to come back to you having me on your sofa. And in any other position you wish. Believe that."*

Riddick swallowed hard. "Get going, Khara," he pleaded. "Please." He was on the ropes, gentlemanly ideals be damned. How he wanted her spread under him, wet and waiting for him. Exhausted and satisfied and unable to think about anyone or anything other than him. He'd never be able to sit on his couch again without picturing her lying there in that sheer black slip, that red dress pooling at her sides, hair spread out like a curly halo across the seat cushion. Those enticing red-painted lips parted. She kissed him—lightly, thank God—told him goodnight, and was gone.

He watched her go, his gaze glued to her ass and the extra sway he could tell she was putting in her hips. As soon as she was out of sight, Riddick let his head drop to the steering wheel and let out a heartfelt groan. That was close. One more word and he might've lost it.

His phone chimed with an incoming text just as he was arriving back home.

Khara: Would you like to know what I said to you?

There was no doubt about what she was referring to.

Riddick: I'm afraid to find out. Was it as suggestive as it sounded?

A winking emoji was her only response, prompting a laugh.

Riddick: Something that would have me breaking land speed records to get you back here with my hand up your dress again?

Khara: Most likely. See you tomorrow night. Bet you look terrific in a tuxedo.

"Damn," he breathed with a smile. Riddick didn't care about the waiting part. When Khara was good and ready, he'd make it so worth the wait. He would lay his game down quite flat.

He felt too keyed up to sleep. His imagination was in overdrive, torturing him with visions of Khara on her knees for him with those plump, ruby-red lips wrapped tight around his cock. Even after taking care of his erection, Riddick was still too wound-up to drop off to sleep right away.

Was she getting under his skin? He wasn't sure how he felt about that.

Chapter Forty-Five

H E DREAMED OF HIS birth parents again.

Falling asleep, Riddick thought for sure he'd have nothing but pleasant dreams after all the excitement of the night before. He'd expected to dream about something along the lines of flipping Khara onto her stomach on his couch and kissing up the back seam of those stockings.

Damn.

The wall clock read 4:09 a.m. No use trying to go back to sleep now. He'd need to be up in an hour to meet Eric at the gym, anyway.

Instead of turning on the news like he usually would, Riddick brewed some coffee and sat next to the big kitchen window, deep in thought. Early morning rain dotted the glass. In the distance, the inky, pre-dawn blackness stretched over Old Town Alexandria with a pensive stillness.

Work was going well. His family and friends were healthy. He didn't think he was feeling stressed about anything in particular. The only thing of significance on his mind was his developing thing with Khara. He hesitated to call it a relationship. They were having fun, that was all. But she was always on his mind these days.

Riddick turned that over. What about that would cause his subconscious to dredge up Evelyn and Jordan again? They were long gone, no threat to him anymore.

He wanted Khara. There was no question there. If she'd said yes last night, he'd probably still be inside her. It had been an immediate full stop for him when she'd asked him to wait. That worry on her face, though, her sudden stiffness—those had pierced him. She'd looked so damn vulnerable at that moment, with uncertainty swimming in the depths of her eyes. Torn, almost. Like an outraged response from him was just inevitable. That didn't sit well with him. Khara was a remarkable woman and should never doubt her appeal.

And her tears. God, he hated that he'd made her cry, however unintentional.

He caught sight of the first drawing he'd done of her, where she appeared to be holding the storm back. Or was it that the storm didn't dare test her? Perhaps that she was protecting him? Riddick felt the urge to draw her again, this time with her lip caught between her teeth as she savored a swallow of wine. That rapturous expression on her face that made him want to kiss her senseless.

You're falling for her, some tiny part of him whispered. Riddick choked on his coffee.

He was not *falling for her*, he maintained, grabbing a napkin from the holder to mop up the droplets he'd splattered on the table. Was that what the dream was about? Riddick wasn't afraid of love, of falling in love. But that was something other people did. He wasn't even sure he was *capable* of falling in love. Khara's smiling face came to mind, and he felt no fear, only... contentment. And an unexpected longing. His heart squeezed as he remembered her looking up at him with those gorgeous eyes glazed with desire.

If he was smart, he'd call it off. This was starting to feel like it had real potential to be dangerous. But he couldn't stay away from her.

When the time came for her to leave DC, they were going to part ways after having a great time together. Just what they both wanted. That felt like a lifetime away. Riddick figured he'd better make the most of the time they had.

He imagined her snuggled down deep in bed, ensconced in luxurious linens fit for a princess. Naked, maybe. Soft and warm. Still turned on.

Riddick smiled to himself. He'd certainly gotten more than he bargained for when he'd taken that first meeting.

Musings distracted him from the start of the workout session, and he didn't pay much attention to the conversation or what they were doing. Eric kept reminding him to focus. Riddick did his best to marshal his thoughts, but his mind insisted on wandering.

What color would Khara's gown be for the fancy do this evening? The Queen had surprised Khara with tickets to the CharityWorks Ball as a token of appreciation for all her hard work as of late. It was a nice gesture, but Riddick thought Khara deserved so much more. He hoped the wrist corsage he'd ordered would complement it. It was old-fashioned and maybe a little corny, but he pictured delight in her eyes at the gesture. And whenever she looked at him like he'd—

"So, I can guess where your mind is." Eric's wry voice cut off his thoughts. Riddick looked up to see him wiggle his eyebrows. "Things seem to be going well with the smokin' hot diplomat."

"It's good. Really good."

"We all loved her, you know. Glad to see you're not practically living at work anymore. How much longer she in town for?"

Was that true? Huh. Riddick waved the thought away. Coincidence. "Another week or so."

Eric peered at him. "You going to make her yours before she goes?"

Riddick felt his face go hot. "What are we—gossiping teenagers now?"

"I'm just sayin'. The sparks you two were giving off...." Eric let out a low whistle.

Despite himself, Riddick chuckled. "We're not there, yet. We're just spending time."

"Uh-huh. Sure. I saw how you were looking at each other in your office the other day. Never seen you look at a woman like that."

"Like you've ever seen me kissing a woman!"

The look Eric pinned him with made him want to squirm. "Man, we've known each other a long time. You'd be surprised what I've seen."

Riddick considered that for a moment and realized it was probably true. "Huh."

"You looked like you wanted to spread her on a cracker."

Oh, Riddick wanted to spread her, alright. Right under him. With those captivating eyes filled with lust as he gave her all the pleasure he possibly could.

"Anyway," Eric continued, "God help you when you *do* get there. You look like you'll set the sheets on fire."

"I gotta say, I'm enjoying the hell out of this lead-up. I've never dated anyone like her. Now, you done bumpin' your gums trying to get out of this set or what?"

"Just waitin' on you, old man."

"My ass."

It was almost time to head out that evening when Riddick remembered to fire off a quick email response to his mother. She looked like she was living her best life in—Riddick had to squint to read the caption on the picture—Puerto Montt, Chile. The mountains in the background were majestic. Parie might have been on to something with this world tour. The notes he was getting from her companions were lighthearted and read like a comedy show. It brought him so much joy knowing she was having a good time.

He pondered telling her about his dream, of getting her thoughts on what it might mean. Decided against it. He didn't want her to worry about anything or read too much into things. If he wasn't careful, he might get her hopes up that there was more to this thing with Khara than there actually was. He was already triple checking each email before sending it, and for sure not sending any pictures of them together. This seemed innocuous enough, though. He sent her a picture of himself decked out for the night instead of anything more substantive. There. Time to go.

Even for her coffee, Khara couldn't get up. Instead, she languished in bed in the morning after a fitful night's sleep. She couldn't face herself in the mirror.

Khara sighed wistfully after spotting the red dress draped over the brocade chair on the other side of the room. That thing should be in a crumpled heap next to Riddick's bed, along with her sexy underthings. They should be lying wrapped around each other. Replete after a night of triumphant coming together. Talking in low voices, laughing together, flirting and playing. But instead of blissed out, she was alone and disgusted with herself. Her secret had deprived them both of much-wanted pleasure. Khara squeezed her eyes shut tight, choking back the sudden tears.

She could not go on like this.

All she'd wanted to do was get her hands and mouth on Riddick's hot body. How she'd wanted to experience every bit of the hard cock causing that impressive bulge in his pants. She'd dreamed about it vividly when she finally got to sleep. It would have been explosive between them, she could tell. Right up until the moment she told him the truth. Khara could lie to herself about how harmless maintaining this little fiction was but making love under false pretenses was just too far.

Her body was at war with her conscience, and the conflict was tearing her apart.

The temptation was there to tell him over text, but that would be an act of true cowardice. She hadn't sunk *that* low.

The text notification on her phone interrupted her guilty thoughts.

Yvanda: So? Did you blow his mind? How did he take it?

Khara: I didn't tell him. I couldn't do it.

Yvanda: WTH, KHAR?!

Khara: I was about to, but the Ambassador showed up. I need to call her and explain.

Khara was too despondent to say more. She tossed the phone down on the bed next to her. There was only one thing to do. She was going to have to suck it up and just spit it out, come what may. An obstinate part of her didn't want to, but it was beyond time. Khara covered her face with her hands and groaned. This was such a mess.

Chapter Forty-Six

F OR THE SECOND NIGHT in a row, Khara nearly stopped his heart when she opened the door to his knock. It took Riddick a few seconds to unglue his tongue from the roof of his mouth. She'd poured herself into a figure-skimming, floor-length gown in a bold rust color. It brought to mind the last burnished rays of sunlight on a fall evening.

"You look quite handsome, Mr. Riddick. You clean up very well."

A thigh-high slit revealed strappy red sandals and an acre of shapely leg when she crossed to the full-length mirror to put the back on her earring. Good God, her legs seemed to go on forever. Most of her back was bare. That long line of smooth brown skin was so sexy Riddick had to make sure he wasn't drooling. The temptation to reach for her was so great Riddick decided he might have to start asking her to meet him in the lobby.

Khara beamed at him when her eyes met his in the reflection. "Would you mind helping me with this, please?" She held up a triple strand of pearls.

After setting the florist's box down on a nearby chair, Riddick draped the necklace around her neck and fastened the delicate clasp, then slid his hands down and up her bare arms. "You use color so beautifully. You look incredible."

The playful smile she gave him was enough to make him thank his lucky stars that she was with him. Again. "I want to do dirty, dirty things to you in this dress. It's not fair of me to say it, I know. But when a woman looks this good, the person she's with better damn well tell her so."

Her eyes widened at the provocative words. But Riddick was already stepping back, trying to put a little distance between them before he did something stupid. The room felt hot all of a sudden. "I think I saw your limo out front as I was coming in. We don't want to be late."

Khara couldn't get the smoldering look Riddick had given her in the mirror out of her mind. She left the expanse of her leg exposed in the car and grew excited seeing how Riddick's appreciative gaze roamed over it. The shoes would be killing her feet later, but so what? Right now, she felt like the most desirable woman in the world. Like a goddess. No one had ever looked at her like Riddick was looking at her now—like she was a mouthwatering morsel he couldn't wait to savor. It was exhilarating. She'd felt great in the red wrap dress, but this was something altogether different. More intense.

Because she was feeling positively badass and not a little reckless, Khara decided to be daring. "What dirty things did you want to do to me in this dress, Riddick?"

The long look he gave her spoke volumes, but he sounded chagrined. "I crossed a line and I apologize."

She cocked her head to the side in silent question. Jiggled her raised foot and watched with satisfaction as his gaze slid down to her heeled sandal.

"I shouldn't have said anything when you've told me you're not ready to level up yet. As I've said before, I respect you not being ready."

"Tell me."

He took her hand and whispered kisses along the back of it. "You sure you wanna know?"

"Absolutely."

"How explicit can I be?"

"Utterly."

"It won't make you uncomfortable?"

"No."

"You're sure?"

"I'm not a blushing virgin, Riddick. I won't get the vapors."

"But you are blushing. Prettily, in fact." He watched the slight rosy flush creep up from her chest and neck to add depth to the bronze of her cheeks. "I'm warning you. None of it's polite."

"Fuck polite. Stop stalling and tell me."

The uncharacteristic profanity almost made him laugh. "I wanted to toss you on that console table in your entryway, push this dress up to your waist, and fuck you so hard you still feel me days later."

Khara swallowed hard. "Well," she breathed.

Riddick's eyes darkened as he gave her a wolfish smile. "I wanted to peel this dress off you an inch at a time. Leave you standing there in nothing but those fuck-me heels and your jewelry as I went down on you. I wanted you soaked and screaming and coming in my mouth, Khara."

"What else?" The question surprised him, but he didn't miss a beat.

"I wanted to bend you over something, shove whatever sexy panties I bet you're wearing to the side and fuck you senseless. Wanted to feel you come while I'm inside you. Woman, the only reason I'm not balls-deep inside you back in the hotel right now is that you're not ready. Understand? Hear me? Shall I go on?"

With her mouth too dry to speak, Khara could only nod.

"I wanted you astride me, riding my cock slow, taking me deep, making yourself come all over me again and again. Taking what you want, using me for your pleasure while I suck on your luscious tits.

"I wanted to hold you up against the wall and take you hard, insistent. With abandon. Both of us out of control. I wanted to take you from behind over the bathroom counter so we can watch ourselves and see how fucking hot we are together in the mirror. I wanted to see those pretty lips wrapped around my cock, Khara. I wanted to watch you tease and suck me until I nearly lost my mind. All of this while you're wearing this sexy fucking dress."

Riddick laughed low in her ear when she drew in a shaky breath. "You like hearing these dirty things, don't you, Khara? Like hearing how I can't stop thinking about how deliciously wet you got coming for me? Like hearing how hard you make me? Like hearing how I want to get my cock inside you so deep you never stop coming?"

A whimper escaped Khara. It was all she could do. He hadn't touched more than her hand, yet he'd aroused her as surely as if he'd spent the last hour with his hands all over her.

"You like hearing how much I want to feel your hot pussy gripping me tight while we fuck?"

Again, Khara could only manage a nod. She was trembling, so turned on she could hardly stand it. She was ready to rip his tuxedo off and have her way with him right then and there.

"I'll be sure to remember how you like my words when we finally come together. When we make love, I'll be telling you how beautiful you are, how much it means. The dirty words are for when we fuck. And we *will* fuck, Khara."

Khara was sure she was going to hyperventilate or spontaneously combust with need. The tiniest moan escaped before she could stop it.

"When we fuck, I'll tell you to take all of my cock, to spread your legs for me so I can fuck that pretty brown pussy of yours however I want. You'll take all of my cock and keep taking it. Oh, we're going to have fun, Khara. You know that, don't you? I want you so satisfied you can't even *think* about me without blushing and getting turned on."

"I... don't think I've ever been so turned on in my life." Her thong was sodden and her nipples felt hard as diamonds. Khara wanted to spread her legs for him now and tell him to fuck her however he wanted to. She wanted everything he'd just described. *Everything.*

"Good. Me, either. When you see me looking at you at this shindig tonight—and I already know I won't be able to take my eyes off you—you'll know I'm thinking about all those dirty, dirty things. Let's go."

Khara hadn't even realized they'd stopped moving. She felt dazed and couldn't move right away when Riddick unfolded himself from the car and held out a hand to her. She took his hand and let him help her out. Time seemed suspended for a moment as his gaze slid over her, from her hair to her toes and back again. The fire in his eyes when they met hers took her breath away.

"Fucking gorgeous," he murmured, then slid his hand over the naked skin of her lower back to steer her inside. His fingertips played there in a gentle, barely there caress. It made her shiver. She wanted to grab him by the lapels and find the nearest closet.

Khara berated herself to focus.

She'd nearly spilled her after-dinner coffee down the front of her gown when she caught sight of Riddick looking at her like he already had her naked and satisfied in his imagination. *You're telling him, no matter what,* she reminded herself. And if he decided she was the lyingest liar who ever lied a lie, completely untrustworthy, and not worth the trouble? Well, at least her last memory of him would be how criminally sexy he was in a tux. All she could do was hope for the best. She'd been entirely too aware of him all evening, hardly been able to sit still through dinner. His gaze dropped to her mouth when she parted her lips to speak.

"The way you keep fidgeting in your seat tells me you can't stop thinking about those dirty, dirty things either, can you?"

Their table companions were none the wiser, for Riddick had draped his arm across the back of her chair and leaned in to speak quietly so only she could hear him. He smelled so good she could hardly focus on his words.

"Tell me, beautiful Khara, if I were to slide a finger inside your panties right now, what would I find? Hmm? Would I find you drenched?"

Khara dragged in a breath and set the coffee cup down on the saucer as gently as she could manage. It still rattled. "I'm so, so wet for you right now."

"My cock's been hard as nails since I first saw you tonight. When I drop you off later, I'm going to take my time and stroke and finger that delicious pussy of yours while you're still dressed. Shoes, jewelry, everything still on. I want to watch you come undone for me, Khara. I want your juices running down your leg."

Lord, the way he kept saying her name. "Oh, God. I'm halfway there already."

"Good. I like hearing I've got you hot and bothered. Hell, I might not be able to wait until we get back to the hotel."

"You want to touch me in the car?"

"Darling, I want to touch you right *here*. Let's dance. It'll be the closest I can get to you for a few hours, yet."

Okay, she'd wait one dance, but no more.

Chapter Forty-Seven

WHILE THEY FLOATED AROUND the dance floor to a schmaltzy big band ballad, Riddick was tapping out on the whole "casual" label.

Holy shit, she'd done him in. Sunk him. Riddick realized it the moment he'd seen her tonight, sweeping around the room almost regally. The dress was vibrant like she was, unexpected. Khara carried herself in a way that suggested she'd been to many fancy dress parties, like she knew what she was doing with getting done up. He imagined she did. The Queen must do this type of thing all the time.

He was no stranger to dressing up himself, having been to his fair share of galas and the like. The pleasure that lit in Khara's eyes when she saw him at the door was unmistakable. She'd looked at him like she wanted to eat him right up and he was here for it. Not a single date he'd ever had could hold a candle to the woman in his arms now.

Khara enthralled him, and he liked just about everything he'd learned about her. But now, with her looking at him like she wanted him to ravish her right here? Like she was thinking dirty, dirty thoughts about *him*? He was about to lose his cool entirely.

Oh, he hadn't meant to start this conversation. Not at all. He was hanging on to his control with a tenuous grip after the two previous nights. He'd been brutally honest with her in the limo and couldn't quite bring himself to regret it. It wasn't fair of him to put it on her that way. No, he shouldn't have been so descriptive, no matter what she'd said.

Then he hadn't been able to stop talking about what he wanted. The talking and her reaction turned him on so much he was having difficulty thinking straight. He could have scared her off. Instead, it seemed they both liked dirty talk.

He didn't want to put any pressure on her, had committed to that. Less than twenty-four hours ago, she'd told him she wasn't ready. When Khara Therin came to his bed, he wanted her sole focus on them and the pleasure they would give each other, not distracted by any doubts or second thoughts. But here she was, looking like temptation personified, more than enough to entice a man away from any lofty ideals he might have about restraint.

The spell was broken when another couple bumped into them. Riddick shifted his body to protect Khara from getting jostled. The sudden movement caused her to miss her footing. He caught her up against him and shook off the man's drunken apologies.

They applauded when the song ended and then those killer curves were pressed to him again as the next one began. She'd done something smoky to her eyes that made them look bigger, even more gorgeous. He was at real risk of being lost in their depths.

A man appeared to be watching them from across the room. Leaning against the wall with his arms crossed, he didn't look happy. In fact, he seemed to be glowering at them. What was that about? Riddick was used to men casting interested glances at Khara—she was hard not to notice. But this felt weirdly personal, not like the guy was just admiring a beautiful woman he happened to see. An instinct made Riddick hold Khara a little tighter.

She squeezed his shoulder, bringing his attention back. "Are you alright?" The man was gone when he looked again.

Yes, this was a much better sight. Lovely Khara with her crimson lips curved into a flirtatious smile just for him. In this drop-dead sexy dress he'd definitely be fantasizing about later.

Riddick had been attracted to her from the first moment, it was true. Spending these weeks getting to know her—her quirks, the way her clever mind worked, what made her tick—made him want her in a way that was damn near visceral. And not just sexually. That was the thing. Sexual attraction he could handle.

She'd gotten under his skin. He thought he'd guarded against this, against letting himself care for her too much. He knew better. Hadn't he convinced himself superficial was the way to go, all they could ever be? Yet something inside him tensed up uncomfortably at the thought of saying goodbye. Of never seeing her smile at him again.

The bottom line was he didn't want it to end here. He'd been kidding himself to think otherwise. Khara was what he hadn't known he needed in his life. And now, here he was, poised to take a risk.

"You're coming to mean a lot to me, Khara." He held her close as they swayed to the music. "I'm happy with how things are going between us."

Her smile was a radiant one. "So am I."

"When we started this, I thought we'd just have some fun while you were here—whatever that ended up looking like—then go our separate ways. That's not what I want anymore."

"No?"

"I hadn't planned on it, but how do you feel about being exclusive?"

"Exclusive?" she echoed.

He tightened his hold on her lower back. His mouth felt very dry. "I've never tried long distance before, never really wanted to until now."

"Are you asking me to be your girlfriend, Riddick?"

He spun her in a quick turn, then drew her back into him, just a little closer than before. "Yes."

Khara's eyes were sparkling as she looked up at him. "What does that mean to you?"

Everything, he thought. His heart was beating hard. She never said what he expected she might. He respected how she was careful and didn't say yes right away. "It means we're in a committed relationship instead of just dating. It means I want you to be the last person I talk to at the end of the day. Let's keep getting to know each other. I really like what I've learned so far, and I hope you do, too. I want to make it officially exclusive."

A brief, nearly imperceptible frown crossed her face. Riddick's stomach dropped. "Shit, too soon?"

Khara shook her head, her fingers tightening on his shoulder. "No, I would very much like to be your girlfriend and have you as my boyfriend."

"Great." Relieved, he dropped a quick kiss on her lips. "It's official."

That quick frown again, accompanied by a ripple of something like fear. "Riddick, I... have to tell you something."

"What is it? You can tell your new boyfriend anything."

She laughed, as he'd hoped. "Give me a moment. I'll be right back."

"I mean it. You can tell me anything."

"I know. And I will. Let me just run to the ladies' room first."

He escorted her, laughing when she caught his hand in hers and kissed it. The ladies' room was being cleaned. A janitor mopping the floor offered an apology for the inconvenience and directed them to another bathroom a few corridors away.

Khara thanked him and they started in the direction he pointed, hand in hand. She gave him a thorough kiss outside the door to the smaller restroom off the beaten path. "Perfect, no line. Your new girlfriend will be right back and explain all."

"Your boyfriend will be here waiting for you."

Another quick kiss and she disappeared inside the restroom.

Riddick knew he was grinning. Who wouldn't? What was Khara going to tell him? He didn't have a clue. He had a girlfriend. He shook his head at his giddiness. Would doodling their names in a heart be next?

Something he couldn't put his finger on made the hair on the back of Riddick's neck stand up, shattering his fanciful thoughts and putting him on edge. He'd started toward the bathroom door to knock and ask if Khara was alright when he heard a soft rustling behind him. He was just turning when he felt electricity arcing painfully through his body.

Taser, he thought, on the way down. There was a bright flash of light as he whacked his head on something. He was unconscious before he hit the floor.

Chapter Forty-Eight

RIDDICK CAME TO WITH a start to a sea of faces glaring down at him. A big, muscular man with a beard and mustache barked at him, "What happened?"

He squinted and then blinked. "Who are you?" Shit, his head hurt.

"Lytuan Guard. What happened?"

Riddick looked around frantically. "Where's Khara?"

"That's our question for you."

"Hold still, please," Another man was kneeling next to him, dabbing at his forehead. "Looks like you hit your head on the way down. You've a superficial cut here."

Riddick shoved the gloved hands away from his face and sat up. The world spun dizzily for a second. "Where is Khara? Someone tazed me."

The man administering first aid had a bald head and a lean face. "We'll get to that. Do you know your name? Where you are?"

Fuck all that. Riddick gave his full name and the name of the hotel.

"No signal yet, *Zildrei*," a tall woman with very short hair said. It was single-name Cenn, the only person around him he recognized.

"That's not good."

"When this is over, I'm insisting on that subcutaneous tracker."

The men and women around him nodded. There were six in total. Riddick made them all as cops despite their formal attire.

"The Queen has declined it up until now." Another woman explained, this one shorter than Cenn, with long micro braids cascading over one shoulder.

Riddick frowned. Realized the woman looked familiar. Hadn't she been in the ballroom, sitting a few tables away? "I don't understand. What does this have to do with Khara? We have to find her. Did someone call the police?"

The mountain of a man who'd shouted at him spoke to the group in rapid-fire Lytuan, then helped him to his feet.

"What are you even doing here?" Riddick asked. This wasn't making any damn sense.

"We go where our Queen goes."

"She's here? Well, I get that, but why aren't you worried about Khara? *She's* Lytuan."

The group exchanged uncomfortable glances and Riddick tensed. "What are you not telling me?"

"Khara is the Queen."

Riddick's brow furrowed. A dull throb was developing behind his eyes. "Say what, now?"

"*Khara* is the Queen of Lytua, Mr. Riddick. Time for you to get caught up. I'm not sure how much she's told you. We're all members of the Queen's personal security detail, known as the Elite Guard. My name is Jaden Everly."

"But she's— What the hell? Queen Lillianna...?"

"That's her formal ceremonial name. Khara Therin is her given name."

Riddick's mind was whirling. "It's okay. I know about the press mi—" Then it hit him. He groaned. Oh. Oh, *shit*. That run-in with the Ambassador last night, the woman at the architecture association mixer. How conflicted Khara'd seemed. That uncertainty in her eyes. Of course, it all made perfect sense now. "Fucking hell. There was no press mix-up, was there? God, I am an idiot."

"Focus, man! We'll sort out the details later. She had her reasons. Right now, we need you to tell us everything you can remember."

Once they'd shown him the identification he insisted on seeing first, he told the assembled group what he could remember. It wasn't much to go on.

When the two of them hadn't returned to the ballroom right away, no one was alarmed at first. Khara had signaled to the team that she was going to the restroom. The Elites figured they were stealing a few moments in a secluded corner somewhere. But after no one had seen the Queen for fifteen minutes, the Guard grew suspicious. They launched an immediate search when she didn't respond to hailing requests. Then the fire alarm went off and the throngs of frightened guests slowed them down.

It was Alene who discovered Riddick on the carpeted floor, unconscious and bleeding, with the Queen's whereabouts unknown. She'd raised the alarm and told Link to bring some smelling salts.

The Queen's evening bag sat undisturbed on the bathroom counter. Her cell phone and ID were inside along with a modest amount of cash and a credit card. It wasn't a robbery. A tube of lipstick was the only item askew, perhaps knocked aside in a struggle. That wasn't good. Uneasy, Jaden reported this to the team.

A small crowd of murmuring party-goers was forming in the hallway.

A slight woman with dark skin and passion twists in a high bun hurried up and introduced herself as the head of hotel security. Her expression was hard. "I'm damned sorry this happened, and mad as hell it happened here on my watch. The hotel's locked down and the Metropolitan Police Department is on the way. My best tech is scanning surveillance footage now. If you'll follow me."

One woman stayed behind in the bathroom to secure the scene and get Khara's purse once MPD photographed it and logged its contents.

At the hotel's security office, Riddick balked when the third woman asked him to wait outside while they watched the recording as a group. His stomach had knotted with fear.

"I want to see it, too."

"We are her security team. We need to see it first."

His frustration was palpable, but he wasn't about to get into a pissing match when Khara's life might be on the line. He didn't force the issue.

Riddick was worried and confused and wasn't quite sure what to do with that. He paced in agitation outside the closed door. Was she alright? She'd better be alright or there would be hell to pay.

A press mix-up. Ha. Riddick grimaced. He'd been so blinded by Khara that he'd swallowed her outlandish tale whole. Thought he knew all he needed to know and hadn't bothered to look any further, particularly since he didn't like her boss. Her. Whatever. *Jesus.*

Frowning, he pulled up the official Lytua website and scrolled through the pictures that showed the Queen wearing an elaborate Carnivale costume, complete with a masked headdress. He'd barely given the photos a glance. He could see it now—how could he have not seen it before? The way she was standing, how her head was tilted, even obscured by the mask. It was so obvious now, of course. He knew how those luscious curves felt against him.

How the hell had he missed all the signs that the goddamn Queen's assistant was more than what she seemed? Questions continued to buzz around his brain.

Surveillance footage showed a stiff-backed, ashen-faced Khara being led from the bathroom at gunpoint. Her captor was a young man in a hotel janitor's uniform. He had a hand clamped on her bare upper arm. The man gave her arm a violent yank when she took a step toward Riddick's crumpled form. She threw him off with a hard elbow to his ribs and dropped to Riddick's side, distress clear on her face. She touched the spot on Riddick's face where he was bleeding, lay her other hand on his chest. The janitor said something that had her shaking her head. It looked like she was arguing or pleading. She put her hands up in a placating gesture when he waved the gun at Riddick. The man dragged her to her feet, and they saw she was wincing at his tight grip in the same place on her arm.

They all gasped in outrage when, unprovoked, the man reared back and struck her in the face with the pistol. Khara stumbled against the wall, her hand on her cheek. The man shook her, then started toward the nearby exit with her in tow. Khara glanced back at Riddick, her face pinched with worry. Another camera angle showed her being shoved into the back seat of a waiting car. The assailants weren't stupid—they'd obscured the license plates and driven a nondescript car.

When the team watched the footage again with Riddick, Jaden signaled Cenn to watch him. It was his first time dealing with Riddick, and he was very interested in the man's reaction.

The footage first showed Riddick's attack. He was leaning against the wall across from the bathroom. Smiling, antsy, and so distracted he didn't hear the man creeping up from behind until it was too late. He knocked his head on the way down and landed awkwardly with a heavy-looking thud.

Jaden crossed his arms over his chest. "Why were you so nervous?"

"She said she needed to tell me something. I don't know what it was. Well, I have a pretty good idea what it was *now*." Realization dawned and Riddick wanted to kick himself. "Goddammit, she's been trying to tell me for days, I think. No wonder she was so defensive of the Queen."

Seeing Khara manhandled incensed Riddick. "Mother*fucker*!" He hissed when the man hit Khara, his hands balling into fists. "Anything we can use from this? What's next? How can I help?"

They were watching the footage once more when Riddick sprang to his feet. "Wait. Run it back a bit."

"Do you see something?"

"There, look. Her necklace is gone. Actually, looks like *all* of her jewelry is gone."

He was right. Every one of the Elites swore as they grasped the meaning of what they were seeing.

"That doesn't make any sense, though," Riddick said. "Why would they take her jewelry and leave her purse?"

"Most of her jewelry has a GPS tracker in it."

"They're not on all the time, though. There's a specific sequence she has to use to activate it."

The truth was sinking in. "So, they knew who she was and took everything before she had a chance. And that spells a different kind of trouble."

"Exactly. They targeted her as the Queen specifically, not because she looks like someone would pay to ensure her safe return."

The group puzzled it out, completing each other's thoughts and sentences. This kind of closeness grew through years of collaborating. The conversation was moving so fast through the room Riddick could barely follow which team member had spoken.

"They knew enough to keep their faces off camera. Showed some savvy by diverting to a remote bathroom closer to the exit."

"Then incapacitated the biggest threat to their plan—Riddick—"

"—who surely would have something to say about her being abducted."

"Smart to take him out of the equation early."

"It's what I would have done."

They all nodded, Riddick included.

If the perpetrators wanted either of them dead, they would be. There was no doubt about it. The opportunity was there. "If they'd tazed Khara, too, they would have had to carry her out. Bastards." Riddick tried unsuccessfully to force the tight muscles in the back of his neck to unclench. He felt hollowed out.

"The fire alarm impeded our search."

"No way was that a coincidence."

"And while we were chasing our damn tails, they were getting a head start."

What did the kidnappers want? And when would they find out?

"Let's regroup. Mr. Riddick? You'd better come with us to the command center." Jaden had spoken. He appeared to be the leader.

Then the group was hustling toward three black SUVs and speeding down I-395. The woman Cenn was driving, Jaden in the passenger seat. He'd recognized her right away. Riddick sat wedged between two women who looked tough enough to scare average men. Everyone was grim-faced. His head was spinning with all the new information.

"So, if Khara is the Queen," he began. "Why would she pretend not to be? I don't understand."

"She had her reasons. You'll have to ask her when we get her back."

"We *will* get her back."

"No one fucks with our Queen."

A few minutes later, another thought grabbed at him. "So all the things she was telling me about Queen Lillianna, was she—?" Riddick broke off. "Never mind. None of that matters now. *Fuck.*"

"Still no signal, *Zildrei*," the woman to his right reported. She had the micro braids and was wearing a black gown.

"What does that word mean?"

"'Sentinel.'"

"That would make you...?"

"The head of palace security and her personal detail."

Cenn snorted. "He's being modest. As usual."

The woman sitting on his left interjected. She had a straight bob and glasses. "The *Zildrei* is the last person shielding our Queen."

"This must grate, then."

Sudden tension filled the air. The three women cast worried looks at each other, then at Jaden. Something like anguish crossed Jaden's face before he glared at Riddick. "I went against my better judgment on this, which I will always regret."

No one said anything the rest of the way to the hotel after that, each lost in their own worry.

Chapter Forty-Nine

R IDDICK SPOTTED TROUBLE ALMOST the moment they arrived. The command center was a large business suite at the hotel, with communications equipment covering every available surface. Team members were busy taking up stations, using laptops and telephones. It was a cacophony of sound and activity.

Jaden called them to order and made quick introductions while they were getting seated. He gave a brief rundown of what they knew so far. It wasn't much. They speculated and discussed observations. The working theory was that this was likely a ransom situation.

The other team members were beginning to look familiar and had been around while he and Khara were out, there to help with the winery purchases. Link he recognized as the one who'd treated his head wound. Another woman he remembered from his first meeting arrived and introduced herself as the Queen's *actual* assistant, Joanne. She provided a bit more back story, that the Elite Guard was a Lytuan Special Forces unit, all internationally trained. The other men and women about were part of the Guard, a prestigious, specialized unit within the Armed Services charged with securing the office of Lytuan Leadership.

It made sense to Riddick. The Elite Guard was like the Secret Service. They protected the Queen herself and the Guard took responsibility for everything else, like logistics, general security, and transportation. Everyone who traveled with the Queen was a member of the Guard. Right down to all the support personnel.

Riddick knew they were speaking English for his benefit, which he appreciated. He'd been told that the entire team was fluent. It was almost jarring when Jaden and Cenn engaged in a short, tense exchange in Lytuan. She had become increasingly agitated.

"Zildrei, I object to having this man involved. An outsider and a civilian? No good will come of this."

"Our Queen cares for him. Do you want to be the one to tell her we froze him out? He has experience that could prove useful."

"He doesn't know our ways. Will he follow the chain of command?"

"We cannot be overly concerned with what he might or might not do. We have one job here: get our Avlah back safely."

"How do we know he's not the one who orchestrated this and had himself tazed to appear innocent?"

"Cenn, enough. Your concern is noted."

Cenn eyed Riddick with contempt as she stalked out of the room, slamming the door behind her. While Riddick couldn't understand the terse conversation, he could read the tone and body language clearly enough. He approached Jaden and asked quietly. "What was that about?"

Jaden sighed and stroked his beard thoughtfully. "Slight difference of opinion."

"She doesn't trust me. None of them do."

"Cenn is... extremely loyal, and the ruse disgruntled her. No one liked it, but we agreed the Queen deserved this. Most even thought it was romantic."

"Not Cenn."

"No, not Cenn. To be fair, it wasn't you, it was the deception. She was quite vocal with *Avlah* about it."

"'*Avlah*?'"

"It means Exalted Queen. Right now, Cenn's concern is that you're an outsider, not a part of this unit."

This Riddick could understand. "Those are smart, valid concerns."

"That's why she's my second-in-command."

"Where did she go? I'd like to speak with her."

"She wouldn't have gone far. Ask Nasha, the Guard outside the door."

The Guard directed Riddick to what looked like a temporary training center. On the far side of the room, Cenn was pulling knives from a target. She gave him an annoyed glance but said nothing. Riddick went to the table and glanced at the collection of wicked-looking knives lined up there. He whistled, impressed. "All these yours?"

"Yes."

There was a lot of subtext in that single word.

"I get why you're pissed," Riddick said. "Your team trains together often, has defined roles, responsibilities, and assignments. You're a unit. You don't need an interloper to muck things up. Am I right so far?"

Cenn crossed her arms, gave a curt nod. Her expression was hard.

"It's red alert right now, and you have a job to do. None of you have time to babysit me."

"Hmph," Cenn grumbled and started putting the knives from the target into sheaths secreted all over her body. Riddick counted eight. Jesus, this woman was probably deadly.

"I can understand that and, if it matters, I agree with you. I worked with a SpecOps team, too. We relied on each other. No room for error. I just want Khara safe, just like you. I'll follow your orders and stay out of your way."

Cenn considered him for a long moment, then surprised the hell out of him. "I see why she likes you." She gave him a small smile at that, and it transformed her face. "Over the years, we've had run-ins, weird happenings. But no one's ever taken her from us before. Not like this. We've drilled this very scenario, though, for years, so she is not unprepared."

That seemed practical. Of course, they would have. It would have been irresponsible not to.

"The Queen and I didn't connect at first. It was my mistake. I underestimated her. She told me off like...." Cenn sighed and smiled at the bittersweet memory. "Anyone trying to harm her will likely also underestimate her. She is not without skill, Mr. Riddick. She'll take advantage. I do believe she could talk her way out of almost any situation."

Now Riddick smiled, even with the fear churning in his gut. "She does have quite the sharp tongue."

"Could outargue the devil himself. She's level-headed and resourceful, not just smart, but clever, too. She'll find a way to get away or get word to us somehow."

Cenn's reassurance made Riddick feel a little better. "Good. Glad to hear that."

"Let's go find my Queen."

Cenn led him back to the main room, and the discussion continued. The MPD SWAT Commander arrived with her team, and they were getting the rundown. Sitting around waiting put them all on edge. These were teams used to acting in a crisis. Waiting on someone else to make a move was unnatural and made them all feel twitchy. The sooner this was done, the quicker they could get back on an even keel.

Optimism waned as the night gave way to morning, and there was still no word. Riddick couldn't sit, couldn't settle. Wished he could do something. Was Khara hurt? Frightened? Cold? These assholes had better not have hurt her. When he got his hands on them, he would—

"Here." Jaden tossed him a black t-shirt to change into. "Have a seat. You're wearing a hole in the carpet."

Riddick offered gruff thanks, then switched his tuxedo jacket and shirt. "Are you as calm as you seem?"

"Oh, I'm not calm. But I do trust her training."

Riddick had taken part in rescue missions before and knew the likelihood of a positive outcome diminished the more time passed. Smart hostages did what they could to keep themselves safe, but it ultimately came down to how far their captors were willing to go. Riddick imagined Khara giving her kidnappers a tongue lashing in that imperious tone of voice. It almost made him smile. "Why isn't the GPS activated all the time? Or remotely?"

"I wondered when you'd ask that." Jaden let out an uneasy laugh as he scrubbed his hand over the back of his neck. "We tried, but she wouldn't allow it. Wouldn't even entertain the idea."

"Yeah?"

"Shut down any mention of it. Said she wouldn't ever live in a police state."

Now Riddick did smile. "That sounds like Khara." God, in all his righteous spouting off about royal exploitation, he'd probably made it harder for her to tell him the truth. *Shit.* "She and I are going to have a serious heart-to-heart when all this is over. I have questions."

"I imagine so."

Chapter Fifty

Trina staged herself perfectly for when the summons arrived. Wearing her crisp dress blues, sitting amongst influential community members, she radiated authority. She'd left her cell phone face up on the banquet table and the incoming call alert was now flashing, "CeCe Alain", along with the Chief of the Municipal Police's official portrait. It was impossible to miss—there she was, flashing a broad smile in front of the Lytuan flag, complete with all the brass on the epaulets. Murmuring apologies for the interruption, Trina picked up with a brisk, "Deputy Chief Krove."

She'd rehearsed her reaction, but not so much that it would come across that way. After listening to CeCe's panicked announcement, Trina was sure to affect a disbelieving tone when she dropped her bombshell. "What do you mean, the Queen's been taken?"

Alarm swept through her table companions as she had a hurried conversation with her boss. There were gasps, hushed conversations, and furious whispers.

"Excuse me, everyone, I need to get to the station." Trina turned to her husband seated next to her. "Corey—"

He shook his head and waved her off. "I'll get home, honey. You go."

A pang of remorse twisted Trina's insides, and she hesitated. She hadn't considered how disruptive her sudden departure would be. "This event was important to you. I'm sorry."

Corey cupped his wife's face. She nuzzled into his hand, guilt churning in her gut. He was looking very dapper in his tuxedo. "This is what I signed up for when I married an up-and-coming police detective."

"You didn't sign up for me running out on your big thing."

"Trina, how many times have I run out on something of yours because of Parliament? You're the deputy chief of police. I know what that means. I love you, and I'm proud of you. Go do your thing."

Trina gave her husband a tender kiss, excused herself, and made her exit. As she hurried to her car, she pulled her formal uniform cap on over her short curls and did her best to keep the giddy smile from creeping into her face. The plan was finally fully in motion. Now all she had to do was play her part. Lillianna's reign was, at last, coming to an end.

Chapter Fifty-One

A LOUD PING BROKE the tense silence in the command center.

"Got it! She's live." A bespectacled tech called it out to the assembled group.

"That's our girl," Jaden said. "Get it on the screen, Melanie."

"One moment, please. The signal is not strong."

"Remember all the false alarms when she was trying to learn the system?"

There was chuckling despite the seriousness of the situation.

Spotting Riddick's confusion, Cenn explained, "In the beginning, *Avlah* had the hardest time trying to get used to all the security procedures. She got flustered easily and ended up repeatedly deploying everyone with the emergency signal."

"She must have done that at least ten times."

Riddick was having difficulty keeping the Elite Guard members straight in his mind, especially now that they'd all changed out of their formal wear into black tactical clothing. He didn't like flubbing names, but it was hopeless trying to suss out who was who from context clues. They knew each other so well there was no need to use each other's names.

The GPS signal triangulated on the wall-mounted television the tech was using as a computer monitor. They all waited while it zeroed in on a building. Riddick tried to slow his racing heart while the tech did her thing. The tech looked up, confusion painting her features.

"My apologies. This must be an error." The young woman frowned and adjusted her glasses before forcing the tracking program to restart. "It's transmitting, but it's not making any sense. Some interference of some kind?" She punched the computer keys once more and when the same information came up a third time, there was stunned silence, then the room exploded in Lytuan.

Lytuan Guard members all over the room shouted, pointed, and rushed around. Riddick and the MPD SWAT team looked on in befuddlement. Then Riddick heard one of the Elites utter a phrase he caught. He thought her name was Alene. "*I don't understand.*"

"What's going on?" Riddick demanded. The whirlwind of controlled panic around him didn't slow. "Somebody tell me what's happening!"

Riddick caught Jaden's arm as he hurried by him, bringing the man up short. "What's happening? Where the hell is she?"

Jaden's eyes were full of fire. "Nicaragua, Mr. Riddick. It says she's in Nicaragua."

To Be Concluded....

The Queen's been taken.
The man she swore she wouldn't love?
He's coming for her.
And if you thought sparks were flying before... buckle up.
Book 2 picks up immediately after this cliffhanger
—because you deserve answers.
And passion.
And more than a few "Did he really just say that?" moments.

Ready to watch him burn the world down for her—**starting now?**
Continue the story in *Queen of His Heart*
—and don't forget to grab *A Matter of Taste* for the full swoon.

Queen of His Heart

If this story kept you turning pages or left you eager for what comes next, I'd be so grateful if you shared your thoughts in a review.

Reviews help more than you know and only take a minute.

Leave a review here: https://www.nikkidavenport.com/international-incident-links-for-reviews/.

International Incident Reviews

**Before *International Incident* and *Queen of His Heart*,
Sparks flew with Jaden and Aimee....**

In the Queen's Service (Crown & Heart Book 3) transports readers to the turbulent early days of Khara Therin's reign. Before Jaden Everly was the devoted husband and father we know and love, he was a grumpy, inflexible know-it-all too used to being in charge.

He's juggling national security and a royal transition, with zero time—or interest—for romance.

Until Dr. Aimee Sebastien dances into his life at his brother's wedding and makes it very clear she isn't here to be impressed.

Challenge accepted.

Coming soon—join my newsletter so you don't miss the release.

Join here.

In the Queen's Service

NIKKI DAVENPORT IS A contemporary romance and romantic suspense author and the creator of the Crown & Heart/Destination: Lytua series—where Wakanda meets *Bridgerton* in a lush, all-Black world of royal romance and unapologetic joy. Her stories reimagine royalty through high-stakes emotion, deep friendships, and characters who fight for love and legacy.

Her debut novel, *International Incident*, became an Amazon bestseller, ranking in the Top 15 of Romantic Suspense and Top 55 of Contemporary Romance, and was selected as a 2023 finalist for the Audio in Color Award. Book two in the series went on to hit #1 in Black & African American Women's Fiction, launching a royal universe readers can't wait to return to.

A lifelong lover of love stories, Nikki holds a BA in History and a Master's in Social Work. She is also the founder of Granite Clover Publishing, LLC, and Granite Clover Author Services, a boutique author-services company offering culturally responsive manuscript support for fiction and nonfiction writers. She works in education by day, paddles with a dragon boat team of fellow breast cancer survivors in her off time, and belongs to a fabulous book club. She lives in Northern Virginia with her husband, a snarky teen, and two spoiled feline overlords—and is rarely without an audiobook or podcast.

Nikki is passionately committed to centering Black love on the page—and isn't stopping anytime soon.

Follow her on Goodreads (37165373.Nikki_Davenport), Book Bub (@nikkidavenportauthor), and Facebook (AuthorNikkiDavenport)!

The Crown & Heart Series

International Incident — Crown & Heart Book 1

A Matter of Taste — A Crown & Heart Novella (Book 1.5)

Queen of His Heart — Crown & Heart Book 2

Season of the Heart — A Crown & Heart Prequel (Book 3)

In the Queen's Service — Crown & Heart Book 3

Worth the Risk — A Crown & Heart Prequel (Book 4)

Healing Reign — Crown & Heart Book 4

Fool Me Once — A Crown & Heart Novella

Also Appearing in Anthologies

Courage: An Anthology to Kick Cancer's Ass — "A Matter of Taste"

Holly & Heartstrings Holiday Anthology — "Season of the Heart"

Crown & Heart Series Guide

Far too many to list independently, but know I love and appreciate everyone who's helped me along on this journey!

Mr. Nikki: you live in the heart of every one of my heroes, my love.

G & Q: nothing gives me more joy than seeing the magnificent young adults you two are developing into. Never stop shining.

The Babes: It's never been just about the books for me. It's being surrounded, supported, and uplifted by a group of such wise, badass, incredible women. I aspire to be half as good a friend as you all have been to me.

Gina: we're a long way from middle school, but damn, those big dreams have come into focus.

Michael: you planted and nurtured that little sprout so many years ago. Your words and encouragement have always stayed with me.

Rose, Nichole, and Mel: keeping me accountable and pushing when I waffled.

Priscilllah, Cindy, Stephanie, Sondari: the best betas an author could ask for. Your insights were invaluable.

Christie, Mariana, and Mpho: Team Nikki editors extraordinaire. Your intuition and guidance strengthened the foundation. Every author should be so supported.

Olivia: for the kickass logos and cover that made me feel like a boss queen even before this book was finished.

Tessa: from margins to widow/orphan control to every single one of the most minute details that vexed me, you got this manuscript in order. Your patience is awe-inspiring.

Kristina, Lucy, Shane, and the Whole Fictionary Community: kindness wins, you all are the best, and Fictionary rocks!

www.ingramcontent.com/pod-product-compliance
Lightning Source LLC
Chambersburg PA
CBHW031210310726
48969CB00001B/295